The Intelligent Gardener

by Monty Mawes

Table of Contents

Chapter 1

Set deep in the rolling Cotswold hill's, a beautiful 200 year old 10 bedroom Cotswold stone Daleridge estate house, was in-fact set in 100 acres of mostly woodland, the land not covered in woodland, was rented out to resident tenant farmers. To the rear of the house were stables and other out buildings, used mainly by the game keepers for storage. The house and all the land was originally owned by Sir Walter Francis who made his millions from the many properties that he owned in and around London's famous square mile. Now deceased, the house, land and his million's were then left in the safe hands of Sir Francis's only son and heir Roger, who at the tender age of 19 impregnated his 16 year old girlfriend Bernadette, who he then married, much to the disgust of his parents. Roger and his young wife Bernadette [Bern] produced their only child, a gifted son, who they named Bobby Francis. Roger and his wife perished at sea as they crossed from the Americas to Africa, the ship and all who sailed in her were never found

Bobby was now aged 18 and lives at the large estate house with his grandfather Fred, on his mother's side of the family, they are both looked after and cared for at the house by Helen, who lives in a quaint thatched roofed cottage that was situated half way down the main drive, if you follow the drive to its conclusion, it leads out onto the main Stow Road.

 Helen had lived next door to Bern when she was a child, they had grown up together and had been the best of friends all through their childhood and schooldays. When Bern fell pregnant she begged her best friend to stay with her, because she was terrified at the prospect of giving birth, that was 19 years ago and Helen still lives on the estate to this very day, she shares her cottage with her husband Charles who was a continental lorry driver and was away for weeks on end. Helen gets very lonely in the cottage all by herself and has made sure that Bobby knows that, saying that he was more than welcome to visit her day or night, saying that her door was always unlocked and there would be a warm welcome waiting for him.

Helen aged 34 is a woman that looks after herself by mainly jogging around the estate wearing the tightest running outfit that she could possibly have bought. Helen stands about 5ft 7, she has long blonde hair that she always wears held high in a ponytail, a pretty face with a slightly pointed nose, her large eyes are pale green that remind Bobby of a cats-eye's. Helen has a nice hand full of tit with permanently hard nipples. Helen cooks and cleans for Bobby and his grandfather for which she was paid a lot of money, so much so that her husband need not work, but she admits that if he was at home with her all the time, she would probably end up killing him.

The green eyed woman likes to walk around her bungalow naked when she was on her own, at the rear of her bungalow are a pair of French windows in front of which she stands most nights, and does her ironing or any other jobs that need doing, she knows that Bobby sometimes stands in the shadows watching her, when she senses that he might be out there, she will walk to the double doors and stand there with her legs wide a part, and stare out into the darkness willing him to have the courage to enter her house, and make love to her. Helen has watched Bobby as he has been sunbathing by the indoor pool, staring at the bulge in his swimming trunks, she has hidden in the shadows and done things to herself that she should be ashamed of, but she wants and needs him so badly it hurts. She is almost certain that Bobby was a virgin and she was desperate to teach him everything that she knows about the art of shagging, purely to help him flourish in the future, and she of course would benefit with him fucking the ass off her all the time that he was learning.

Bobby Francis stands 6ft tall and has shoulder length wavy brown hair with blond highlights, he was a handsome man with startling blue eyes, his lean, muscular body was well toned and lithe. He has an IQ that was well into three figures, speaks French, German and Spanish fluently and scored A star in every subject that he sat at the very expensive well known private school that he attended. With all of his fine education and high intelligence all he wants to do was work with his grandfather Fred in the gardens of the family home. Fred has another job that he attends to every day, for 40 years Fred has worked at the Pine Trees School for young women, in his capacity as the manager/maintenance man of the well-tended gardens. The school was situated on the edge of the Daleridge estate and was initially a 15 century manor house, with enough rooms to house 50 young women, all aged between 16 and 18. Now semi retired from the gardens Fred was still in overall charge, every evening he and Bobby would walk the gardens to decide what needed doing the following day. Fred would stop and explain things to his grandson such as what jobs needs doing, why and how the task should be carried out, they would then go to the gardeners hut, where there was a white board situated on the wall, and hung from a length of gardening twine, was a black felt pen. On the left hand side of the board are four names, Bob, Harry, Ray and John, next to each name was a long space in which their next day's tasks were written. All the gardeners are elderly and have worked with Fred for a life time.

Fred knows each man's ability and assigns each task accordingly, that job done they turn to leave the hut to see pinned to the back of the door was a brown envelope with Fred's name on it. Fred reads the note inside, tutt's a few times, he then glances at his grandson and says.
"C'mon youngun we have been summoned." The pair walked through the front doors of the very exclusive school. There are pretty young ladies walking stiff backed and silent along the well-lit corridors, every pair of female eyes devour Bobby as he walks next to the wizened old man in his flip flops, tight jeans and skin tight tee shirt. Fred stops outside a brown oak door with Matron emblazoned on it, Fred stops and taps the door and waits to be told to enter.

The two men walk into the room to breathe in the smell of old age, old books and decay, to see a stick thin old woman with her grey hair pulled back severely and fixed in a bun that was held tightly behind her head, her face looked like a slapped ass as she stared at Bobby through eyes that seemed to have a pale film over them, she then looked hard at the old man and said. "Ah Fred, before we start I don't want to see that young man in my school again, just in case he should turn any of my young ladies heads." [she looks hard at Bobby] Now, I have a job for you that needs some thought, she stands and walks to the large bay window and looks out into the grounds,
 "That clear patch of grass at the end of the garden, would it be possible to erect some swings and other such things to give my young ladies somewhere to go and relax?" Fred moves to the old ladies side and looks to where she was pointing and says, "aye, it can be done, but it

will be a job for the youngun here, leave it to him, he will get it sorted for thee."

Fred returned to Bobby's side and waited for the Matron to speak, the old woman turned and stared at Bobby for a full minute before saying,

"So be it, but I warn you young man to stay away from my young ladies, they aren't for the likes of you."

Bobby felt himself tense and he leaned over the table, he held his face inches from the old woman's pinched face.

"Who do you think you are fucking talking to Matron, my family owns this school and all the land around it, so don't tell me that your young ladies aren't for the like of me ever again, or I promise you that you will be out of here quicker than you can imagine and I will then personally turn this place into a hotel. Got it?" With that he turned and walked out of the silent room, before she had a chance to speak.

When Fred found Bobby he was standing on the patch of grass that the Matron wanted renovating. Fred stood by his side and began to chuckle.

"I've always wanted to put that old witch in her place, I've never had the nerve to do it. The reason that the gardeners here are all old was to protect her young ladies, if you want my advice young'un, if you get the chance, fuck each and every one of them young ladies and the teachers as well." The old man began to chuckle again as he walked away. Bobby looked back at the Matrons office, before turning away and joining the old man as he walked out of the school gardens.

Chapter 2

Bobby was fuming as he drove down the along the long drive in his black BMW X5, he slowed down as he passed Helens cottage, not seeing her little red car there he carried on up to the house, he walked into house to see Helen on a tall pair of steps dusting the top of a large picture, Bobby rushed over and held the stepladder for her, she looked down at him and said.

"Thank you kind Sir." He smiled up at her which made her blush a deep crimson, when she turned back to her task, he looked at her tight ass in her faded blue jeans, when he felt his cock jerk in his own jeans, he thought to himself fuck it and asked.

"Can I come around for a chat tonight, I could bring a bottle of wine?" Helen looked down at him trying to figure out what he meant, did he just want to chat or did he want to rip her clothes of and ravish her? She wasn't sure, so she said.

"Why don't you come around for something to eat about 7, I can put up something for old Fred, so we won't have to worry about him." All Bobby could do was nod his head in agreement and think to himself hopefully,

"Was this the night I finally lose my virginity? I do hope so"

Bobby had showered and changed his clothed three times, was this how a teenager felt on his first date he thought to himself, finally ready he chose a nice bottle of red wine and drove nervously down the long drive to Helen's cottage. When he arrived at her cottage the door was slightly open, so he pushed the door open and called out her name.

"In here" she called out. Bobby followed the wonderful cooking smells into the kitchen to see Helen standing by the Aga stirring something in a copper saucepan, Helen turned and smiled as he walked into the kitchen, Bobby smiled back and could tell that she had made as much of an effort as he had, because she looked as sexy as hell, she had naked feet and legs that disappeared inside a thin flowered summer dress, her freshly washed blond hair hung loosely down her back, she had on just enough makeup to finish herself of perfectly. Bobby went over to her and kissed her lightly on her cheek, they both took a deep breath of the others scent before he said.

"That smells good but not as good as you." He could have kicked himself for what he had just said, but he needn't have worried, because she said.
"My aim was to please you kind sir." She blushed and turned her attention back to stirring the sauce. For something to do he searched a few drawers to find a bottle opener, having found one he stood opening the bottle and could sense her looking at him, he glanced up to catch her looking at the bulge in his jeans, she instantly blushed and turned away. Bobby poured them both a glass of wine and sat down at the table watching her slowly moving the wooden spoon around in the pot, wondering what she was thinking, hoping that she was thinking the same as him. Helen took some warm bread out of the warming oven and placed the bread on the table. She then dished up the Spaghetti Bolognese and they chatted while they ate, both nervous at first but slowly relaxing with each other. The meal finished and with the washing up done, the dishes were left to dry. They were still chatting nervously, but by now the sexual tension in the room hung heavily in the air. The clearing up all done and now forgotten, they stood looking at each other.

Helen took the bull by the horns and taking his hand she led him into the bedroom, she closed the door behind them and stood leaning against it, looking at her soon to be young fit lover Helen began to undo the buttons on her dress, she began at the top and undid every button on the dress, leaving the dress closed but unbuttoned the rest was up to him, she looked up at him and waited, she was so wet and swollen between her legs that if he didn't react soon, she would have to put two fingers into her wet fanny and take care of herself, one way or another. Helen looked down at the bulge in his jeans, his hardness was starting to stretch down his leg, just as she had hoped he was definitely big down there. She now knew that Bobby was a virgin so she removed the thin dress from her shoulders and let it fall to the floor, she now stood naked in front of this man that she had wanted for so long, still he didn't move but his eyes took in every inch of her fine body, lingering on her recently shaved fanny. Helen walked to him and lifting his hands she placed one hand on each breast, he looked down at his hands as they caressed her firm breasts, she slid her own hands under his tee shirt and onto his hard torso, she took his nipples between her fingers and twisted then bringing forth a moan so deep she thought he had just cum in his pants. Bobby took the hint and began twisting her nipples, she lifted his tee shirt and he reached up and removed it and dropped it on the floor, she lowered her lips to his nipples, as she began sucking and chewing his man nipples, bringing even deeper moans from him. Helen looked up into his face and moved herself against him, pushing her naked fanny against his hard cock, as she began rubbing herself back and forth she realised that he was literally seconds away from coming, so she pulled away from him.

Bobby stood there with his eyes closed, his hips moving back and forth. Helen reached down and undid his belt, tiny groans were coming from him so she undid his top button and drew his zipper down, reached inside and gripped his thick cock. At her touch his cock began to jerk in her hand, she dropped to her knees and took the head of his jerking cock into her hot mouth. Bobby grunted and exploded, Helen swallowed every drop of his virgin cum, that he had to offer, she continued to pleasure him until he was standing full hard again, standing up she took his hand and led him to her bed, she let go of his hand and lay down on the soft bed, he removed his clothes and lay down beside her.

Bobby went to speak but she put her fingers to his lips, smiled, turned him onto his back and whispered.
"Lay still my love and let me teach you how to make love to a woman."
With that she lifted herself up and straddled his hard body, she moved above him and when she was in the correct position, she reached beneath herself and gripped his long thick cock. With the head of his big cock held at her entrance, she closed her eyes, held her breath and slipped slowly down his thick shaft, stretching her inner self more than ever before. Helen now fully embedded on his whole length of his massive cock, moved her knees closer to his body, she lowered her right breast into his mouth and let him suck her nipple to its hardest, she repeated this with the other nipple and placed her hands either side of his head, she waited for him to look into his eyes before she began to slowly ride him, she watched him carefully and using her skills she stopped riding him when he was close, she would stay still and allow him to calm down enough for her to carry on. Helen stopped and whispered,
"Hold my tits and bend your knees up, when I start going faster I want you to thrust upwards as I sink down on you" his response was to grip both of her tits and bend his legs up, now he was ready, she closed her

eyes and began to ride him slowly but deliberately. Helen could feel her orgasm getting ever closer, so she picked up her speed, Bobby did as she had asked, and was soon grunting himself.

The lovers met each other stroke for stroke, Helen was now sat upright her hands gripped in her hair, urgent moans coming from her throat, his first deep spurt of his hot cum brought forth her own powerful orgasm. They rode each other perfectly until she finally sank down onto him and rested her hands on his chest, she blew loose hair from her sweat soaked face and thrust her hips back and forth as quickly as she could bringing forth another very strong orgasm. When she opened her eyes, he lay there with a broad smile on his face and whispered,
"Thank you darling Helen, you know that was my first time don't you?",
"Yes, I know my love, but it won't be your last, let me teach you everything I know, that way you will know how to give pleasure, as well as receive it" she said, his only response was to nod his head and whisper thank you. She lifted herself from him and drenched his limp cock and inner thighs with a mixture of warm cum as his thick cock flopped down onto his thigh, she climbed from the bed and wiped herself with a tissue as their warm love juices ran down both of her legs, she moved back to the bed and looked down at her perfect young lover, she reached out and gently gripped his sticky limp cock, she pulled the foreskin back to look at his huge purple knob, she moved her hand up and down his shaft and looked into his eye and said.
"I'm going to get it hard again and then you can do it to me from behind, [when he frowned, she said] don't worry I will talk you through it." She then lowered her mouth and began to lick his cock clean, starting at the base and finishing up on his knob, he was half hard already, but as soon as she began to move her warm mouth up and down his shaft, she felt him grow and grow, she lifted her eyes to look at him. Bobby rested himself on his elbows and watched this wonderful woman, giving him new untold pleasure.

Helen was satisfied that he was as hard as he could be, she lifted her head from his cock and climbed onto the bed, she turned her back to him and placed herself on her hands and knees. She looked back at him, he had moved up behind her on his knees, and she could tell he was trying to figure it out for himself, so she left him to it. Bobby soon worked it out and had his big knob at her entrance, she reached behind herself with her right hand and pulled him into her willing body. Now buried deep inside her he just held himself still, so she told him to grip her hips and move his own hips back and forth. It was like switching a light on as Bobby was soon ramming his big cock into her for all he was worth, there was no finesse just years of stored up questions and sexual wondering, this was simple animal lust, he was fucking her for all he was worth, and she had to admit that she was really enjoying it, she had cum twice and was closely heading fast towards another strong orgasm.

Helen began thrusting back at him, now this was turning into the fuck of her life. Suddenly Bobby called out and exploded inside her, her response was to scream out at the top of her voice and enjoy her own very strong orgasm, she gripped his cock with her fanny muscles which made him groan deeply, to give him yet another first experience she began gripping and releasing his shaft. This drove him mad and he began ramming his cock into her again, she didn't quite know how but he was rock hard again and fucking her hard, she had to say this for Bobby, he was a fast learner. Helen let herself go limp in his strong hands and enjoyed getting a good fucking for a change. Charles was a good lover at the beginning, but just lately he was always too tired for sex, but now she had brought Bobby out of his shell, she would fuck him where ever and whenever she could.

They slept together that first night, the next morning at breakfast she asked him what he knew about sex and the female body, Bobby lowered his eyes and said.
 "What you thankfully showed me last night was the total sum of my knowledge, I'm sorry if I was a disappointment." She reached out and touched his hand, his fingers curled around hers as she said. "Stand up Bobby" he stood and she moved around to sit on the edge of the table in front of him, she then opened her dressing gown and sat there naked, she placed her feet onto the table and parted her knees. Helen took her time and told him what did what and what went where, she used her hand to guide his fingers as they explored her most intimate place, inside and out. Helen asked him if he wanted to know anything more, he sort of hesitated but at her insistence he said.

"I watched a film once at a friend place and there was this bloke using his tongue down there, will you show me how to do that to you?" Helen smiled and said.

"With pleasure, pull up a chair and sit down." Helen then talked him through every step of giving a woman oral pleasure, she pointed out all the sensitive parts and places. When he had the knowledge in his head, he carried on and with a fair amount of practice, gave his first lover an orgasm with his mouth, when he heard her scream out in orgasm a thrill shot through his body, he lifted his head and look at the prone woman. Using his new skill he stood up and put his big knob at her entrance, he could see that he had to lift her legs, doing so he then pushed his cock mighty cock into her, she reached out and gripped the edge of the table with both hands and her on.

She didn't even open her eyes to look at him, he took his time and when she lifted her legs onto his shoulders, he automatically gripped the insides of her thighs and at each thrust he gave her, every hard inch that he slid in and out of her willing body was gratefully received. Helen began moving her hips in time with him until she was close to her goal, she then lowered her legs and held them out as wide as she could, and screamed out at the top of her voice as she had the strongest orgasm of her life.

Bobby was so deep inside her body that she thought the he was almost touching her heart,

"Do it harder." She shouted. He didn't need telling twice, he gave her the orgasm that she so desperately desired, as soon as she slowed her hip movement, he followed suit and slowed his thrusting. This fuck was their best yet, Bobby was a very fast learner, in less than twenty-four hours he had gone from virgin to a controlled lover, he slowed when he needed to and he increased his speed when she needed him to, he had learned in such a short time how to read her bodies' most intimate signals, he had learned a gift that some men never mastered in their whole lifetime.

Chapter 3

Bobby was at the school working on a tractor, he was making holes in the hard ground for the poles that would create the extra-long swing, it was a hot summers day and he was working shirtless when a group of young ladies seemed to magically appear from no-where, they were all standing around watching him work when a woman in her early thirties shooed them away. Bobby stopped the tractor and looked at the young woman.

He climbed down from the tractor to speak to her, her eyes were instantly devouring his hard body, as he walked over to the good looking petite woman in her grey business suit and looking to her firm tits, he asked.
"Can I help you miss, I am so sorry if I have done something wrong?" The woman was flustered as it has been a long time since she had been this close to a half-naked man, she stuttered.
"No, no there is nothing wrong, but what are you doing and does the Matron know about all of this?"

He smiled and said
"The Matron has asked me to build a relaxation area for your young ladies, this particular piece will be swings, miss?." She looked into his sparkling blue eyes, the slightest touch from this wonderful man and she would cum on the spot, she could feel the dampness in her pants, which was a feeling she hadn't had in a very long time.
"Charlotte Brent but people call me Charlie, what's your name?" She asked. He placed his hand into the small of her back and eased her towards a trestle table, at his first touch he felt a tremble go through her body, and if from what Helen had taught him, Miss Charlotte had just cum in her pants.
"Bobby and people just call me Bobby." They both laughed out loud at this,
"Let me show you the plans for the small park." They leant over the table, Charlie made a point of leaning against him. Bobby went through the plans and said "I should have the swings done by tonight, if you want to come back just as it is getting dark, I will give you a ride." He

smiled and she blushed deeply getting his double meaning. Charlie didn't answer, she just turned and walked away back towards the school.

Bobby was sat on the highest crossbar tightening up the last of the bolts that held the swings in place, it was just getting dark and he was thinking about his supper when a quiet voice said.
"Is it ready to ride on yet?" He had forgotten about the lovely Miss Charlotte, he looked into the gloom and could just about make her out, so he climbed down and went to one of the swings and held the ropes,
"Take a seat and I will push you." The young woman sat on the swing and allowed him to push her, she laughed out loud as they did this for a good couple of minutes, when she began to drag her feet trying to stop herself, he grabbed the ropes and used his strength to pull her to a stop. Bobby held the ropes and she just sat there so he lowered his mouth to her neck and began kissing her around her ears, he reached around and felt her right breast through her thin clothing, she turned to him and whispered,
"Not here, take me somewhere where we can do it properly." He took her hand and led her to his car, as soon as they were underway her hand was in his lap stroking his big cock.

When they arrived at the big house, he climbed out of the car but she stayed where she was and when he opened her door, she asked him.
"Do you live here?" Helping her out of the car and smiling he said,
"Yes, just myself and my grandfather, you can choose any room you want". He took her from room to room, she would walk into each room with her hands behind her back and have a good look around and if she wasn't happy, she would just turn and walk back out again. When they walked into the master bedroom, she smiled and went and sat on the bed and began undoing the buttons on her white blouse.

Bobby said he would take a quick shower as he was all sweaty, she looked at him and shook her head,
"I like a man to be all sweaty and ready, look Bobby it has been a long time since I have had a man, close the door and get your clothes off" they watched each other as they undressed, she had nice firm upturned tits with long thin nipples that were as hard as they could possibly be, she was now sat on the side of the bed in her small white pants, he

stood by the door in his boxers his cock at half-mast and straining at the thin material of his under clothe, he placed his fingers into the sides of his boxers and waited, all the time looking at her, she knew that game, stood up and put her fingers into the sides of her pants, as if by some silent signal they pushed down at the same time. Now both naked he walked towards the bed. Her eyes never left his half hard cock as it swayed from side to side every step that he took, and as if by magic her hand reached out and gripped his thick shaft and began to urgently wank it to full hardness. He lowered his right hand and she opened her legs and pushed her hips forward in anticipation, his fingers went to work inside her tightness, using his free hand he pulled her head down towards his big cock, she resisted him so he stopped pushing, she looked up and said.

"I never have, but I know what you want me to do to you, maybe after we have done it, I will try then?" he nodded and eased her back down onto the bed, he gripped her hips and eased her bottom towards the edge of the bed, she automatically lifted her legs and opened them wide for him, he gripped his hard cock and glanced down at her neatly trimmed fanny hair. Charlie had really swollen fanny lips that were already covered in pale cum, as he pushed his big hard cock into her slim body, she grunted, arched her back and gripped the bed clothes, he managed to get three quarters of his big cock into her before she tried to pull away from him. He placed his arms under her slim legs and gripped her inner thighs, in turn she reached out and gripped the edge of the bed, he began with short but firm strokes, she grunted at each of his firm thrusts but was now game for whatever he wanted to do to her, in under a minute she began to buck underneath him, she lifts her head and bared her teeth as she went through her first proper orgasm in a very long time.

When Charlie had calmed down she placed her hand on his chest and said.
"Please stop for a minute, I had forgotten what it was like to have a cock inside of me, turn me over and fuck me as hard as you can" so he pulled out of her and in a flash she turned over and backed towards the edge of the bed, he gripped his sticky cock and guided it back into her, only this time she took all of his length in one thrust, before he could start thrusting again, she turned and said.

"Please Bobby, don't cum inside me if you can help it" he smiled and gave her a deep thrust to get her mind back on the job in hand, he could see her clenched fists as they gripped the bedclothes. Bobby used all the skills that he had learned from Helen and fucked her perfectly, he rode her at a steady rate until she showed signs of being close to her goal, he would then speed up and take her through her much needed orgasm. After her third orgasm she seemed to be tiring, so using his strength he lifted her bodily from the bed,

"Grab a pillow" he said, when she held the pillow in her hands, he literally carried her over to the table, still buried to the hilt inside her, she laid the pillow down lengthways and he then lowered her down onto shiny surface, he waited for her to grip the sides of the table, as soon as she had he began riding her again. Bobby looked down to where her almost transparent fanny skin was stretched tight around his thick shaft. Helen had told him that he was a natural shagger, he smiled at the thought and made a decision, the next time she came, he would stop and try something else.

He was ramming his cock into her so hard he thought that the legs on the table were going to break, she went limp on the flat surface so he stopped moving and just held himself still inside her, he looked down at her prone body as her back heaved, as she took deep breaths, when he pulled his cock out of her she gasped out loud and turned to look at him and said,

"Where did you learn to fuck like this, I ain't used to all this, I need a rest" so he moved back and let her stand upright, she instantly looked down at her fanny juices as they ran down her legs, he gripped her hand and took her to the wide window sill once she was sat down he pulled her to him, and lifted her up bodily and said.

"Reach under yourself and put it back in, once-more and then you can rest" she did as he asked and when she slipped down his thick cock this time, she groaned out loud because she was so sore. Bobby took hold of her and used his body strength to lift her up and down on his cock, he had done this with Helen and particularly liked this, Charlie began groaning but gripped him around the neck, she closed her eyes as he abused her tiny body. When his first spurt exploded inside her, it burned her insides, she screamed out at the top of her voice, but she gripped his cock hard with her fanny lips as he pumped his hot spunk into her, when he stopped spurting she leaned back and ground herself against him all the time groaning as her orgasm, seemed to rumble on forever and ever.

Charlie finally collapsed against him and cried, her back heaving as giant sobs racked her small body. He held onto her with his right hand while he stroked her with his left hand, his own heart thumping in his chest from his exertions. His cock slipped from her stretched fanny followed by a loud fanny fart, which seemed to startle her for a second or two, she eased away from him to look down between their bodies to see sexual fluids freely running from her body and. Dripping onto the wooden floor, she moved away from him and went into the en-suite to clean herself up.

When she came out of the small room she seemed to be a bit shy all of a sudden, in her hand she carried a wet flannel and a towel, she cleaned his cock and wiped it dry, she looked up into his eyes, smiled, saying,
"I have never had sex like that before, where did you learn to do it like that, it seemed to last for hours and I am so sore up inside" he smiled and said.
"That's a real shame because I had other ideas for you" she shook her head and said.
"I'm sorry Bobby but I don't think I could do it, maybe in the morning if we meet up somewhere?" He frowned and said. "Does this mean that you aren't staying the night?"
"I can't, I have to get back to the school soon, I'm on call tonight, I'm sorry I didn't tell you, but tomorrow night I can stay all night if you want?" he looked down and lifted his limp cock, shook it from side to side and said. "But look, my friend is all disappointed" She looked at his limp manhood, smiled and said. "It wouldn't be much use like that anyway, would it?" He pulled her to him and eased her down to her knees and then holding his cock out to her, she instantly knew what he wanted, so she lowered her head, but just before she closed her mouth over his big knob, she looked up into those to die for eyes and said. "If I don't do it right will you tell me?" He nodded and she lowered her head and took his tender knob into her warm mouth, she lubricated his big knob with spittle before she slowly managed to get him hard again, once hard he lifted her head from his lap, she looked into his eyes quizzically. Bobby pulled her up and took her to the soft bed, he lay down first and eased her down on top of him, he placed her knees ei-

ther side of his head and waited until he felt her hot sweet lips close around his cock, he then returned the compliment by placing his mouth onto her very sensitive fanny. He began by licking her slowly from bottom to the top, over and over until Charlie was moaning out loud. When he placed his puckered lips over her hard clit, she groaned out loud and lifted her mouth from his cock, as she moaned out loud and enjoyed another glorious orgasm. Once over her climax she lowered her head back to her task only now she was much more urgent, as she tried her best to please him, she felt his fingers open her entrance and his long silky tongue enter her most intimate part in search of her heavenly cum.

Her head was now bouncing up and down his shaft, she could tell by the noises that he was making that he was close, she herself was close again as he continued his deep search. She readied herself for what was about to come, this was the part that she had dreaded the most, but she would do her best to swallow it all, when he pushed his hips up high and grunted she lowered her mouth down his shaft as far as she could to try and allow his seed to shoot straight down her throat, in the hope that she didn't have to taste it. Her plan seemed to work until he began thrusting his hips up and down almost choking her. He realised what he had done and lay still and let her do her thing, when she could no longer suck his cock because her jaw ached so much, she lifted her head and looked back at him. They smiled at one another as she lifted herself from him, turning around she lay by his side and rested her head on his hairy chest, she could hear his heart pounding in his chest and then realised that her own heart must be doing the same thing but there was one feeling that she had that she would always remember and that was the way that her fanny was tingling at this precise moment in time.

Bobby brought up the possibility of her being pregnant, she shrugged her shoulders and told him not to worry, she would take care of it in the morning, with the morning after pill. He dropped her off near the school with the promise to meet up again soon for a repeat performance, he smiled two days later when he received a text from her, telling him that she had sorted out their problem, and that she herself would be out of action for a few days, but if there was anything that she could possibly do for him, he only had to name the time and place.

Bobby was working flat out on the ladies rides, some of the young ladies had begun using the swings and had been trying to engage him in conversation, but he had decided to try his best and stay away from them, if he possibly could. A blond haired young lady was being pushed by her friend and unusually she was using the swing facing him, she had tried talking to him, but he had ignored her until she said.

 "Are you gay mate?" he squatted down on his haunches and looked at the young lady and said. "No I am not gay; far from it but I would hate to scare you with what I have." The two girls whispered to each other and then the girl on the swing eased her bum forward on the swing, she took a look around and seeing no-one looking, she opened her legs and let him get a good look up her skirt, he shook his head and said.

 "I've seen a pair of pants before young lady, it will take more than that to turn me on" he went to start work again, when she said.

"Wait, [she took another look around then continued] if I show you, will you show us yours?" he shook his head and shrugged, the two girls whispered again, then the one that had been doing the pushing turned around and held her skirt out, the young lady on the swing put her hands up her skirt and gripped the sides of her pants and pulled them down and off, she passed them to her friend and then opened her legs again, he could see the top of her pubic hair but that was all and said so, she spoke to her friend again, reassured she turned to face him again and lifted her feet onto the swing and opened her knees as far as she could, he nodded and said very nice, she lowered her feet to the floor and said.

"Your turn." He nodded to them to follow him, he went to his van and opened the side doors, behind them was the thick woods when he opened the doors it acted like a shield.

Now that they were somewhat out of sight he looked at the swing pusher and said.

"Let me see your tits" she took a quick look around but quickly lifted her top to show him a fine pair of young, firm tits. He put his hand on his belt and undid it, he started on his zipper but stopped and asked them.

"Are you sure about this?" both girls nodded enthusiastically, so he opened his jeans and pulled his big thick cock out, both young ladies gasped out aloud, the pant less one asked.

"Is it heavy, can I hold it?" he folded her hand around his cock and began moving it back and forth, he watched as she held her breath as it began to grow in her hand, her friend said.

"Quick, let it go Suzy it's scary" but Suzy was having none of it and kept her hand moving up and down his thickening shaft, he told Suzie's friend to check that no-one was coming, she was gone for only seconds, when she was back she stood watching the scene in front of her. Bobby asked how old they were, both said 17 so he reached out and put his hand up Suzie's skirt and rubbed her bum cheeks, she didn't seem to mind so he tried to get his fingers underneath her bottom to her fanny, she realised what he was trying to do and pulled away from him and turned sideways on to him, which placed her young wet fanny against his hand.

Bobby pushed his finger along her slit to her entrance, he had to encourage her to open her legs with the back of his hand, she opened her legs for him to allow him to push a finger inside her, he began to frig her and within a minute she anointed his finger with her virgin cum. She shuddered all over, gasped out loud, she hugged her friend and said

.

"Fuck me Liz you have got to try that, it's fucking great." Liz was a bit nervous but Suzy checked that no-one was coming and went back behind the van, he had managed to get her hand around his cock, he had tried to get his hand up her skirt, but she had pulled away from him, Suzy saw what she had done and said.

"Let him do it to you Liz, you will love it I promise" she didn't hesitate in putting her hands up her friends skirt and pulling her friends pants down, Suzy stepped out of her blue pants, so he placed his hand between her legs and did the same to her with his finger, only when she came, her knees bent and she almost passed out on the spot.

Suzy held her friend until she had calmed down and then said .

"We had better be getting back." He said "Whoa there ladies, you can't leave me like this can you, I made you both cum now it was my turn" the two ladies began whispering again until Liz went and looked around again to see if the coast was clear, she nodded to her friend who turned to him and said. "If I let you do it to me do you promise not to make me pregnant?" he smiled and said. "Only if I can shoot it over Lizzies tits" another quick whispering session and the deal was made, she just stood there so he eased her around and told her to bend over and grip the side of the van, when she was ready he lifted her skirt over her back and then eased her feet apart, he took up position behind her.

Bobby had to physically lift her small frame of the ground to enable him to enter her tight fanny, his first push took him to her barrier, his second push took her screaming into womanhood. Suzie screamed out as he forced his giant cock deeper inside her small frame, the young woman did well for the very first time, he gave her a few seconds to recover before he began to ride her, she was soon into fucking in a big way, she moaned at every thrust he made. He was now pulling her back to meet his forward thrusts, he knew that she had cum at least twice, but she was so tight that he knew that he would not last much longer. He turned to Liz to see that she had her fingers inside herself and was close to her own orgasm, he watched her finish and pulled her forwards. "Get your tits out quick." She lifted her top and he bent her forwards, he grunted and pulled out of the one young woman, and shot his hot cum over the tits of the other.

All three were in a state of total disarray, Suzie recovered first and looked out to see if the coast was clear, she came back and leaned against the van and blew loose hair from her face, she glanced at her friends naked cum covered tits and did no more than began licking her tits clean. Liz realised that he was watching them and pulled her top down quickly, grabbed her friends hand and they were gone, leaving him slightly stunned but with two pairs of et pants on the ground and a huge smile on his face.

Chapter 4

The next few days were uneventful as far as his sex life was concerned, he hadn't seen the girls again, but he knew that they would be back for more, Charlie was away on a course of some kind, she texted him most days saying that she missed him and couldn't wait to get back and into the big bed again. He was at the present towing a trailer up the M6 towards Crewe to collect another fairground ride for the young ladies and with a bit of luck he should be back by early evening, maybe he could call in on Helen and have another lesson. He followed the sat-nav down a narrow lane country lane, he stopped at a pair of large green iron gates, hanging from the gate was a large iron ring with a hammer tied to it, so he hammered the ring and stood there waiting until what looked like a middle aged woman with short black hair came to the gate and said.

"Yes, can I help you?" He was shocked when she came closer, because she was maybe late 30's early 40s not pretty nor ugly, she wore a big coat so he couldn't see her body but had dismissed her sexually anyway. She opened the gate and walked in front of his van as she showed him the way, the ride was dismantled and under a blue tarpaulin which she pulled off with ease. He stood there looking at all the big pieces and wondered how he was going to get them onto the trailer on his own, but he need not have worried because the black haired woman said,

"Let me get changed and I will give you a hand." When she came back she wore a pair of tight green shorts and a blue tee shirt, he noticed instantly that she was bra less, she saw him looking and her thick nipples instantly became hard, he had better rethink his ideas as she may not be the best looking woman in the world, but she had a body to die for.

They loaded the trailer and tied the load into place, he took a roll of cash out of his pocket to pay her, she looked at the money and said.

"You best come up to the van where I can give you a receipt." He followed her into a new static home, inside was neat and tidy and very well furnished, he took a seat while she poured two glasses of cool cider. She passed him a glass and sat opposite him and said "my names Fran and I live here with me dad, he has one half and I have the other, he is out for a couple of days buying some more rides so if you want to keep in touch, maybe I can show you some more." She seemed to blush slightly at what she had said, to hide her embarrassment, stood up and went to the table and bent over to write out his receipt, he could see under her loose tee shirt as she bent over writing, her ample tits were hanging like two ripe melons, she glanced back to see if he was looking, seeing that he was she stood up and turned to him and said.

"Look Bobby, as you can see I don't get to see many men, what with me being cooped up here on me own all the time, I love sex but don't get much, so if you want a fuck, let's get on with it" when he stood up, she turned and walked to a door at the end of the van, when he followed her into the room, she had already removed her top and was now sat unabashed with her full breasts on view, she was undoing her shorts.

He began removing his clothes and when he opened his jeans and exposed his big cock, she smiled and said.

"I hope that you can use that big fucker?" his cock grew as she undressed further, he took a step towards her as she pushed her pants down her legs, when she stood up he thought that his cock would begin to shrink, because as she had the biggest patch of pubic hair in the world, the curly hair began at her bellybutton, it spread down in a thick line getting wider and thicker, the nearer it got to her fanny, she had thick hair at the top of both thighs, that spread a good 4 inches down her legs, she had enough pubic hair to make any man a toupee, he was about to pull away, when she sat down, reached out for his shaft, exposed his big knob and slipped big purple bell end into her mouth, he closed his eyes as she began to suck the life out of him, he reached out and gripped her hair at the side of her head and began to fuck her mouth, when a clanging sound filled the caravan, she pulled her mouth from his cock and said ."Who the fuck is that?" She stood up and got dressed, he watched her leave the caravan and go to the gate.

Bobby didn't hesitate he dressed and was soon back in the BMW, he made a sign that he would ring her as he drove past her, but the two young lads that were talking to her, would surely make up for his absence, he was sure of that as he drove on with a touch of relief in his heart.

Bobby was again working shirtless on the new ride that he had collected from Crewe. He had laid the base and was now on a digger trying to lower the top section onto the ride, he had noticed a tall thin blond girl watching him from over by the swings.

He lowered the top of the ride in place, but had to get down from the digger, lay down on the grass to look up underneath the ride to see if everything was in line, he had been lay there for maybe only a second, when the tall thin girl was suddenly stood by him, she was standing with her legs wide open so that he could see right up her skirt to her tiny white pants, that were definitely wet, he sat up and looked up at the thin girl and said.
"Can I help you miss?" she looked around and said. "Are you Bobby?" He said that he was as he stood up, and using one of the levers on the tractor to lower the top down onto the ride, he lay back on again just to recheck the ride when the girl almost stood over his head, he looked up the long body, he had a good look under her skirt before standing up, wiping his hands on a piece of cloth he stood there looking at this tall gangly girl, she must have been getting on for six feet tall.
"I made them tell me what you did to them, those two slags now I want you to do it to me, or I will tell the Matron what you did to them" she said.
"What if I don't want to do to it to you, maybe I don't fancy you one little bit what
then?" He snapped. "But you have to do it to me, you must." She was almost crying by this point, he then realised what was going on, this tall girl/woman was the school bully and had told all of the other girls that she was going to get fucked by the school handyman, he took her by the hand and took her behind his van, he sat her down on the side of his van and looked down at her and then said. "You can stop here for five minutes and then go back, what you tell them is up to you, but I ain't going to do it to you just because you bragged that I would." She had her had bowed and tears running down her face as she said. "But you can do it if you want to, I don't mind honest" he shook his head and asked her. "Look tell me, what's your name?" "Zoe," she said.

He knelt down in front of her and placed his hand on her leg, she almost jumped a mile at his touch, he stood up and looked down at the thin girl and asked her. "What have you said to the others Zoe?" she lowered her head again and sort of said. "I bragged that I had done it before, and your big cock didn't frighten me, so you see I can't go back without doing it can I, everyone will laugh at me." He pulled her up and said. "Look undo a couple of buttons on your blouse and do them up again wrong", he then went behind her and reached up her blouse and undid her bra, he then told her to take her pants off and put them In her pocket, he placed his hands on her shoulders and looked her in the eyes and said. "Now go back and tell them what you want to tell them, and when you are ready yourself to do it, and you will know when, come back and I will make you a woman, I promise ok?" She nodded and looked him in the eyes and said. "Thank you Bobby, will you at least kiss me so that what I tell them won't be a complete lie?" He pulled her up and took her in his arms and began to kiss her, she clung to him like a limpet, he pushed his tongue into her mouth and she shuddered in his arms, he put his hands on her ass and pulled her fanny mound hard against his hard cock, he moved her back and forth along his length, she was almost ready, but not quite because she pulled away from him and looked down at his had cock. She then reached out and gripped it once before she turned around and ran back to the school.

Which left him with a hard on, so he took out his phone and texted Charlie the words [ten minutes] within seconds a message came back [I will be there] Bobby smiled and climbed into his van, he drove down the lane to where they had arranged to meet, Charlie stepped out from behind a wall and climbed into the seat next to him and said
"I haven't much time Bobby, can we do it in the van only I have to stay close to the school" he turned into a gate way, when he had pulled to a stop she had her blouse open and her tits on view and had her hands up her skirt, trying to get her pants off, she looked across at her lover and said. "Come on Bobby get that big cock out and get it into me quick.

 He kicked his flip flops of and undid his shorts, as soon as his cock sprang into the open, she gripped it with her right hand and began wanking it furiously, he pulled her near naked body to him and pushed his bum forwards on his seat, he pulled her into position in his lap and eased her upwards, she reached under herself and gripped his thick head and placed it at her entrance, she then slid slowly down his length until she was fully embedded on it, she then moved her knees closer to him and the leaned back slightly until she was leaning against the steering wheel, he began fondling her tits, she closed her eyes and gripped him around the neck and began to ride him, she began slowly at first moaning every-time she reached full depth on his magnificent cock.

Her orgasms were reached by closing her eyes and fucking him with her fanny muscles clenched tight around his thick cock, she had cum numerous times when he lifted her up bodily and began ramming his cock into her for all he was worth, this was now his turn only this time she wanted him to cum inside her, she wanted to feel him cum again, she wanted to feel his hot cum burn her insides. Charlie screamed into his ear as he released his soldiers into her willing body, they thrust against each other for all they were worth, until he slipped unceremoniously out of her, followed by a gushing of mixed love juices.

Within seconds she was sat in the passenger seat putting her tits away and doing the buttons up on her blouse, she took a handful of tissues out of her pocket and rammed the tissues against her fanny and pulled her pants up her legs, checked her face in the mirror, kissed him and she was out of the door and gone. Bobby sat there with his wet sticky cock lay across his thigh wondering if everyone's sex life was as complicated as his was?

Chapter 5

When Bobby walked out to his van the next morning there was a brown envelope under his windscreen wiper, he unfolded it to see that it was from his grandfather saying simply Matron want's thee, so he drove towards the school with a head full of dreaded thoughts about who had said what to whom.

Bobby walked into the school with a heavy heart, the young ladies were all at lessons, which was a good thing, he tapped on the door and waited, the tiny voice invited him into her office, he walked in and sat down, the withered old spinster continued to write for a full minute before she took her time to screw the top onto her fountain pen and then place it in a precise position on her blotter, she then threaded her finger into each other and cleared her throat and looked up at the handsome young man sat in front of her and said
"seeing that we cannot get rid of you and protect our young ladies from you, it has been decided that we make better use of you inside the school, you see we need all the lighting changed in every classroom, we need you to change the naked bulbs to fluorescent light fittings and when that is done there is a list of other jobs that need doing, now the work must be carried out after lessons, now was that at all possible?" he looked up at the bare light bulb in her office, smiling said that he would start in her room.

Bobby walked around the school and looked into every classroom, much to the joy of the young ladies, he saw Lizzie and Susie both girls gave him a wave and blew him a kiss, before being shouted at by the teacher, he turned and looked at the teacher standing at the head of the class, she was young maybe only mid-twenties, she was very beautiful, even though her hair was pulled back so severely, just like all of the other teachers.

She stood maybe 5ft 8 very slim and looked daggers at him because she had caught him looking at her ample tits, she began waving him away from the window, but before he knew it she had stepped out of the classroom and was saying "you-there, what are you doing?" he had on his tight shorts and flip flops with a skin tight tee shirt, as he walked towards her eyes were locked onto the bulge in his tight shorts, he stood very close to the teacher and said "I have to change you lighting at some point and I just wanted to see how desperate you were to have it done" he looked at his notepad and wrote

"Desperate" the teacher blushed a deep red and stamped her foot, turned away and returned to her classroom where the room fell silent, he stood and looked at her through the window, she pretended not to look at him, but she blushed all over again.

Bobby ordered what he would need to change all the light fittings in the old schools classroom's, one or two of the girls had asked him if he would be doing the bedrooms as well, his answer was simple

"Yes, if you are very lucky" he began work on the lights, choosing the rooms that were empty, but he was biding his time to catch a certain young teacher working late or on her own. He was maybe three quarters of the way through the classrooms when he saw the young teacher that he had his eye on, sat on her own in the classroom marking papers, he tapped the door and walked in carrying a large set of step ladders, she ignored him when he first walked in, but he had his shorts on again, the ones that showed his cock of the best.

Bobby began work and when he was at the highest point on the steps he asked her

"excuse me miss, do you think you could hold the steps for me please, just while I do this bit?", she looked up at him and he pretended to wobble the steps, the beautiful young teacher made a tutting sound, but stood up and walked over to him, she looked up to see his big cock outlined in his shorts, just like he knew she would, he finished doing what he needed to do and climbed down the steps.

Bobby stood looking at her until she sat back down at the desk again, and began to do her work,

"Thank you miss?" she never looked up at him but said

"It's Mrs Tombs, Sylvia Tombs and I want you to know that I am very happily married, thank you" he smiled and sat on the edge of her desk, so that his big cock was nearest her and she couldn't help but look at it,

"How about a drink one night Sylvia, just for a quiet chat?" she placed her pen down and turned to look at him and said

"I know what you are after Mr Francis and you will not get it from me" she awaited his reply which when it came it made her smile

"Why don't you call me Bobby like everyone else here, then we could be friends, I only want to be your friend Sylvia" she shook her head and said

"But Mr Francis I have told you that I am a happily married woman, and I am not interested in the slightest" she glanced at his cock as she said this.

"Just maybe, I could come around and see you with a nice bottle of wine, we could have a nice chat, tell me where you live Sylvia" she looked up at him and said

"I live with my husband Brian in Rose Cottage just at the end of Barbers Lane, but please don't come around, my husband wouldn't be a happy man if he caught you there" she lowered her head back to her papers and began work. He finished his work and placed his mouth by her ear and whispered,

"I will walk past at about 9 o'clock tonight and if I don't see a car in the drive, I will knock on the back door" she didn't answer him so, she didn't exactly say no did she?.

Bobby parked a little way down the lane from Rose cottage, he knew the way to the back of her cottage from his younger days, and from where he was standing he could see that there was no car in the drive, so he walked down the lane to the back door of the cottage and tapped the door, she opened the door and stood there holding the door saying "You just don't give up do you Bobby Francis, but I will not be letting you in" he waved the bottle of red wine and said,

"Be a shame to waste this fine wine, just one drink, eh?" she stood back and let him enter her kitchen, she turned and went to do something in the sink.

She may not have admitted it, but she had made an effort in her appearance, she had let her dark hair hang freely down her back and she had on a flowered dress that if the sun was in the right direction you would be able to see right through its thin material, finally her blue shoes brought her almost up to his height. Bobby stepped up behind her and placed his hands on her waist and gentle leaned against her, she

didn't resist him and when he pushed his cock into her bottom she couldn't help, but push back just a tiny bit, he placed his lips to her ear and nibbled her earlobe, a deep moan escaped her throat. He pushed his hands under her arms and gently caressed both of her breasts.
Sylvia Tombs was lost as she closed her eyes, she had decided to give herself fully to this beautiful man, when she felt his hand move up her naked leg, her heart began to race and she opened her legs in readiness. Sylvia turned her face and placed her lips onto his, letting him know that she was all his. When his finger slid along her swollen fanny lips to her opening she pushed her hips forward to allow him to slip his fingers inside her most secret place.

When his fingers entered her, she reached for his hard cock and felt him through his trousers. She was able to grip his thick shaft and moved her hand back and forth, she had never wanted a man this bad in all of her life before. Sylvia snatched his hand out of her pants and took a step away from him, looked into his eyes and said
"I draw the line at his bed, so if we are going to fuck it will have to be in the sitting room" with that she took his hand and led him into the other room, she closed the curtains and locked the doors and when she walked back into the sitting room she found him sat on the settee. She went to him and said. "Please let me see it." He undid his belt and then his trousers and reached in and pulled his big hard cock out, she reached behind her back by her neck and undid a few buttons and pulled the dress over her head and dropped it onto the floor to land in a heap. She stood there in a white pair of pants that were so damp he could see her pubic hair through the thin wet white material, he placed his fingers into the side of her pants and pulled them down to the floor, she showed no sign of embarrassment in her nakedness.

He eased her down beside him and made a point of removing his clothes in full view of her, she reached out and gripped his hard cock and began slowly wanking it. Standing in front of her he moved her hand and pulled her mouth towards his exposed head but she turned her head away and said. "I refuse to do that for my husband, so I will definitely not do it for you" he lowered himself down to his knees and opened her knees wide, he then reached forwards and pulled her bottom towards him making her lay back as he did so. Bobby lifted her knees and positioned his big cock at her entrance, he pushed forwards and his big cock slid inside her body, stretching her insides wide for the first time ever in her short life. When her husband had taken her virginity, he hadn't stretched her at all. She had used a vibrator on herself in desperation, while she had waited months for him to fuck her and when he finally got around to it, she had to admit that she was very disappointed, to the point that as soon as he was gone to work she took her biggest vibrator out of it's hiding place and gave herself another right fucking. Now this beautiful man with his big cock was stretching her beyond belief, she let her legs flop over his arms and was now willing him to begin hi work.

Bobby was a fine energetic lover, he rode her to her first ever orgasm with a real cock. He was a considerate lover and thought about her pleasure more than his own, he slowed down when he needed to and he increased his speed when required to take her through orgasm after orgasm. Sylvia Tombs had cum more on this wonderful night than ever before in her short life and still he hadn't cum. Bobby stopped and gently turned her over onto her hands and knees, when he re-entered her he was so beautifully deep inside her body that she wanted this fuck to last forever, he dug his strong hands into her soft hips and began fucking her with his big thick cock, she closed her eyes and lost herself in glorious feeling of perfect sex. Bobby was getting close himself and asked her if he should pull out, her only response was to shake her head and began thrusting back at him for all she was worth. The new lovers met each other stroke for stroke until he exploded deep inside her body, spurt after spurt erupted inside her and she had to admit that it was the best feeling that she had ever had in her whole life. Sylvia had dreamt of being fucked like that and now that she had been, she didn't care if she was never fucked ever again, but if he wanted to fuck her again, she would give herself to him willingly, where ever and however he wanted.

They were locked together as tight as could possibly be, he was deeper inside this woman than he had ever been before and his knob felt as if it was about to explode all over again. His slowly shrinking cock finally slid from her fanny and a mixture of their love juices ran freely from her and ran down both of her legs. The well fucked teacher hadn't moved a muscle, her head hung down so far that she could actually see the mixture of pale spunk bubbled from her gaping fanny, he flopped back onto his haunches, his limp cock lay twitching across his left thigh. He looked at her wide open fanny, with its pink twitching inner workings, as warm pale fluid oozed from her and dripped from her matted pubic hair, her back heaving from the effort of perfect love making. It was a few minutes before she turned and sat naked on the floor and smiled at this man who had given her so much pleasure, she reached out and pulled his lips to hers, they kissed like young lovers tongues fighting first in her mouth, and then in his. They rolled to the side and lay on the wooden floor, both bodies intertwined, pushing and thrusting against one another.

She wanted him back inside her and was prepared to do anything to get him there again. Sylvia pushed him onto his back and began kissing him from the throat downwards, she gripped his limp cock in her right hand and began wanking him hard and fast, he placed his hand on top of hers and eased her hand to a stop, he didn't say anything to her, she took it on her own back to lower her mouth to his exposed knob, she closed her mouth and gave him such good mouth sex, that he soon began to respond and get hard again, he could tell that she had sucked a cock before, but maybe she had had a bad experience in the past, and it had put her off, he wasn't sure but she was well and truly back in the saddle again now.

When he was as hard as she could get him, she turned from him and waited to be mounted again, he moved up behind her, but before he had even touched her she had tiny goose bumps all over her back. Bobby gripped her left hip and with his right hand he slid his hard cock back inside her, when he was deep inside her again, he gripped her other hip and spreading his knees he began to fuck her, this time he used deep longer, strokes bringing deep moans from her throat. They fucked as one, perfectly as only well practiced lovers can. Sylvia had strong orgasm after strong orgasm, each time he rode her perfectly to her climax, this time when he erupted inside her she screamed from somewhere deep in her throat, each spurt brought another loud scream, she sensed that at that precise moment, she had become pregnant. He pulled her back as hard as he could, but still she managed to squirm against him, this time when he slipped from her she got up off the floor and turned around and pulled his mouth against her gaping fanny, she gripped his hair and moved her fanny up and down his face, all that he could do was push his chin out as far as he could, this action alone brought an instant deep sensuous moan from her throat, her head was thrown back and she was howling at the top of her voice as yet another vicious orgasm, racked her tortured body. Finally she was done and slipped down his body until they were face to face.

She could see their love juices smeared all over his face, she took her time and licked every single drop from his beautiful face, she looked deep into his eyes and said
"I love you Bobby Francis and any time that you want me, you can have me, all you have to do is ask, now please go." She kissed him hard on the mouth and then stood up and walked naked from the room, leaving him there on his knees smiling, but well and truly fucked.

Chapter 6

It was a few weeks before he heard from Sylvia again, he saw her at the school, she was sat in front of a group of young ladies on the lawn, reading to them from a book, she sat facing him and he caught her looking up at him more than once, he wanted her again and he knew that she wanted him, but every time that he had walked past her cottage her husbands car had been on the drive. He chose his moment carefully, as she stood and followed her young ladies into the school, he just happened to be walking by her side, she dropped back slightly so that she was out of earshot of her charges and said.
"We need to talk Bobby, I will stay behind and do some marking in the garden, come to me then" and with that she turned from him, and followed her ladies into the school.

Bobby pushed a wheelbarrow full of tools into the garden and sat down by her side, she turned to him and pushed her thigh hard against his, and making sure that they were on their own she said
"I'm pregnant Bobby, but don't worry I will take full responsibility, my husband is overjoyed as he has wanted a child for a while, the child is yours Bobby, but that fact will stay between us, the only thing that I ask is for us to be together again, next week my husband has to travel to Germany for four nights, maybe we could spend the whole night together, if you don't want to come to mine we could always meet somewhere else?". Bobby's heart was pounding in his chest, he was going to be a father, but who could he tell without causing ructions for Sylvia and her husband. He wanted to meet her, he wanted to feel her trembling in his arms again. He said. "Which would be the best night for you Sylvia?" When she told him, he said that he would book a room at the Lygon Arms hotel in Broadway and meet her there. With the evening of sexual pleasures planned he left her there, smiling expectantly in the late summer sunshine.

The night came that promised them both sexual adventures but for Sylvia a chance to learn new things, when she arrived at the hotel he was sat at a corner table. He stood as she joined him, she glanced around to make sure that there was no-one there that she knew, but he had chosen the venue well. Not only was the Lygon a long way from the school, the hotel was discreetly situated. They enjoyed a fine meal together, even if the sexual tension hung heavily in the air, when the desert was done with, she touched his hand and whispered. "Can we go up now please?" Bobby smiled and picked up the champagne bucket, two flutes and stood up, Sylvia was instantly by his side, they walked to the lift together, she wanted to touch him there and then but there were cameras in the lift, so she would have to wait even longer, she was so wet and swollen between her legs and her hips had begun moving slowly back and forth in anticipation of the sexual marathon to come, whatever was the matter with her, she had never felt like this before about any man, but Bobby, she was just so desperate to feel him inside her again.

Once in the room he walked to the table and placed the champagne down and then turned to her, they stood looking at one another for a few seconds. It was Sylvia that spoke first, she said. "I have thought about nothing else other than this night Bobby, it is only fair on my husband that this will be our last night together and I want you to make love to me for as long as you possibly can. I will always love you Bobby Francis but I will never tell our child the truth about who her father is." With that she began to slowly remove her clothing, he stood and watched her every movement, and when she pushed her white silk pants down her slim legs, he gasped out loud at her recently shaved sex, at his gasp she looked up smiling broadly, she then parted her legs proudly and swooned at his stare, he suddenly became urgent and began almost tearing at his clothes.

Now naked and his readiness standing proudly in front of him she went to him, swaying seductively from the hips every step that she took, he tried to place his hand between her legs but her needs were more urgent than that, she brushed his hand away and walked to the end of the bed, gripping the frame of the four poster bed, she then bent forwards, parted her legs and closed her eyes in anticipation. His long thick cock entered her slim body easily and she was instantly lost. She began thrusting back at him in her urgency for the long awaited release of her glorious pent up orgasm, the groan when it came started somewhere deep inside her and when it left her throat, sounded almost animal like. He rode her for an age, moving her to the bed itself, then to the table and when he finally exploded inside her he was mounted on her from behind, she was on her hands and knees on the deep Indian rug, she knelt there with her head hanging down, her back heaving as he tried to get some oxygen into her lungs, he knelt behind her looking at her open fanny, her pink insides twitching and throbbing, mixed sexual fluids bubbling inside her cavern and oozing from her fanny and dripping onto the expensive carpet. Both needing to rest they crawled onto the bed, he lay down on his back and she covering him in soft tender kisses, now confident she closed her mouth over his tender cum covered purple knob and pleasured him to hardness again.

Sylvia kept him where he was and mounted him confidently, sinking down his thick shaft in one movement, she pulled her knees in close to his body and rode him as if she had ridden him a thousand times before, totally unabashed as she had climax after climax, she pleasured herself on his perfect hard cock, pulling her own breasts in all directions, gripping her hair in both hands, even touching her own clit in her moment of ecstasy, lost in the most glorious sexual moments of her life. Finally sated she curled herself around him and lost herself in the afterglow of perfect sex, it was then that she suddenly replayed the way that she had reacted to his lovemaking and fleetingly thought about the silent sex with her husband, her only response ever as far as she could remember to his efforts was a kiss on the cheek, when he had finished, she would then go into the bathroom on the pretext of cleaning herself up and take her vibrator out of it's hiding place and fuck herself stupid, but now that she had had Bobby Francis, she will need to send for a bigger, thicker longer, rubber cock.

They held each other in the soft bed and slept, when he woke in the morning she was gone, the only sign of her ever being there was the soreness of his big knob and her white silk panties that were lay out neatly on her pillow. They did speak quite regularly, but she had promised that their love making would never be repeated. He watched her blossom in her pregnancy until she was too big to work, he did hear that she gave birth to a beautiful daughter, whom she name Roberta.

It took Bobby quite a while to get over Sylvia, apart from the odd visit to Helen when circumstances allowed, his sex life had stagnated. But with the birth of his daughter an invisible weight had been lifted from his shoulders and he began to look at the young ladies again for his pleasure, he had seen the tall Zoe hovering at the edge of the gardens, it seems that she was trying to build up courage to approach him, because she knew that if she did go to him, then he would definitely fuck her this time, she just had to make her mind up if that was what she wanted. Over the next few days Zoe seemed to be there more and more, spending her break-times watching him work, he took the bull by the horns late one afternoon when she should have been in class, but had obviously skipped her lesson, she was hovering at the edge of the gardens by a large rhododendron so he climbed into his van and drove to where she was standing, he stopped by her side and reached over and opened the van door, she hesitated for a fraction of a second before climbing into the big front seat, neither spoke as he drove off, he looked across at her once to see her chewing her top lip.

Bobby stopped by the side of the stables and got out of his van, he went to her door, opened it and stood looking at the tall thin girl and said. "Do you want to do this Zoe? I won't do anything that you don't want to do" she looked at him as she made up her mind and climbed out of the van, he closed her door and took her by the hand. He led her into the stable and closed the door behind them. He took her into the end stall where the bales of hay were kept, he eased her back against the bales and began undoing the buttons on her blouse. With all the buttons undone on her blouse he lifted her bra up to reveal her small but firm tits, her nipples were long and thin, she took an intake of breath when he took a breast in each hand and began fondling them, he tried to kiss her but she kept her lips tight.

Bobby stopped what he was doing and looked down at the pretty tall girl and said
"Do you want me to stop Zoe, it is your choice, I can stop or I can teach you, but if I am to teach you, you must relax and follow my lead" she chewed her lip for a second and whispered. "Please teach me Bobby." He looked at her to make sure that she was sure, he looked at her naked tits and slid his hand up her skirt, he immediately felt her tense, he rubbed his finger along her fanny lips through her wet pants, she didn't resist him but then she didn't help him either. "Open your legs for me, Zoe." She parted her legs and when he began to press his finger harder against her virgin fanny, she reached up and gripped him around the neck, when his finger went just into her entrance, she

gasped out loud, he took his time and rubbed his finger back and forth long her slit before he lifted his hand and eased it inside her pants to her virgin fanny. Her pubic hair was very short and almost downy but her fanny lips were swollen and when he placed his finger at her entrance, it slipped easily inside her. As soon as he began moving the long finger in and out, she visibly relaxed, he felt her hold her breath and shudder as she came on his finger. This brought a smile from the tall girl and she began to relax altogether, he reached out and took her hand and placed it on his thickening cock. "It's to big" she whispered, he moved her hand back and forth over his hidden cock.

She tried to ease him away from her, so that she could look at his cock, and he asked her.
"Do you want to see it first?" She nodded, so he undid the top of his jeans and then the zipper, he reached in and pulled his half hard cock out, stared at it at first, she then reached out and folded her tiny hand around its thick shaft an automatically began moving her hand up and down, she proudly looked into his eyes and smiled. He reached behind her waist and unbuttoned her skirt and pulled the zipper down. Zoe wiggled her hips so that the skirt slipped to the floor, he placed his fingers into the top of her pants and pulled then down. Again she wiggled her hips and when they hit the straw covered floor she stepped out of them and looking at him again and asked. "Will it hurt me Bobby?" He said "Maybe when it first goes in, but only for a second." She nodded and pulled his cock forward and lifted her left leg and tried to get it into her fanny.

Bobby stopped her and lifted her up and sat her bum on a straw bale, he tried to open her legs wide, but still there was some slight resistance, so he lifted her legs over his arms and pulled her bottom forwards, he placed his knob at her entrance and pushed forwards, she screwed her eyes up and held her breath. When his knob slid just inside her she visibly relaxed, he pushed forwards until he reached her barrier and stopped, he looked into her eyes and said. "This next bit will hurt slightly but only for a second." She nodded and closed her eyes and when he pushed forwards and took her into womanhood, she gasped and then as his big cock stretched her insides, she opened her legs wider to try and ease the wonderful discomfort. He managed to get maybe three quarters of his length inside her before stopping. He asked her if she was ok, she smiled in response and nodded, he began to slowly ride her, going deeper and deeper with each stroke until he was all of the way inside her, she was instantly into it and placed her lips tightly against his lips, he used the tip of his tongue to part her lips, suddenly it was as if a light had come on in her brain, as she began thrusting against him, her orgasm when it hit her frightened her at first and then the beauty of the experience flooded through her and she wanted more of the same.

Bobby uncurled her arms from around her his neck and laid her back on the straw and pulled her bodily towards him, he then adjusted his arms and began to fuck her at a great rate, she was so tight that he knew he wouldn't last long but then there was plenty of time to fuck her again, her small tits bouncing back and forth in time with his thrusts. Bobby stopped and made her jump, she looked up at him and said. "Did you do it inside me?" he shook his head and said. "No, I just want to turn you over." She looked at him quizzically, he pulled his big cock out of her and pulled her up onto her feet, then he picked up his jeans and laid them out on the straw and eased her forwards, he used his feet to part her legs and when he pushed his knob back into her, she went up onto her tip toes. He pushed forwards and she called out into the dusty stall, he gripped her hips and began fucking her, Zoe loved this position and groaned at every thrust that he made. She came and came.

She began calling out for him to do it harder, it was as though she had gone from virgin to nymphomaniac in the space of a few minutes, he was close but knew that he couldn't cum inside her, he left it as long as he dared and then pulled out and shot his hot cum all the way up her back. Zoe screamed out at the top of her voice, reached behind herself and rubbed his warm cum all over her back, each spurt brought more frantic rubbing from the tall woman, he stepped back and leant against the side of the stall breathing heavily, the now young woman slowly turned and looked at the naked man that had just given her pleasure be-yond her wildest dreams, his big cock twitching and her cum sparkled as it covered his manhood. He reached out and pulled her to her feet and pushed her down onto her knees. She looked up at him not know-ing what he wanted. He lifted his half hard cock and pushed it at her mouth, she had read about what he wanted her to do to him, she had the need to please him as much as he had pleased her, she closed her mouth over his naked knob, but just held it there so he gently talked her through the process of giving a man mouth sex. Bobby was getting hard again so he pulled her up to standing, he pulled at her blouse, so she stopped what she was doing and stripped the rest of her clothes off, now standing naked in front of a man for the very first time, she seemed to have lost all of her inhibitions.

She reached down and began wanking his almost hard cock again, now looking into his eyes she stepped close to him and said. "I am so glad I came here today, it was much better than I thought it would be, when can we do it again?" Bobby looked down at her thin hand wrapped around his cock, he reached forwards and placed his hand onto her hairy mound, this time when he slid his finger along her slit, she willingly opened her legs for him, he didn't hesitate and pushed two fingers inside her opening, as far as he could, as soon as he began to frigg her, her knees seemed to spread on their own, she let go of his cock and gripped him wide mouthed around the neck.

She clung onto him with bated breath as he took her to a fierce orgasm, her love juices flooding from her and running down his fingers to pool in the middle of his hand, he stopped moving his fingers and when he withdrew them she almost collapsed and gasped. "Whatever did you do to me then, I have never felt anything like it before." He lifted his hand and showed her the sticky pale cum all over the fingers and in the palm of his hand, she looked at the pale love juice and said. "Is that all mine?" he nodded and said. "Why don't you taste it?" she wrinkled her nose up at the thought, but he said. "Now, poke your tongue out." She did as he asked and when he wiped some of the warm cum over the tip of her tongue, she took her own cum into her mouth and tasted it but she wasn't keen and made a spitting action as she tried to get rid of the taste. Bobby just happened to look behind the young woman and said. "Now Zoe, would you like to try something else?" She looked puzzled and asked. "Like what?" He reached up and took some reins from a hook and said. "How about I tie you up and do it to you like that?" He could see her thinking about it and she asked. "You mean like rape?" He shrugged and she shrugged, so he tied reins around each wrist and going to the other side of the bales of straw he tied her to the slats in the stable, she was now bent forwards with her arms outstretched, he

leaned over and said. "So do you like the idea of this?" she shook her head and whispered. "I'm not sure if I do like it, if I don't will you let me go?" He took a step back and looked at his handy work, he could do what he wanted to her now and there was nothing that she could do about it, he reached up and took a riding crop down from a hook and swished it through the air, she was straining to see what he was doing and when she saw what he intended, she wasn't at all keen and said so, he ignored her pleas and ran the thick end of the riding crop along her fanny lips bringing deep moans from the restrained young girl, he pushed the handle of the crop into her fanny and began to fuck her with it, Zoe had suddenly become a wanton woman and wanted him to fuck her as hard as he could, her hips were bouncing up and down as she came on that leather handle.
He pulled the handle out of her and pushed his big knob at her entrance, when he held his knob just inside her she pushed back as far as she could in her desperation to get him back inside her fanny.

He relented and gripped her hips and proceeded to fuck the ass off her. At one point she called out for him to stop but he was raping her after all, so he kept going and when he stopped, he pulled put and shot his cum up her back again, she screamed out into the dusty stall. Bobby finally staggered away from the crying girl, she had her thin legs crossed and she was sobbing out loud, he finally pulled himself together and untied her, she slid down to the straw covered floor and lowering her head down onto her knees, and cried her heart out. Bobby went and sat by her side and held her while she slowly calmed down, she finally stopped crying and he asked what was wrong, she looked at him with tear filled eyes and said. "It felt to much like real rape Bobby, I wanted you to let me go so that I could have watched you cum over my tits, but now I may never see it.

You see that was my dream for today, that was my fantasy and you ruined it for me" Bobby reassured her that as soon as she was ready to meet up again, he would be only too happy to meet her and they can do whatever she wanted, it would be her time, her choice as to what they did, and where they did it.

Zoe finally calmed down and pulled herself away from him and began to get dressed, she was fully dressed before he himself began to dress.

She walked towards him as he pulled his shorts up his firm legs she gripped his limp cock and moved her hand back and forth.

She lifted her eyes to his and said. "Can it really be my choice as to what we do and where we do it?" He looked down at her hand as it move back and forth along his thickening cock, lifting his eyes to hers he said. "As I promised, your time, your place and your way." A wicked smile crossed her face as she let his cock go, turned away from him and went and stood by his van waiting to go back to school.

Chapter 7

Bobby was back at work at the school, building more rides for the young ladies, he had received a few texts from Zoe the last one saying. "Soon; be afraid!" He swallowed at the thought of the text and wondered what she had in mind.

Bobby was deep in thought as he worked on the latest ride, he jumped when a voice said. "HI Bobby are you busy?" he looked up to see Susy and Liz only this time it was Liz on the swing and Susy pushing, Liz opened her legs wide and he could see that she was pant less, but that was all he could tell and said.
"You will have to open your legs wider than that, I can't see anything" the two girls whispered to each other before Susy said.
"Can we come behind the van again Bobby?" He nodded and said
"Please, help yourselves, I will be there in a minute, I just want to finish this bit, why don't you two start without me?" They looked at one another and giggled out loud, after checking that the coast was clear they gripped hands and ran behind his van.

He could hear them whispering and he could tell by their feet that he could see under the van door that they were standing facing each other and were toe to toe. When he walked behind the van door the girls jumped apart, but he could tell by their clothing that they had been playing with each other's tits, he sat down in the side of his van and said.
"Don't let me stop you." Both girls looked at one another and as usual it was Susy that made the first move, she went to her friend and pushed her hand up her friends blue jumper and began feeling her tits, but Liz wasn't interested and pulled away from her best friend saying.
" No Su, that sort of thing is just between us, you know that and you know why we have come here?" Bobby not being slow in coming forward asked.
"And why have you come here then, girls?" Liz instantly blushed, but her friend said
"She wants you to do it to her Bobby, just like you did it to me." Liz slapped her friend on the arm and said. "Su, you don't have to be so

crude." Bobby pulled the nervous girl to him so that she was stood between his parted thighs, he then put both of his hands up the back of her skirt and began fondling her tight ass cheeks, he looked up into her eyes and said. "Get your tits out for me Liz, I want to suck your nipples." When she hesitated her friend moved up behind her and lifted her clothes up to reveal her friends firm tits.

Bobby kissed and sucked both nipples as he squeezed her firm buttocks, moving his hand to the front and slid his finger along her swollen fanny lips bringing a loud moan from the young woman. He moved his finger to her opening and slid it inside her, she instantly opened her legs so he inserted a second finger, and when he began frigging her she began thrusting her hips at him, looking down she placed her left breast into his mouth. Bobby took her to her orgasm and standing up he looked at Susy and said.
"Check that the coast is clear" The young woman came back and nodded at him, he did no more than undo his shorts and pulled his big hard cock out, he bent Liz forward and lifted her skirt onto her back, he then moved up behind her, gripping his hard cock in his right hand he placed his big knob at her entrance, he was surprised when his huge cock slid easily into her, she groaned out loud and spread her knees wider as he stretched her inside. He gripped her hips and began fucking her, she wasn't as tight as her friend but she liked being fucked just as much, he pulled her back to meet every thrust he made, something he hadn't done with her best friend.

He looked at Susy and she was stood staring at them with her skirt clutched high around her waist. Her right hand was like a blur as she fingered herself, showing no embarrassment as he watched her. Bobby watched the watcher take herself to her orgasm and said.
"Check that the coast is clear, if it is take all of your clothes off." She looked around the van door, she must have been happy because she began removing all of her clothes. She was stood naked in front of him waiting to be told what to do next. He said
"Go down onto your knees and lean back, I want to cum all over you." She did exactly like he asked, the only thing she did that he hadn't asked for was she began to play with herself again. She closed her eyes as she began to cum again, Liz was going mad in his arms as she had cum god knows how many times, it was all too much for Bobby and he grunted

and pulled his cock out of her, just in time as he shot his hot cum all over the naked young girl, she watched and waited for each spurt and as the spurt landed on her body she rubbed it all over herself. Liz turned to see what was happening and stared at her friend as she had her eyes closed and was obviously coming again. Bobby turned to Liz and said. "Take all of your clothes off." A quick look around the door of the van and she began to remove all of her clothes, when she was naked she looked at Bobby who said.

"Rub your body all over hers." This time she didn't hesitate and within seconds they were holding each other as their young bodies writhed against each other, Bobby said.

"Kiss each other." And they did just that, it was then that it was obvious that they had done this before. "Put your fingers in each other's fannies." They didn't hesitate and soon both pairs of legs were wide open as he watched them frigging each other, Liz came first but it was only a matter of seconds before Susy groaned out loud as her orgasm shook her body, they both turned their heads slowly to look at him, so he moved forwards and lowered his half hard cock between their heads.

Susy didn't hesitate and began to lick his cock all over which encouraged her friend to join in, when Susy took his big knob into her mouth and began to bounce her head back and forth, Liz looked on fascinated, his cock was now rock hard again and Liz eased her friends mouth out of the way and took him into her young mouth and did just as her friend had done, he reached down and took Susy's hand and folded it around his shaft and encouraged her to wank him hard and fast. Bobby was close again, he hadn't experienced anything like this before, but wanted to again and very soon, he grunted and shot his first spurt into Liz's mouth she immediately lifted her mouth from his knob but Susy soon too her place, and swallowed every drop of his warm salty cum.

All cleaned up and dressed again they all stood around looking at one another, it was him who asked.

"Can you two get away from the school on Saturday afternoon ?" The two girls looked at one another and Susy said. "Yes, we can say we are going into town, why?" He smiled and said. "How would you both like to come to my house for more of the same?" the girls looked at one-another and both nodded so he said. "I will wait for you by the main gates at one o'clock, ok?" They said that they would be there and with that they were gone and Bobby couldn't wait until Saturday, he would make sure that the house was empty and he would give them a fucking that they would never forget, but first he wanted to see them fuck each other, maybe he should take a look on the internet and see what he could find.

Saturday finally came around and he was sat in his BMW waiting for them by the main gates, when they came into view his cock jerked in his shorts, they both wore tiny red shorts with white crop tops, they climbed into the big car and he drove away, no-one said a word until he turned into the drive that led to the big house, he pulled up outside his home, and both girls sat in the car looking up at the huge house in awe. "Do you live here Bobby?" asked Susy. He smiled and said.
"Yep, all by myself, so if you want to explore, you go right ahead." The girls climbed out of the big car and ran hand in hand to the front doors but they stopped and looked back at him, he just waved them forwards. They opened the big oak doors and rushed in, when he entered the house he could hear them running from room to room so he took a seat and waited for them to calm down, they finally walked towards him hand in hand.
"This is a huge house Bobby, why do you live here all alone?" He shrugged his shoulders and said. "I don't know really I just do, fancy some champagne?" Both girls nodded their heads so he went to a side cabinet and removed a large bottle of chilled champagne, he poured them all a large glass full, the girls both gulped at the sparkling liquid and both sneezed and said that the bubbles tickled. When he picked up the bottle he walked towards the stairs and said. "Shall we." Neither girl spoke they just followed him up the wooden stair case, when he walked into the master bedroom he stood to the side as the girls entered, they both placed their glasses on a sideboard and ran and jumped onto the huge king sized bed and began bouncing up and down giggling at the top of their voices. He sat down on a chair and watched them as they held onto each other and bounced up and down, he was more inter-ested in watching their young tits bouncing up and down in their tight tops. It was Susy who stopped bouncing and looked at him, he looked from one to the other and said. "Strip each other naked." Susy began pulling at her friends clothes and soon had her friends tits out, in under two minutes they were both naked and looking at him, he looked from

one to the other and then stood up and stripped himself naked and sat back down. Susy asked.

"Aren't you coming over to join us?" He said.

"No, I want to sit here and watch you two do to each other, what you would do when you are on your own, and if you are good, I have a nice surprise for you"

As usual it was Susy who started things off but Liz was soon a willing participant, still standing they were kissing urgently with tongues in each other's mouths, hands were fondling tits and bums and when Liz placed her hand between her friends legs, Susy opened her legs for her best friend and allowed her to take her to a beautiful orgasm, as soon as she had cum Liz sank down to the bed and opened her legs and arms and waited for her friend to join her, Susy knelt by her friends side and with her right hand she began frigging her friend and with her other hand she pulled her friends firm tits hard and in all different directions, Liz had her eyes closed and he watched fascinated as her hips moved up and down as she was being pleasured by her best-friend, in a well-practised move, as she was about to cum Liz lifted her mouth to her friends mouth, they kissed urgently as Liz pushed her hips up high and moaned out loud.

Now both girls had cum they held each other for a minute or two before they both looked at him as he sat there with his hard cock sticking out in front of him.

"Are you coming to join us now?" He shook his head and said.

"In a minute, but first I have to reward you both for a wonderful show, [he nodded to a cardboard box on a dresser] that is for you two to keep, but I want to see what you make of them first?" Susy jumped from the bed and grabbed the box, she shook it first and smiled at the sounds coming from inside the box, she tried to cut the tape with her nails but failed, so he tossed a pair of scissors onto the bed, the two girls tore at the box in their excitement to get at the contents, when the box was open the girls looked at the contents and then looked at him, he said.

"One each; you choose which one, now I want to see you use them on each other, if you like them, they are yours to keep." Susy lifted up a thick black strap on rubber vibrator, she turned it this way and that, examining the rubber cock closely, Liz reached out and touched the shaft to discover tiny bumps all along the full length, Liz reached into the box and picked up a red strap on a rubber vibrator. Both were the same length and thickness only the red one had thick veins all along its length, they swopped and examined each other's and when Liz turned hers on and it began buzzing, she dropped it onto the bed. Susy switched hers on and began teasing her friend by rubbing the tip all over her tits, soon the girls were giggling as they teased each other.

Susy reached into the box again and pulled out a long thin tube with 'lubricant' printed on the side, she opened the tube and squirted some onto her finger, both girls smelt the jelly like substance. Susy reached into the box again and came out with the instructions for the vibrators, he sat and watched as they knelt side by side and read the instruction leaflet, when they had read it they both examined their chosen vibrator and looking at the straps, they began to slip the rubber cocks up their legs and into place. It took them a while but with a bit of help from each other they finally got them into the right positions, they both stood up and had a pretend sword fight with their new toys, laughing out loud as they did so.

Susy picked up the lubricant and squirted some onto her cock and rubbed it along its whole length, the two girls looked at the now sparkling rubber cock, she turned to her friend and said
"Turn around then Liz, let's try it out?" Liz looked a bit sheepish at first but turned away from her lover and dropped onto her hands and knees, Susy moved forwards and placed the rubber head just inside her best friends fanny, she reached down and switched the vibrator on and then pushed forwards, Liz screamed out and shouted. "Fucking hell that's nice, do it harder." So Susy pushed forwards and gripped her best friends hips and began to give her friend a real good fucking, he watched on as Liz knelt there with her eyes closed and her mouth wide open, as she automatically moved her body back and forth, her first or-gasm came in seconds, but she wouldn't let her friend stop.
"Keep going, keep going." She shouted.

He watched as her slight body became covered in goose bumps as she began thrusting back and forth which became ever more urgent, he watched her cum at least four times before she asked her friend to stop, when Susy pulled the buzzing cock out of her friend, the tip and most of its length was covered in her friends thick creamy coloured cum. Both girls looked down at the cum covered rubber cock, Liz whispered. "I couldn't believe it Susy, it just feels wonderful, better than anything that we have done before, put some of that stuff on mine and I will do it to you, just you wait and see" Susy covered the thick veined cock with the lubricant and Liz moved behind her kneeling friend, Liz switched the cock on and unlike Susy, Liz placed the head at her friends entrance and pushed forwards, Susy gasped out loud as the rubber cock slid inside her, her mouth was held wide open and she opened her knees as wide as she could.

"Fuck, fuck, bloody fucking hell" she shouted as her friend gripped her hips and proceeded to give her the fucking of a lifetime. Bobby sat and watched the two young girls as they fucked each other time and time again and realised then that he had made a huge mistake, he should have given them the cocks after he had fucked them both, and he wondered now if he would get to fuck them at all.

Both girls lay panting on the bed, both hand in hand staring at each other, cum covered rubber cocks still standing proud, they were more in love now than they had ever been before, it was at that point that Bobby knew that he had made a mistake in giving them the rubber cocks so soon. He sat on his chair still naked only now his big cock hung limp hung between his legs, he sat and watched the two girls as they whispered to each other, their lips almost touching as they talked.

They stopped whispering and Susy turned her head and looked at him, she then reached out and with her fingers beckoned him to the bed, he sat by her side and looked at the two perfectly formed young bodies, he reached forward and unclipped the straps that held the rubber cock in position, she lifted her bottom and let him pull the vibrator down her legs and drop it onto the floor, he did the same to the other girl. They both looked at him with glazed eyes, he said.

"You two really do love each other don't you?" Both girls nodded at his question, he looked from one to the other and said.

"You two have discovered a lot today, but there is one thing that you need to discover before you can be truly intimate female lovers, do you want me to show you?" Again both girls nodded, so he stood up and lifted Susy to a kneeling position, he then moved her around so that the two girls were top to tail, he then moved Susy so that she was kneeling by her lovers head, he lifted her right knee and placed it over the head of her lover, he then pushed Susy's head forwards so that her mouth was near her friends fanny. He stood up and said. "From what I have seen of this, I will show Susy what to do first and see how we get on, (he looked at Liz and continued) if Susy does something to you that you like, then you do the same to her, the rest is up to you two." He sat down by Susy's head and eased her mouth down to her friends fanny, he then talked her quietly through the art of fanny kissing, as he had been taught by Helen.

When Susy seemed to be struggling he reached under Liz's leg and using two fingers he opened her lovers fanny lips, he told Susy to lick all over but to pay particular attention to the little lump by his finger tip, as soon as she touched the tiny button, Liz moaned out loud, so her lover did it over and over again until Liz was on the verge of her orgasm. He whispered for Susy to close her lips over the tiny button and suck as hard as she could. As Liz came she almost lifted her lover off the bed with her head. Just as soon as her orgasm began to subside, she quite happily returned the compliment. He did have to point out the tiny button to Liz but the rest she figured out for herself. Susy almost screamed out loud as she came, her orgasm was much more intense than her lovers.

When the girls had calmed down enough they both looked at him with huge smiles on their faces, he smiled back and said. "I think that you have learned enough for one day if you want to learn some more tricks, then we will have to meet up here again "the girls looked at one another and nodded enthusiastically, he went to get of the bed when Susy stopped him with her hand on his arm and said.
"We would like to thank you Bobby for changing our lives, but we have something to give to you as well. Did you know that when you began working at the school, the Matron sent each girl a small box and a letter, warning us all of the consequences of mixing with young men, but if any of us did fall, then the pills in the box would take care of any mistakes, should they happen. Well, what we have decided together is that we want you to do it to both of us and to shoot your stuff into us, we will then take the pills as directed and solve the problem, but we want to feel what it is like for you to do that to us, it may be the only opportunity that we ever get." He looked from one girl to the other and both

girls were smiling at him, Susy reached out and lifted is limp cock and said

"We will have to do something about this poor chap first." The girls parted and eased him down onto the bed, they began kissing him all over, driving him mad with desire, he lay there with his eyes closed and when he felt a pair of hot lips slide over his knob he almost came on the spot, one of the beautiful young girls; he didn't know which one, lowered her fanny onto his mouth, he took great delight in giving her as much pleasure as he could, his only problem being he wanted to make her cum before he shot his hot cum down the other girls throat.

He needn't have worried because he felt the girl sat on his face tremble and rub her fanny up and down his face, as soon as she lifted herself from his face he sat up to see Liz sucking his cock for all she was worth, he reached out and lifted her head from his throbbing knob, she looked at him pleadingly, but he moved around the bed and positioned himself behind her, she took up position and waited for him to mount her. As he slid his big thick cock into the young girl, he felt her groan out loud, he gripped her hips and began to fuck her at a great rate, he knew that he wouldn't last long, as he was taken to the edge by the wonderful mouth of this girl he was now fucking for all he was worth.

He opened his eyes to see that Susy was kissing her lover hard on the mouth and with her left hand she was fondling her hanging breasts. He grunted out loud and shot his hot cum deep into the young woman who screamed out loud as each spurt scolded her insides. The girls stared at one-another as he shot his seed deep into the young willing body. Bobby hung onto Liz for as long as he could, she had sort of lowered her front half down and the girls were kissing again, he could see their tongues as they fought first in one mouth and then in the other, his cock slipped from the young girl and she flopped to the bed, only now the girls were locked together by their mouths. Bobby sat back on his haunches and watched the young girls as their hands were all over each other, their hips rising and falling.

As if by some hidden signal they parted and looked at him and eased him down to the bed again, this time it was Susy that sucked his cock, she seemed to go deeper down his shaft than her friend, Liz stood up and looked down at him and picked up the red vibrator, she stepped over his head and spread her knees, he watched her closely as she closed her eyes and eased the thick vibrator into herself, the red cock was buried to the hilt inside her young body, she then fiddled with the end and managed to switch it on, her nipples suddenly grew rock hard and she was covered in tiny goose bumps. Her right hand began to ram the rubber cock back and forth, he glanced down at Susy and she was watching her lover as well, he couldn't see her right hand, but he guessed from the look on her face that her fingers were doing their thing in her fanny, he watched as Liz too took herself to her orgasm, the sensual moment seemed to last for a long time as she slowed the hand movements on the vibrator, she now used long slow strokes and long groans came from the young girl.

He was hard again and wanted to fuck Susy, just as soon as possible, he eased himself out from under the two women and pulled Susy from the bed, he took her to the end of the bed and bent her forwards, so that she gripped the iron work of the bed frame, he pushed her feet wide and gripping his hard cock with his right hand he pushed his cock deep onto her young body. Bobby lifted her bodily from the ground, he held her weight easily as steadied himself and gripped her hips and began to give her a good fucking. Susy groaned, moaned and thrust back at him, she called out for her female lover who was stood to their side watching them fuck, she had her legs wide open and was fucking herself with the black vibrator. Liz dropped the rubber cock on the floor and went to her lover, who pulled her to her and made her stand in front of her. Now standing with her back to the bed Susy pulled her lovers lips to her own. The two women hung onto each other as he rammed his cock into Susy who was by now almost crying with pleasure.

Bobby was fascinated by the two young girls who were so obviously deeply in love for girls so young, he looked at Liz and pulled her around to him, he then pushed her down to her knees. She knelt there looking up at him, her closed his eyes and began his race to a finish Susy sensed he was close and increased her backward thrusting. Bobby grunted and shot his first spurt of his hot cum into the young girls willing body who screamed out at the top of her voice, each spurt brought another scream. Susy suddenly went limp in his arms and he lowered her down to her knees, he turned to Liz and gripped her hair as he pulled his steaming hot cock out of her lover and pushed it at her mouth, she didn't hesitate and sucked hungrily on his still hard cock, he gripped her hair on both sides of her head and began fucking her mouth, when she gagged and tried to pull away from him he realised what he had done, and released her hair and let her carry on at her own pace, the only thing he did was lift her hand to his shaft and move it back and forth a few times to show her what he wanted her to do for him.

Bobby wasn't surprised when Susy recovered and came to join her friend in cleaning his sticky cock, like true friends they took it in turn to suck his cock, His cock finally gave up the ghost and shrank to nothing allowing the girls to stop what they were doing and lay down on the bed and rest, both well and truly fucked. Bobby lay across the bottom of the bed whereas the two girls were lay lengthways, he looked up between them and they were holding hands again, but both girls were lay with their eyes closed. They all seemed to doze off for a while, Liz woke Bobby with a gentle shake, when he sat up both girls were still naked but they had been down to the kitchen and made sandwiches that were neatly laid out on a small table. Susy had filled glasses from a bottle of chilled lemonade. Susy passed him a plate with a thick cheese sandwich on it and they all ate quietly.

When they were finished eating Susy said. "We would like to thank you Bobby for what you have done for us, we have learned so much today, if there is more that you can teach us, then we are willing to come back in two weeks' time, but be honest with us Bobby if you don't want us to come back please tell us." He looked from one girl to the other and said.
"If it was at all possible, I would have you both living here with me so that we could become permanent lovers for the rest of our lives, but as for two weeks' time, yes there are still other things that I can teach you, and I would be honoured to share a bed with you both again. So shall we say the same time and place in two weeks?" both girls nodded and then smiled at one another.

Bobby asked if the day's activities were over and both girls said that they were too sore for anything else, but if he wanted them to give him more mouth sex, then they would both try their best. He smiled and declined saying that his knob was in a very tender state and he couldn't manage a hard on if his life depended on it.

So that was the end of their days shagging, they were in no hurry to re-turn back to the school, so he ordered a take away to be delivered and they spent the day relaxing together, the girls were completely relaxed with each other even though they both had a body full of his seed.

He dropped them off close to the school, he sat and watched them walk through the front door and as he was driving off his phone buzzed in his pocket, he opened the text to see this message.
"We love your big cock Bobby and are both looking forward to seeing you in two weeks, sleep tight lover. XXXXXXXX." He smiled as he drove along the drive to his house, he was knackered, but it was a nice knackered.

Chapter 8

Bobby was working hard laying turf to create a grassed area for the little darlings to rest their weary bones on, he had a pile of timber stacked off to one side to make picnic benches with, he could hear a tiny voice somewhere close by, talking in German, the voice was repeating the same thing over and over, but at different speeds, he followed the sound to the other side of the stacked wood, a dark skinned young woman of no-more than sixteen or seventeen was sat with her knees up by her chest with a book resting on her knees, he stood there watching the girl as she moved her finger along the line of words in her German book, he coughed quietly which made her jump.

She gasped and looked up at him, he smiled and told her how to say the words that she was trying to read out of the book, she repeated what he told her and asked him.

"Do you speak German then?" he told her that he was fluent in the language and if she needed any help, he would be only too willing to help her, she only had to ask. She frowned and said.

"Are you Bobby?" He said that he was, the girl stood up and began walking away from him, he stopped her by saying.

"Are you frightened of me then?" she turned and it was then that he saw her big chocolate coloured eyes, she was a stunningly beautiful young woman, she stopped and said.

"I have heard of your reputation amongst the other girls, they say how big you are and how long that you can last, but I am a virgin and intend to stay that way until I get married, just as my religion demands." He shrugged and smiled and said.

"That seems to be a terrible waste to me, just think of all the fun you could be missing out on, and your husband may be a bad lover with a small manhood, if that happens then you will regret missing out on some fun and games with me." She shook her head and smiled

"A very nice try, but your sweet words will not work on me, I am immune to them." Bobby said. " At least tell me your name so that I can at least carve your name next to mine in a heart on the oldest tree in this wood behind us?" "Mia, my name is Mia, goodbye Bobby." She said "Bye Mia, if you need any help with your German or change your mind with the other, just leave me a note in the woodpile or when I have done the benches, leave me a note and phone number under one of the feet and I will text you straight away, bye beautiful Mia[as she walked away he called after her] I will dream about you tonight and every other night, sleep tight my darling Mia." She turned and smiled at him as he watched her walk back to the school building, she was small but perfectly formed with small tits and a tight ass. As she opened the door to the school she looked back to see if he was still watching her, he made the sign of a phone at his ear, Mia smiled and disappeared into the school.

Bobby spent some time on the internet watching girl on girl porn, to get some ideas on what he could help his young lesbian lovers with, he was fascinated with what he had seen and had a plan for the next time that they met. Bobby started work the next morning on building the benches to place on the grassed area, he lifted the top plank of wood to find a folded piece of paper with a phone number written in red ink, underneath the number it said. "Please ring me Bobby as I would like to be further educated." His heart jumped and he smiled to himself as he put the number into his pocket, he would text his dark skinned beauty when he stopped for a coffee.

He poured his coffee and sat down on his newly erected bench and took his phone out, he installed her number into his phone and sent her a message saying. "Is this your number my dark skinned beauty, if so what can I do for you?" It was maybe two hours before a reply came back it read.
"Yes it is I, I have thought about what you said and maybe you are right." He smiled and wrote back. "Do you want to meet up and discus it?" Disappointingly he didn't hear from her for the rest of the day. He woke in the morning and showered, he sat down for breakfast when his phone buzzed, the message read.
"I would like to meet you, but I am very nervous." He sent a text straight back saying
"Then let us meet at Mc Donald's at lunch time, one day this week?" Her reply came straight back. "I have a violin lesson in town on Thursday, I could meet you there after the lesson say at 12.30." He replied saying that he would be there.

Thursday lunch time came and Bobby was sat in Mc Donald's when she came through the door smiling, she wore a bright yellow summer dress and yellow sandals, her jet black hair was caught up at the back by a brightly coloured butterfly clip. She sat down by him and he asked what she would like to eat and he fetched them both a meal, they sat and chatted about her violin lessons and how often she had them, she told him that she had a lesson every Thursday, sometimes a double lesson depending on how she felt.

Their meals finished he, asked her.
"So Mia, tell me what I may be right about, this thing that you mentioned in your text?" she blushed crimson and looked down before saying. "Oh, you know, what you said about all of the fun I might be missing out on, I don't want to miss out on anything, not if I can help it." He looked at her for a while before asking.
"And what is it that you are prepared to do Mia?" She looked around before saying
"Look Bobby, I have told you that I am a virgin, what I know about such things is very limited, what I do know I have read it in books, I know what goes where if it is that that bothers you?" He smiled and said. "Look Mia, I don't want to frighten you or make you do anything that you don't want to do, maybe you should wait for a while?" She looked disappointed with him. "Did you think that it was easy for me to leave you my number, by doing so I was agreeing to give myself to you, or had you not thought about that?" She sucked the last drops out of her paper cup and with a tear rolling down her cheek she stood up and was about to run out of the restaurant, he placed his hand on her arm and she sat back down, she looked at him and he nodded.

"I hadn't realised what it must have taken for you to leave your number, I am so very sorry,[he stood up and said] shall we go then?" She stood up and walked out of the restaurant, he opened the passenger door for her and she climbed into the black BMW, she looked tiny in the big seat of the car, he drove down the drive to his house and saw Helen working in her garden, so he knew that he would have the house to himself.

He stopped outside the house and took Mia inside, she still carried her violin in her right hand, he took it from her and placed it on the table in

the living room, she stood looking around at all the full length pictures
of his long lost relatives on the walls. He sat down in a deep leather
chair and watched the beautiful young girl as she made her way slowly
around the room, when she came into the living room he reached out
and eased her into his lap. She looked nervously into his eyes and said.
"Please don't hurt me Bobby" he pulled her trembling lips to his, she
kissed him with her lips closed tightly, he pushed his tongue at her lips
and she pulled away and looked at him, he whispered. "Trust me Mia,
let me teach you how to love" this time when he pulled her lips to hers
she seemed to be a little bit more relaxed, he pushed his tongue at her
lips again and she open her mouth slightly, just enough for him to get
the tip of his tongue into her mouth, within seconds she was sucking
hungrily on his tongue.

Bobby placed his hand onto her right breast, as she didn't object he
placed his hand onto her naked leg, she began to tremble again and as
he moved his hand higher to her damp pants she seemed to tense, he
moved his hand between her legs which she held tightly closed, he used
his finger tip to tease the top of her slit, he had to use the back of his
hand to ease her legs apart, when her legs were open enough he could
then run his fingers along her slit, tiny purrs were coming from her as
he reached up and slid his hand down inside her pants to her hairy
mound, at his first touch on her fanny lips, she opened her legs wider
for him, he slid his finger to her opening, he pushed his finger into her
fanny as far as he could, she suddenly went stiff and held onto his neck
with both hands.

As soon as he began moving his finger back and forth she relaxed instantly, he tried to get a second finger inside her and had to ask her to
open her legs wider, she made the decision and opened her legs wide
for him, he took her to her first ever proper orgasm which seemed to
scare her when it happened, she looked into is eyes and smiled when
she said.
"I have read about that, but the real thing is much better than what
they say in the books." He eased her from his lap and stood up, he took
her hand and led her to the stairs, they climbed the stairs hand in hand,
he took her into the first bedroom that they came to, he closed the
door behind them and went to her, he lifted her pretty yellow dress
over her head and placed it over a chair, she stood there trembling in a

matching yellow bra and pants that stood out perfectly against her olive coloured skin, he reached behind her and undid her bra, when he uncovered her firm breasts, she was perfect, her nipples were thick and hard, he placed his hands onto her breasts and she looked down at the big hands as they fondled her breasts, when he rolled her hard nipples under his thumbs she closed her eyes and purred like a kitten.

He placed his fingers into the side of her pants but she stopped him by saying. "Show me your thing first" he stripped his shirt off and undid his shorts, he reached into his boxers and pulled his half hard cock out, Mia gasped out loud and said.

"You are much too big for me, Bobby" and went to step away from him, but he reached out and placed her hand around his thick shaft, he moved her hand back and forth, Mia looked down at her dark skinned hand as it folded around his growing white cock, he slid his hand down into her pants again and pushed his fingers back into her tight fanny, he began frigging her and her hand moved faster back and forth along his hardening cock, he eased her backwards towards the bed, when her legs touched the bed he eased her down, she lay back and stared up at him, he reached to the side of her pants and pulled them down her legs, her pubic hair was dark, thick and wiry, even though there wasn't much of it, he removed her pants and opened her legs, he looked down at her virgin fanny and pulled her to the edge of the bed, he placed his knob at her entrance and she closed her eyes and chewed her top lip as she waited to be deflowered.

When Bobby pushed forwards, she groaned out loud and arched her back, he came to her barrier and gave a gentle push, Mia groaned out loud, but as his thick cock forced it's way inside her, she seemed to relax slightly, she asked him.
"Is it all inside yet?" He looked down at her fanny skin stretched tight around his thick cock and said.

"Almost, just one more little push and you will have it all." She smiled and waited for him to push the rest of his big cock into her young virgin body. Now he was fully embedded inside her willing young body he lifted her slim legs onto his arms and begun his journey, Mia grunted at each of his firm thrusts, it took him less than a minute to give her first ever orgasm with a cock, she looked up at him and hissed at him through gritted teeth as she came hard.

Bobby made her cum three times before he stopped moving inside her, she looked up at him and said. "Please don't stop yet Bobby" he smiled down at her and eased his hard cock out of her and said. "Turn over my dark skinned beauty." She turned over and he pulled her into the position that he wanted her in, when he entered her again, she instantly began scratching the bedclothes and became very vocal as she called out her pleasure, orgasm after orgasm flooded her young body before he could hold himself back no-more and grunted out loud and pulled his jerking cock out and shot his hot cum all over her back, causing her to scream out loud.

The new lovers lay side by side on the bed, both panting heavily from their sexual exertions, the young girl reached out and gripped his hand which brought a smile to his face. Mia lifted herself onto her elbow and looked at the grown man who had just given her pleasure beyond any- thing that she had read about in any of the books, she reached out and lifted his sticky limp cock and examined it, when she pulled his foreskin down and exposed his purple coloured big knob, she giggled and said. "It looks funny, doesn't it?" He reached out and moved her hand up and down, she was eager to please him, but when he put his hand on the back of her head and pushed her mouth towards his exposed knob she looked confused, he looked up at her and said gently. "Put it in your mouth and suck it." She shook her head and said. "No way, that is gross.

"He shrugged and could have insisted, but he didn't want to scare her so he lay back and let her use her hand to get him hard again, when his cock began to grow in her hand she became excited and called out. "Look Bobby, it's working, it's growing again." He lifted his head and watched her as she increased her efforts, when he was hard again, he pulled her on top of him she automatically opened her legs and tried to move backwards trying to get him inside again, he lifted her up into a sitting position, he lifted her up bodily and said. "Reach under yourself and put the end inside yourself." She struggled at first, but got the tip of his cock inside herself and smiled at him, she then waited to be told what to do next, he let go of her and said.

"Now slide down it until you are comfortable." She closed her eyes and slid slowly down his hard cock, when she had maybe three quarters of his cock inside herself, he moved her knees closer to his body and gripping her thighs, he lifted her up and down a couple of times.

Mia smiled and nodded, she rested her hands on his chest and moved her hips up and down his thick cock, she soon had it all inside of her young body and was now riding him at a fair rate, she closed her eyes and began humming a tune, which became louder and louder until she shuddered and called out loud as she came on his massive cock. Mia opened her eyes and smiled down at him and said. "Play with my tits, please Bobby" He did as she asked and as soon as he had his hands folded around her tits she closed her eyes again, and lost herself in a tune as she began humming again. Her second orgasm was a lot stronger than the first and when she had cum he gripped her hips and held her down with his cock fully embedded inside her and moved her hips back and forth.

Mia called out. "Fucking hell Bobby, this is bloody nice, I could ride your big cock all day long." She closed her eyes again and she was riding him flat out again, this time when she came she sank down again, but he gripped her hips and moved them in a circular movement, she still had her eyes closed as she ground herself against him, he reached out and lifted her into a sitting position, this she liked best of all, he said. "Play with your tits Mia." She didn't hesitate and her hands went to her tits, she pulled them all ways, she gripped her thick nipples and pulled them hard, he was getting close himself and watching her now was driving him mad, he encouraged her to start riding him again a said. "You will have to get off soon or I will cum inside you." She smiled down at him and said. "I don't care Bobby, I want you to shoot it all into me, she gripped his cock with her young fanny muscles and increased her speed, he couldn't help himself and shot his scolding hot cum into her. Scream after scream escaped from her as she sat up and ground herself against him, as he filled her young body full of his hot seed.

She stayed sat on him until his cock slipped noisily from her, she then flopped to the side and lay back with a huge smile on her face, her body squirming around on the bed as she continued to enjoy the feeling of his seed inside of her young tender body. He sat up and looked at the young girl and asked her. "Why did you do that Mia, I wanted to pull out, but now you may be pregnant." She didn't even open her eyes when she said. "That is my problem Bobby not yours, let me worry about it." He took that to mean the gift from Matron will sort it out again, he really ought to start buying condoms, it would save him all these problems.

Bobby dropped the dark skinned school girl off at the entrance to the school, they kissed urgently and promised to see each other soon. He went back to work but all he could think of was the olive beauty with her big brown eyes, he wanted her again so much, he dropped his tools and walked off into the wood and kept walking, he had a feeling of foreboding creep over him, he took out his phone and sent Mia a message, it read. "Don't forget to take care of things Mia, I want to see you again soon. XXX." He didn't hear from her for almost three weeks, his phone buzzed late in the evening, the message said.
"Bobby, meet me at the Grange, Friday evening at 8pm." There was no name but it was Mia's number. He was dressed smartly and was sat in the Grange at the appointed time. He had a bottle of red wine on the table with two glasses, he watched the door as he waited for her, a slim woman of late thirties entered the bar, it was obvious that she was a relation to Mia by the colour of her skin, she stared at him and sat down in front of him, she didn't speak but poured herself a full glass of red wine, she then stared at him long and hard and drank half of the glass of wine in one go.

He knew that he was in some sort of trouble, but how much he didn't know. She steadied herself and said. "What were you thinking of forcing yourself on my beautiful daughter and making her pregnant, let me give you fair warning, young man, my husband is an important diplomat and when he hears about this he will have you arrested and jailed for what you have done to our daughter." He sat up straight and said. "Whoa there, what has Mia been saying to you then?"
"Kim, my name is Kimberley, but people call me Kim, as for what she has told me, she told me how you dragged her into your car, took her to your home, dragged her into a bedroom and forced yourself upon her." He shook his head and said.

"Will you listen to me while I tell you my side of things." She nodded, he took his wallet out of his pocket and opening the wallet he took out the piece of paper with Mia's number and name written on it and placed it in front of her, she picked up the note and read it twice and scrunched up the note and looked down into her lap, he took out his phone and leaning forward, he showed her every message that had passed between them.

 Kim read every message and sat there looking like she was chewing a wasp, she was so bloody angry, she whispered.
"The bloody little madam, she never told me about these messages, her version of events were much simpler than this, and when the school rang me and said that she was pregnant, I sat and cried and I have to admit I wanted to see you punished for what you had done to her, but I can see now that it isn't all of your fault, I am truly sorry Bobby for accusing you like that, I had no right without knowing all of the facts." She picked up her glass and drained the red liquid, he refilled her glass, which she picked up and drank from again.

She carried on. "We have taken care of the problem and we are removing Mia from the school out of harm's way to avoid a scandal, her father will hear nothing about this and as far as I am concerned the matter between us is over and done with, but I will be having a word with that young lady, just as soon as I get her home." He smiled his relief and asked. "Are you hungry Kim because I am starving and the food here is very good." She glanced around the bar come restaurant and nodded. "Yes, I am quite hungry as it happens, I haven't had much time to eat today worrying about what I was going to say to you." He passed her a menu and making their selections he ordered their food and another bottle of wine, she emptied her glass and held it out for a refill.

Mia now seemed to be forgotten as they chatted like old friends, the food was exceptionally good and they seemed to relax in each other's company, they had emptied the second bottle of wine and he went to order another when she giggled and said.
"Please don't order any more, I have had too much all ready and feel a little bit frisky." He looked at the waiter and called her over and or-

dered two large Brandies, Kim didn't argue, and when the drink came she drank half of the amber liquid straight down, he asked.
"Where are you staying Kim, only I will order a taxi for us and drop you off" she swirled the liquid around in her glass and said.
"I hear that you have a big house with plenty of spare rooms, maybe I can stay at yours" he smiled and his cock jerked, he said. "As you wish" he ordered two more large brandies and asked the waiter to order him a taxi, she was impressed that he didn't have to tell the waiter where the taxi would be going, and when they stood to leave he didn't pay a penny.

The taxi was waiting outside and when they climbed onto the back, the driver didn't say a word, he just drove, in the darkness Kim slid her hand into his lap and rubbed his leg, she looked into his face and moved her hand higher and with the tip of her little finger she rubbed his thickening cock, as she felt him grow she gripped him through the thin material of his trousers, using her other hand she lifted his hand and placed it between her parted legs, she tried to pull his zipper down, but couldn't manage it so she changed tactics and pulled the hand that was between her legs all the way up the to her fanny, she pushed her bottom forwards and opened her legs wide, he rubbed his finger along the thin thong that was buried between her swollen fanny lips, she groaned and placed her mouth to his ear and whispered.

"Make me cum Bobby." She reached under her dress and pulled the thong from between he fanny lips, he had to turn slightly, but he man-aged to get his fingers just inside her fanny, with her hip movement and his fingers doing their thing, she shuddered in the darkness and snatched his hand from under her dress, she whispered into his ear. "I hope that that was the first orgasm of many this wonderful night." She then began to nibble his earlobe, he was relieved when the taxi stopped outside his home, he paid the driver and when he looked around, she was already entering through the front door.

He walked in behind her, she turned to face him and asked.
"Are we on our own in this big wonderful house?" He nodded and she did no more than slip her dress off her shoulders and let it fall to the floor, her naked tits were just like her daughters with thick hard nipples, she pushed her thong down her legs and let that fall to the floor, she

stood naked in front of him with her hands on her hips, his eyes were locked onto her hairless fanny, she said.
"Well, are you going to fuck me or are you going to stare at me all night?" he removed his clothes slowly, because she watched every move that he made, when he pushed his boxers down his legs she said.

"Wow, fucking hell Bobby, that is a big cock." She walked to him and gripped his shaft and began wanking him, he returned the compliment and pushed his fingers along her hairless fanny lips to her wet entrance, he pushed two fingers inside her and began frigging her, when he bent his fingers forwards and increased his speed she let go of his cock and gripped him around the head and groaned her orgasm into his ear, her hips moving back and forth in her urgency, she stepped away from him and went to a thick black leather chair, she sat down and opened her legs wide and eased her bottom forward and watched as his huge cock swayed from side to side as he approached her.

He dropped to his knees in front of her and using his right hand he eased his hard cock into her, she arched her back as he stretched her further than she had ever been stretched before, and the depth that he reached, *my god he was so deep*, she thought. Gripping her inner thighs he began to ride her with slow long deep strokes, she knew that he was going to be her best ever lover from the way he began to fuck her, he was thinking of her pleasure just as much he thought of his own.

When she came she lifted her bottom off the chair and held herself stiff as he rammed his mighty cock into her, taking her through her orgasm, he soon took her to her second orgasm with the same reaction as be-fore, he then slowed down and stopped, she opened her eyes and said.
"You didn't cum did you?" He shook his head and smiled at her, pulled his cock out of her and stood up, He reached out for her hand, she took his hand and when he pulled her forwards he intended to pull her to her feet, but she stopped and reached out and gripped his thick cock, she exposed his knob and slid her mouth over the top, she gripped his shaft with her lips and began bouncing her head up and down, she gripped his shaft with her right hand, and gave him the best blow job that he had ever had.

He had to stop her or he would have cum in her beautiful warm mouth, because he wanted to cum inside this gorgeous woman, she lifted her head from his cock and asked

"Why did you stop me, I wanted to taste your cum?" he moved her to the side of the chair and bent her forwards and said "I am going to fuck you hard and shoot my spunk as far inside you, as I can" he pushed his cock into her and gripped her hips, she spread her feet and gripped the arm of the chair, now he was into his stride he rammed his big cock into her as hard and as fast as he could.

Kim made a whining sound which ended in a grunt every time he reached full depth, his first spurt of hot cum made Kim scream out into the empty house, each spurt brought another scream, he pulled her back as hard as he could while he pushed forwards, as hard as he could, even though they were tightly held together she still managed to move her fanny against the base of his cock. After a short while she asked him to let her go, he did as she asked and she instantly turned and fell to her knees, she gripped his still hard cock and took most of it down her throat, Kim took up where she had left of before and tried to suck the very life out of him, she kept him hard and performed the perfect mouth sex on him, he reached down and gripped her thick black hair either side of her head and with closed eyes he began to fuck her mouth, Kim loved this and held her head still as she somehow closed her throat to stop him choking her and at the same time gripping his cock as tight as she could with her lips and let him fuck her mouth.

Bobby grunted and shot his hot cum into her mouth, she made a gurgling sound as she swallowed every drop of his cum, when she had swallowed all that he had to give, she lifted her mouth from his fast shrinking cock, she stood up and placed her mouth onto his, she opened her mouth wide and let him search her mouth with his tongue, at the same time she rubbed her mound against his still slightly swollen cock. Kim finally pulled away from him and said. "Please take me to bed Bobby, I want you to fuck me all night long." He took her hand and led her to the stairs just as he had with her beautiful young daughter.

Kim was insatiable, as soon as they were in the bedroom she had his cock in her mouth again doing her best to get him hard, she finally achieved her goal and went down to her hands and knees and looked back at him as he took up his position behind her, she arched her back as he entered her, all the time that he fucked her she scratched at the Indian rug that she was knelt on, he was well knackered, but he wasn't going to give up, he reached forward and grabbed a handful of her thick black hair and forced her head back, she began moaning out loud but on and on he rode her, she came time and time again each orgasm seemed to give her renewed energy and enthusiasm to make him last longer.

Bobby finally filled her with his seed again and was relieved when his cock slipped from her, he stood up and collapsed backwards onto the bed, his arms and legs spread wide, in a second she was kneeling by his side, she lifted his cum covered cock and exposed his tender knob, a huge blob of hid pale spunk oozed out of his piss hole, she did no more as she puckered her lips and covered the tip of his knob, then made him moan out loud as she proceeded to suck every last drop out of him. She licked her lips just before she took great pleasure in licking his cock clean, when she was done, she curled herself around him, but he was already asleep.

Bobby woke in the morning to a most glorious feeling of soft warm lips around his already hard cock, he looked up to see Kim's head bouncing up and down, she lifted her eyes to his and smiled, she lifted her mouth from his cock and crawled up his body, she spread herself over him and placed her mouth over his, she squirmed all over him as they kissed passionately, she lifted her mouth from his and said.
"Lay still lover, I am going to ride you to a finish and if you are lucky, I will stay another night." With that she lifted herself up and reaching underneath herself, she used her hand expertly to guide him into herself, she sank down on his length, with him now fully inside her she placed her hands either side of his head and moved her knees in closer and began to slowly ride him, she would dangle her breasts into his mouth and let him suck on her nipples like a baby.

Her orgasms were still as intense as they were the night before, after her second orgasm she stopped and lifted herself from his cock and like a crab turned herself around and remounted him back to front, now she gripped his shins and rode him again, when he looked down he could now see her fanny stretched tight around his big thick cock, she rode him towards another orgasm and slowing down, she turned to him and said. "I want you to help me this time, I want you to slap my thighs as hard as you want." She pulled his knees up so that they were bent and leaned on them, he used both hands and slapped her hard on both thighs, she called out in pain, but did not complain so he hit her again, and again.

Kim was like a demented wild cat as she bounced up and down on his mighty cock as he neared another orgasm, she began calling out "I'm coming, I'm coming" he lifted himself up onto his elbows and waited his time. Kim picked up speed and began moaning out loud, she shouted. "Get ready Bobby boy." She suddenly stopped and held her body dead still, he began to ram his big cock upwards into her, Kim was going mad, she began shouting all sorts of strange stuff like.
"Go on Bobby, ram that big cock into me, I am riding your big cock Bobby just like Mia did, I want your baby Bobby, shoot your spunk into me, Bobby." That was exactly what he did.

She sank down on him and screamed out at the top of her voice as she ground herself against him, he watched her stretched fanny as it moved around his hard cock. Kim final lifted herself from his cock and turned around and began sucking his cock again, he looked down once and could have sworn all of his mighty cock was down her throat. He closed his eyes for a second and when he opened them again, she was nowhere to be found, her clothes and every trace of her was now gone, he sat down and didn't know if he was relieved or not, she was a lot of woman maybe too much for any one man.

Thankfully he never heard from her again, sadly he never heard from Mia either but she would always hold a very special place in his heart.

Chapter 9

Bobby was sat at one of his wooden benches trying to sort out a box full of hammocks that he planned to hang in the trees that were on the edge of the wood, when Sylvia sat down opposite him.

She had parked her pushchair by the side of the bench, she looked up at him and said.
"Hello Bobby, I thought it only fair to let you see your daughter." With that she reached down and lifted the blond haired child out of the pushchair and sat her on her lap, she then said.
"Roberta, meet your father Bobby, Bobby meet your daughter Roberta." He reached out and touched the babies hand and said. "She is really beautiful just like her mother." Sylvia blushed a deep crimson at his comment and said.

"I have taken the baby into school to introduce her to the other teachers, I heard some bad things about you Bobby, they tell me that you got a sixteen year old girl pregnant, and she had to leave the school out of embarrassment, is it true?" He shrugged and said.
"She told me that she was seventeen and that she would take care of it with the pills that the Matron had given out." She looked around and said.
"Why can't you use condoms like any other normal human being, it would save you a lot of trouble." His answer struck a chord with her when he said.
"Like you Sylvia, she wanted to feel me cum inside her and I like to oblige." She lowered her head and said.

"I miss you Bobby and I miss your big cock, will you do something for me please,[he nodded] when I am ready for another child will you make me pregnant again, I will come to you if you want, but no-one must ever know." He nodded and said
"I miss you to Sylvia and I would be honoured to do as you ask, but what if I called around in the mean time when the coast was clear, would you turn me away?" She shook her head and said. "You know that I wouldn't turn you away because you know that I love you Bobby, but if you do come around please bring some protection with you, that

is the only way that I will let you do it to me." She glanced back at the school and said that she had better be going.

She placed the baby back into the pushchair and looked back at the man that she loved and said. "I will be seeing you soon then, if you come to the back door and the hanging basket is hanging on the left of the door, then the coast is clear, but if the hanging basket is on the other side, that means either my husband is due home or I am having my period, is that clear?" He nodded and said. "Very soon Sylvia, maybe before the end of the week?" She nodded and said as she walked away. "See you then, then." And with that she was gone.

When he arrived home later that evening, he sat down and logged on to the site that he had used when he bought the girls their strap on cocks, he chose to white butt plugs for the girls and for himself he ordered 100 assorted condoms, some were flavoured, some had little nobbles all over them, there were blue, red, yellow, pink even black ones. As soon as they arrived he planned to go and have a look at a certain hanging basket.

The parcel arrived and he was like a kid with a new toy, he put the batteries into the small white butt plugs and switched them on and held one in each hand, they were really quite good for something so small, he couldn't wait to see the girl's reactions, only two days to go.

Bobby walked along the path that led to Sylvia's house, it was just getting dark and she had left the outside light at the rear of the house, he could see the hanging basket hanging on the left hand side of the door, he walked to the back door and tapped it twice. Sylvia opened the door in her flowered dressing gown, she kissed him on the lips and turned away from him, he closed the door and followed her into the living room, she sat down on the settee and watched him walk towards her, as he sat down by her side she said. "I had given up hope of you coming round tonight, I was just thinking of my favourite vibrator and an early night."

With that she undid the belt on her dressing gown and left the next move up to him, he eased her face to his and kissed her warm soft lips, when he pushed his tongue to her lips, she opened her lips willingly and accepted his warm tongue into her mouth. His hand slipped inside her dressing gown to her naked breast, as soon as he touched her nipple she groaned somewhere deep inside, the nipple grew to its fullest extent and when he slid his hand down her slim body she opened her legs in anticipation, he slid his fingers down to her shaved fanny, as he slid his fingers along her slit, she groaned out loud and placed her hand on his hard cock, she tugged at his belt telling him that she wanted him to undo his trousers. He stood up and stripped his clothes off, when his big cock came into view Sylvia reached out and gripped it, she then moved her hand ever so slowly up and down his thick shaft, he reached forward and pulled her dressing from her body, and let it fall to the floor.

 Sylvia sat back down, he went to sit by her side but she stopped him and pulled his knob to her mouth, she closed her mouth around his knob and slowly licked all around his rim before she began to bounce her head back and forth, he closed his eyes and lost himself in sheer delightful because of the loving, sensual feeling that she was giving him, he opened his eyes and looked down at her mouth at the same time as was looking back at him but she was smiling with her eyes, because she could see just how much pleasure she was giving him. Bobby stopped her head and pulled his cock from her beautiful warm mouth, she said.

"I don't mind if you want me to finish you off with my mouth?" He shook his head and bent down for his trousers, he reached into a pocket and pulled out a hand full of condoms. "Please choose one my darling, any one you like." She closed her eyes and picked one at random, ripped the end off and reaching forward she slid it down his long thick cock and said.

"It has got little nobbles all the way down its length", he lowered himself down to his knees and opened her legs, he looked down at her swollen fanny and placed his knob at her entrance, when he pushed forward she arched her back and grunted out loud, when he was fully inside her she stopped him and said .
"That was like losing my virginity all over again, now fuck me like you did that very first time, make me cum over and over." She then closed her eyes and waited for him to begin fucking her.

Bobby lifted her legs up to his shoulders and gripped the insides of her thighs and began to ride her, for the first time in his short sex life, he wanted to make love to the mother of his child, he even thought that he may well be in love with this woman. Sylvia was totally relaxed as he made love to her, her only movement was her fingers as she squeezed her breasts, he could tell by her lifting her chin and holding her breath that she neared her first orgasm, when her hips began to move up and down in rhythm with him, he picked up his rate and took her through a powerful orgasm, as she came out of the other side she smiled to herself and then relaxed her body again, as she waited for the next climax to build. Sylvia loved sex with this beautiful man, after this night if she never ever had sex again, she wouldn't care.

As for sex with her husband, it happens but it is over so quick that she has never really been involved with it, after he had fallen asleep she goes into the spare bedroom and takes out her special 10 inch black vibrator and fucks herself stupid. But now that she has had Bobby's big cock inside her body, when she goes into the spare room, as she slips the rubber cock into herself the only person that she would be thinking off was Bobby Francis, this beautiful man that was deep inside her body, at this precise moment in time, making love to her, fucking her, giving her pleasure that she has longed for all her life.

Her second orgasm was much more intense than the first, she placed her hand on his chest and stopped him, she gently pushed him out of her and sat up, he moved back and she dropped to the floor in front of him and then turned away from him, he moved up behind her and slipped his mighty cock back into her, he then gripped her hips and began to make love to her again, he loved this position mainly because he had total control over the pace but also because he was very deep inside her, in this position as with any woman he was as deep as he could be.

He was snapped out of his thoughts by Sylvia scratching the carpet and moaning out loud, her back was covered in tiny goose bumps as she began thrusting back at him, forcing him to go just a fraction deeper, just as quickly as she had begun thrusting hack at him, she stopped and held herself dead still and let him take her through her orgasm.

When he began to ride her again he knew that he wouldn't last much longer, she sensed this and gripped his cock with her fanny muscle and held her breath, he was now flat out and grunting at each thrust, she began calling out as she wanted to cum with him.

The noise that they were making was enough to wake the dead, he finally exploded into the rubber condom but still she screamed at the top of her voice in ecstasy, as they came together. That one fuck was enough for Sylvia, she said he could come back anytime he wanted to, but for tonight she had had enough, a single tear ran down her face as she left the room and went to bed, he cleaned himself up and left her house locking the door after him.

As he walked back towards his car, he felt that he was more in love with her now, than he had been before, and couldn't wait to go back again.

Chapter 10

Bobby was sat waiting outside the gates of the school for his two favourite 17 year old girls, Susy and Liz who he had arranged to meet, even though they were still very young, they were deeply in love with each other but willing to learn more about the art of sex from him, he had given them one lesson two weeks ago, but today was their second lesson, he had surfed the net finding out about girl on girl love, so that he can pass on the information to them, his reward was that he gets to fuck them both. His face broke into a smile when they came into view, both girls smiled and waved at him. Both girls wore tiny little shorts and loose tee shirts, they climbed into his car. Susy was sat next to him and leaned over and kissed him hard on the lips.

Liz sat with a bag on her lap and held her lovers hand. Bobby started the car and drove towards his home. Susy said. "We have been really looking forward to this, haven't we Liz?" He saw Liz squeeze her lovers hand and said.
"Oh yes Bobby, we can't wait do it again with you, but we want to learn some other things as well." He squeezed Susie's leg and said. "I have some new things to teach you, but I also have a nice little surprise for you both as well." He reached into the side pocket and passed then a brown paper bag, they looked inside and giggled, Liz said. "They are a bit small aren't they Bobby?" And both girls began laughing as they reached into the bag and took out the butt plugs, Susy switched hers on and began teasing her best friend with it, when Liz turned hers on as well they played like little kids laughing and screaming out loud.

He stopped the car outside his house and climbed out of the car and went up to the big oak doors, he looked back and the girls were still sat in the car looking at him, so he went back to the car and stuck his head through the open window and said.
"What?" Susy looked at her lover who nudged her and told her to ask him, Susy looked back at Bobby and said.
"Can we please do it outside in the fresh air?" He smiled and said. "Just give me a minute and let me think about where we can go, in the mean-time you two go into the kitchen and make a picnic and I will go and fetch some blankets and stuff." The girls ran into the house and he

drove off in the car to a barn that they used for storage. Liz had left her bag in the car, so he had a quick look inside and saw the two strap on cocks and the lubricant. He found what he needed and loaded it all in the back of the car. He drove back to the house and when he went into the kitchen the girls had made enough food to feed the five thousand, he found a large basket and helped them put everything inside. Back in the car he drove down some bumpy tracks towards a Dutch barn that was half full of straw, he stopped outside and the girls were out of the car in a second and began jumping up and down in the loose straw, kicking it up in the air, laughing and shouting at each other. Bobby took a pile of blankets out of the back of the car and dropped them on the floor, the girls stopped playing and spread the blankets out to make a square about twenty feet square, he took some cushions out of the car and tossed them onto the blankets, the girls soon picked up a cushion each and began play fighting.

Bobby took the picnic basket out of the car and placed it on the edge of the blankets and sat down and watched them screaming and laughing at each other, he leaned back against a large cushion and smiled at their antics, when Liz caught her lover on the side of the head and she fell over laughing, Liz dropped her cushion and dropped down on top of her lover and best friend, within second they were kissing and their hands were all over each other, soon two pairs of tits were on view and they were trying to open each other's shorts. Bobby said. "Girls, girls, just stop for a minute." The girls stopped but didn't break apart, both young women turned to look at him, he said. "Why don't you stop what you are doing and take all of your clothes off?" The girls looked at one another and pulled apart, they sat on the blankets and stripped their clothes off, he watched with interest as his cock was growing in his shorts, Susy looked at him and said.

"You as well." He casually removed all his clothes and when he pulled his shorts down his big cock resembled a large banana, both girls began giggling at the funny sight, so he jumped up and gripping his half hard cock in his right hand he began chasing them with it, both girls screaming at the top of their voices, he caught them and grabbed them both and they all fell down in a heap laughing out loud, they all lay flat on their backs looking up at the wooden rafters in the roof of the barn. Bobby just happened to be in between the two girls, he placed his arms

under each girl's shoulders and that is how they stayed for quite a while, there was no urgency about the sex, they all knew that it would happen, when it happened. Susy said .
"Please tell us about those little white vibrators?" He said. "It might be better if I show you rather than try and tell you, that way it will be more fun." Susy nudged him and said.
"Go on then show us, we are desperate to know what they are for." He went to the car and fetched the paper bag, he sat back down, looked at the girls and said.
"We could do with some of that lubricant that I gave you." Liz jumped up and went to the car and came back with her bag, she opened it and took out the lubricant and passed it to him, he took the butt plugs from the bag and lubricated them both, he looked from one girl to the other and said. "Right you two, get on your hands and knees side by side and look forwards."

They did as he asked, he moved up behind them and spread their knees, he put some lubricant on his fingertip and rubbed it around both bum-holes, both girls looked back at him to see what he was doing, he pointed for them to face forwards again and when they were looking forward again, he picked up one of the white butt plugs and holding Susie's bum cheeks open, he slipped it easily into her bum-hole, he did the same to Liz who resisted a little at first, bit but he managed to get them both all of the way inside, he reached and switched Susie's on first and she burst out laughing, when he switched Liz's butt plug on she groaned out loud and her hips began bouncing back and forth, she was really into it in a big way.

Liz reached under herself and began rubbing her own clit, she was coming and she didn't care who knew it, her lover sat and watched fas-cinated as she masturbated openly in front of them. Liz called out her orgasm and flopped to the blanket whispering
"Please turn it off, leave it in but turn it off." He reached forward and did as she asked, Liz lay there panting eventually saying quietly. "Bloody fucking hell, I have never felt anything so bloody sexy in my life, can I keep it please?" He turned to Susy and said
"Why don't you go and put on one of the strap on cocks and we will give our Liz here a right good seeing too." Liz lay and watched as her lover pulled the big red strap on cock up her legs and snapped it into

place, Bobby passed her the lubricant and Susy rubbed some all over the big rubber cock, he stacked two of the biggest cushions on top of one-another, he then pulled Liz up and leaned her over the cushions, he placed Susy behind her and she moved into position, when she put the tip of the rubber cock at her entrance, he reached forward and switched the butt plug on, which brought an immediate reaction from Liz, she groaned out loud as Susy pushed the rubber cock into her lover, she gripped her hips and began fucking the very life out of her.

Liz was going berserk, she was thrusting back at her lover as well as making all sorts of noises, she was almost in tears. Bobby moved to Liz's head and held his hard cock out to her, he pushed it at her mouth, which she parted her lips, he pushed the head of his big cock into her hot mouth, with her action from being fucked from behind, he just knelt there and let her movement do the work, the young girl was getting it from every angle and was loving every second of it, she spat his cock out each time she screamed out her orgasm, as soon as she was through it, she opened her mouth again for him to push his cock back inside. Susy was doing her nut at the scene in front of her and she was desperate for some action of her own and was groaning out loud as she was so close to her own orgasm, in her urgency she began ramming that rubber cock into her lover as hard as he could, Liz lifted her head and screamed out loud as she came yet again, as soon as she had cum she begged them to stop, she wanted to rest and flopped forwards, she lay there shaking all over.

Susy on the other hand still knelt exactly where she was, her eyes closed and her hips moving back and forth as she remembered the sight of that big rubber cock as it went in and out of her lovers fanny as, he couldn't help himself as he moved behind her and bent her forwards, he didn't hesitate as he pushed his cock all of the way into her, which instantly brought a deep moan out of her, a moan like he had never heard the like of before, he had planned to use a condom on both of the girls, but the point of no return had long past, his first spurt of hot cum made her scream out and reach out for her lover, who had turned around and was now watching them fuck. Susy pulled her lover to her and they held onto each other while he filled her with his spunk, he pulled her hard back against him and at the same time he pushed his big cock into her as hard as he could. Both girls had begun crying but he didn't care, at that precise moment in time someone could have cut his head off and he would still have pushed his still hard cock into her. It was Liz that brought him out of his urgency by shouting at him saying that he was hurting her best friend, he pulled his cock out of the young girl and the girls fell forwards and held each other tightly, he could see that Susy was crying her heart out, he went to them and curled himself around them.

They stayed like this until Susy had calmed down, her body still gave the odd sob but she was almost back to normal, Liz had begun whispering to her lover, he couldn't hear what she was saying, but whatever it was she was responding, Liz looked at him and said
"Can you turn these things off and take them out now?" He had forgotten all about the butt plugs and did as they asked, when they were out he tossed them to one side out of the way. Bobby got up and opened the picnic basket, the girls had packed a bottle of champagne, he opened the bottle and poured them each a large tumbler of the bubbly liquid, they sat there and silently sipped at the fine wine, he looked at Susy and said how sorry he was if he had hurt her, she shook her head and said. "I hurt up inside Bobby, I don't think that I can do it again today" he pulled her to him and held her tight, she whispered how sorry she was for being such a wimp, he shook his head and said that it was him that should be sorry for being so selfish.

Liz broke the spell when she said out loud. "But that was the best thing that we have ever done, it was as sexy as hell, an army of soldiers could have lined up and fucked, me and I would have let every single one of them cum inside me." She opened her legs so that they could both look at her fanny and she said
"Just look at me, I am so wet my stuff is literally running out of me." Susy reached forward and using her finger-tip she scooped up some of her lovers cum and placed it into her mouth, she sucked the cum from her finger and went in for a second helping, saying. "Hhmmm you taste so nice Liz, why don't you try some Bobby?"

He took some on his finger tip and placed it onto his tongue, before he had time to speak Susy pushed his head towards her lovers fanny, Liz fell backwards and opened her legs wide, he lowered his head down to the young girls fanny and quickly gave her an orgasm with his mouth, he licked her ever so slowly, just as he would lick an ice cream, he flicked his tongue at her clit, as soon as she reacted he closed his lips around her tiny button and sucked for all he was worth. When she had cum he went in search of his reward, he dipped his tongue as deep into her fanny and searched everywhere he could for her offerings, when he lifted his mouth from her fanny, she lay back down with a huge smile on her face.

They all relaxed and ate some of the vast amount of food that the girls had made, he looked from one girl to the other and asked.
"Should we not discuss what happened, because I don't want to hurt either of you again" Susy spoke first and said.
"You were so deep inside me Bobby I think that you may have split me, if I don't start bleeding I can get involved again, but I can't have you inside me again today, sorry." He nodded and said. "I owe you an apology, because I actually brought some condoms with me today and fully intended to use them so that you didn't have to use those pills again" Susy smiled and said. "It's a bit late for that now Bobby, but I know why you did what you did, we were both so desperate for some sort of release, we would have done anything to get what we wanted." All three of them nodded their agreement.

Susy turned to her best friend and said. "And what about you then Liz with that thing up you other place?" Liz blushed a deep crimson and said. "I have never felt anything like that before, but if I am honest I want to do it again, it felt so good." Susy placed her mouth to her lovers ear and whispered something that made Liz look at his limp cock and smile, the two girls looked at one another and smiled at one-another, they then both turned and looked at him until he said smiling. "What are you two up to then?" they both crawled towards him and one went either side of him Susy lifted his limp cock, and Liz picked up a tumbler of champagne and between them the managed to dip his big knob into the champagne.

Liz closed her mouth over his bell end and sucked all of the champagne from it, they did it again only this time it was Susy that sucked him dry, this went on for a few minutes until he was hard again, Susy jumped up and went to the car and was out of sight for a while when she came back she was wearing her shorts, he looked disappointed, she shrugged and said. "I'm bleeding, but don't let me stop you two enjoying your selves." He was laying there and Liz was lazily wanking his big cock with her right hand, he was worried about Susy and asked if she needed to go somewhere for some treatment, she shook her head and said. "I will give it a couple of days and see what happens, but don't worry about me, if anything was wrong I will text you, now let me watch you fuck my girlfriend.

" Liz crawled over the blankets and lay over the two cushions and opened her legs, Bobby moved up behind her and slid his big cock into her young willing body, she groaned and lifted her head back as he forced her insides to stretch, Susy moved around and sat in front of her lover and took Liz's hands in her own and enjoyed the fuck with her best friend, when she was close to coming, Susy would begin kissing her, Liz said something to Susy, but he didn't know what it was, Susy stood up and walked away, he didn't see what she was doing but when she came back she had one of the butt plugs in her hand all lubricated, he stopped moving and Susy inserted the white vibrator inside her lovers bottom and switched it on, the effect on Liz was instant, she began moaning out loud and gripped onto her lover for all she was worth and began thrusting back at him, he watched as Susy reached under her lover and squeezed her tits hard which just increased the young girls pleasure, Liz was lost in a world that she didn't fully understand, she wanted something that she was too embarrassed to ask for, she looked pleadingly at her lover willing her to understand, willing her to read her mind and do what she wanted.

Susy said.
"What is it Liz, tell me what's wrong?" Liz shook her head but she was getting desperate and shouted out.
"Please Susy, make him fuck my ass with that big cock" Susy frowned and looked at her lover and asked her.
"Are you sure Liz?" Liz nodded her head and said. "Please make him do it, I want him to, I want to feel his big cock up my ass." So Susy stood up and went and fetched the lubricant, he looked at Susy and wondered what she was up to, Susy stopped him and he pulled his sticky cock out of the young girl and looked up at Susy who pulled the buzzing white vibrator out of her lovers ass and rubbed some lubricant all around her brown hole, she then gripped his hard cock and held his

knob at her brown hole, he pushed forward and his big cock stretched her anus, it was so tight around his big knob that he thought he would shoot his load there and then.

Liz sort of screamed out as his cock slipped easily inside her ass, he gripped her hips and fucked her brown hole for all he was worth, she was so tight that he knew that he wouldn't last much longer, Susy went back to her lovers head and took her hands in hers again, Liz opened her eyes and looked lovingly at her lover and said.
"It's so good Su, it feels so big up there, I want him to cum up my ass Su." She closed her eyes again and began thrusting back at him as another orgasm flooded her young body, Susy went to Bobby and standing by his side she placed her right tit into his mouth, he sucked hungrily on the hard nipple, she looked deep into his eyes and said.
"Cum up her ass Bobby, she wants you to."

She went behind him and gripped his swinging balls and squeezed them, he instantly grunted and shot his cum up the young girls ass, making her scream out into the clear blue sky, each spurt of hot cum brought another loud scream from the young girl, he wanted to push his cock into her but he had already split one girl today, he didn't want to damage the other, so he let her make the decisions, he could feel himself going limp and Liz pulled away from him, his big cock slipped from the young girls body and when he looked down all sorts of funny stuff was running from her brown hole.

Liz didn't move, she just lay there with her eyes closed, silent tears running down her cheeks, her lover and best friend rubbing her back and trying to console her as best she could, Liz looked at her lover and said, "I'm sorry Su, but I just wanted it so badly, I don't know why but it felt so bloody good and when he came up there, well it burned my insides, it felt different from the other way for me anyway." Susy stroked her friend and said. "You can do whatever you want Liz, if that was what you wanted when we get back, I will do it for you with our toys, I would do anything for you, you know that, you know that I love you so much, now we had better get back, you can help me sort myself out." Susy nodded.

In the car on the way back to the school, they arranged to meet in two weeks, because he hadn't got around too showing them his new tricks, Liz tried to get him to tell them what it was, but he was having none of it, if he told them they might not want to meet up again and he didn't want that. Susy had begun holding her stomach and moaning, he offered to take her to the hospital but she was having none of it, when he dropped them off they walked away from him with Liz almost dragging Susy along. He drove home worried about the young girl and what he had done to her. He would never forgive himself if anything happened to her.

Bobby drove home and when he was driving down his drive he saw Jill Pouch the local restaurant owner walking her golden retriever along the side of his drive, he was surprised as in all the years that he had known her, she had never once walked her dog on the estate near the house before, he had seen her across the fields before but never near the house, he waved as he passed her but she just stared at him and when he looked at her in the rear view mirror, she was just standing there staring at the back of his car.

He never gave Jill another thought, he sat and ate his evening meal and thought about the afternoon's somewhat strange activities, especially Liz and the ass fucking thing, he   hadn't got a clue where that had come from, but if that was what she wanted then that is what she would get. He was sat on the settee watching the television when his phone bussed in his pocket; he took it out and read the message. "Susy in hospital, pick me up at the gates, soonest Liz." He jumped up and ran out to the car, she was waiting there when he arrived and jumped in the car and he drove off, he asked Liz what had happened and she said that. "Susy was pouring blood and curled up on the floor in agony, so I fetched the nurse who on taking one look at her phoned for an ambulance, that was nearly an hour ago, but they wouldn't let me go with her, I hope that she will be ok Bobby?" He tried to reassure her but was worried to death.

When they arrived at the hospital, they were told that Susy had been assessed and was being prepared for minor surgery, and no, they couldn't see her under any circumstances, they would have to wait. It took two hours before anyone came to see them, they were taken into a two bed ward where Susy was on her own, she looked tiny and so fragile in the big bed. Liz went to the far side of the bed and held her lovers hand, he sat the other side and held her other hand, they had been told that everything had gone well and that she would be out of it for a while and to let her sleep. It was at least two hours later that her eyes fluttered open; she looked at Liz and whispered. "Hello there lover."

Liz had tears running down her face in relief, he squeezed her best friends hand, she slowly turned her head and smiled at him and whispered.
"My two most favourite people." A sister came in to check the charts, Liz asked if Susy was going to be ok?. The sister looked at Susy and said. "The lining of her stomach had split, it can happen sometimes with strenuous exercise, she has had key-hole surgery to repair the tear, [she looked at Bobby and said] she will have to be a bit more careful next time she exerts herself like that again." She placed the chart back on the end of the bed and was gone.

Liz giggled and said.
"She knows how it happened doesn't she?"   Bobby shrugged and answered
"It would seem so, maybe we should give things a rest for a while, at least until Susy is fully recovered?" Susy squeezed his hand and said.
"No, I don't want that, anyway you two can carry on as if nothing has happened and I can watch, maybe I will have to try the other hole like Liz?" He reached across the bed and took Liz's hand and said. "We are three, we are a team, we will wait until we can all be as one again." They all agreed and the sister came back in and told them to leave, as the patient needed her rest.

He dropped Liz off at the school, and knew that he could have stopped the car and fucked her, she had almost said as much, but he wanted to keep his word to Susy, if he could. He had dropped her off and was driving home, it was quite late and he saw something that he had never seen before, Jill was walking her dog by the gates of the estate, he peeped his car horn and waved, she waved back and as before when he looked back, she was stood dead still watching him drive away *strange* he thought to himself.

They visited Susy at every opportunity, he had filled her two bed room with flowers and she had that much fruit on the table by her bed that she could have opened a fruit and veg stand. Susy was well on the road to recovery and feeling a little bit frisky on this particular evening, she asked him to draw the curtains so that no-one could see in, when they were closed she turned to Liz and said. "Show me your tits Liz, I have missed you so much." Liz smiled and lifted her top and showed her lover her fine tits, Susy reached out and fondled both breasts, Liz moved closer to her lover and kissed her hard on the lips. Susy looked at Bobby and said. "You don't mind do you Bobby?" he shrugged and said

"Carry on, I don't mind watching." Susy told him to lean against the door to stop anyone coming in, he did this and Susy removed her night shirt to leave herself naked, Liz was on her in a flash, she had her legs wide open and her face buried in her best friends fanny. Susy was groaning in ecstasy, it was as if she hadn't had any sex in months, he coughed and when Liz looked up at him he said. "Use your fingers at the same time as your tongue." She nodded and bent over to her task, the fingers were making a vast amount of difference and Susy was soon crying out in her orgasm. Liz lifted her mouth from her lovers fanny and planted her lips hard on Susie's lips, he watched as Susy searched her lovers mouth for a taste of her own cum, he watched as Susy reached her hand under her lovers short skirt and pushed her hands down the back of her pants and squeezed her ass cheeks. Liz reached back and pushed her pants down her legs, now almost naked she looked at Bobby and climbed onto the bed.

Susy eased her lover up so that she was knelt either side of her head, he could hear Susy sucking on her lovers fanny; as for Liz she had her eyes closed. Susy reached around behind Liz and pushed a finger up her bum hole, the reaction from Liz was amazing, she reached out and planted her hands flat against the wall and rubbed her fanny up and down her lovers face, as she called out in orgasm. When she had cum, she sat there crying out loud before she lifted herself from her friends face, Susie's face was covered in her friends sticky cum, Liz said sorry and went and fetched a damp cloth and washed her lovers face, she went to wash her fingers but she shook her head and slipped them into her mouth and sucked them clean. Susy slipped her night shirt back on and pulled the bed clothes over herself and said.

"That's better, I needed that, it was better than any medicine that the doctor can give me." She looked at Bobby who was still leaning against the door his hard cock clearly on view in his trousers, she turned to her lover and said. "You had better go over there and take care of our teacher, he looks a bit excited to me."

Liz looked at his hard cock and walked over to him, her tits were still on view and she was still naked underneath her skirt, she stood in front of him and looked up into his eyes as she undid his trousers, she pulled his zipper down and reached in and pulled his hard cock out and began wanking him, she said. "Do you want me to suck it or do you want to fuck me?" He looked at Susy and then back to Liz and said.
"Fuck, but how?" she took his hand and opened the toilet door and then used a chair so that the door stayed open and Susy could watch them doing it. She went into the bathroom and undid her skirt and taking it off she hung it on a hook on the wall, she looked back at Susy, leaned forward and gripped the sink.

He moved up behind her and placed his big knob at her entrance, when he pushed his big cock into the young girl she moaned out loud. Bobby didn't want to get caught, so he gripped her hips and began ramming his big cock into her as hard and as fast as he could, with-out knowing it he had lifted her bodily from the ground and held her weight easily, he glanced back at the patient and he could see her hand moving under the bedclothes as she pleasured herself.

Liz had called out her orgasm at least twice before he shot his hot cum deep inside her young body, she groaned at each spurt burned her insides, he still held her whole body off the ground, but still she managed to grind herself against him as he pushed himself as far inside her as he could. The bell sounded for the end of visiting, she had to shout at him to put her down, as soon as she landed on the ground she reached for some paper towels and pushed them between her legs and pulled her skirt back on, she walked back to the bed while he was sorting himself out. Liz was pulling her pants back on when Susy beckoned him to her, Susy said to her lover. "Stand by the door for a minute please" Liz did as she asked and he went to the patient who sat up and leaned towards him he hadn't managed to put his cock away because he hadn't cleaned it, he need not have worried Susy licked him clean before sucking any remaining seed out of his cock, all the time her hand was doing its work underneath the bed cloths. When Susy was finally satisfied that he was clean she looked up at her lover to see that she had her pants down by her knees and her fingers busy inside her fanny as well.

Bobby and Susy watched and waited for Liz to finish, she finished and pulled her sticky fingers from her fanny and looked at them, she pulled her pants up with her other hand and went over to Susy and pushed her sticky fingers into her best friends mouth, which Susy sucked hungrily. When the fingers were clean Susy pulled them from her lover's mouth Susie's eyes were sparkling as she said. "I could taste you both then, I have dreamt about that all day, it was perfect and now I want to go to sleep and dream but before you go can you pass me some paper towels as my pants are soaking wet." They all laughed out loud and after they had all kissed each other, Bobby and his young lover left. They walked across the dark car park hand in hand and as soon as they were in the car she asked him to kiss her properly.

He pulled her to him and pushed his mouth onto the young girls mouth they were soon tongue fighting, he had his hand up her top and had her left breast in his hand she had her hand on his hardening cock. She pulled away from him and said.
"Find somewhere quiet Bobby." She then reached under her skirt and removed her pants again. He drove out of the car park and down the main road, his eyes scanning for somewhere quiet, she leaned into his lap and with a bit of help from him she managed to get his hard cock out and began sucking it for all she was worth. He pulled off the road into a lay-by, and switched the car off.

He pushed his seat back as far as it would go and she climbed into his lap but facing away from him, he lifted her skirt and felt her firm buttocks when she said. "Please fuck my ass again Bobby" he hadn't expected this but any port in a storm, he licked his finger and rubbed it all around her bum-hole, he then rubbed a lot of spit all around his knob, as soon as he put his knob to her brown hole she began lowering herself down, his cock slid into her quite easily and when he was deep inside her she began moaning out loud, she had gripped the steering wheel with both hands and was bouncing up and down on his hard cock, they fucked flat out both desperate for the same end, and that end was for him to cum deep inside her, her orgasms had come and gone, but now it was his turn she sensed he was ready to explode and gripped the steering wheel harder, he grunted and erupted deep inside her brown hole which made her scream out at the top of her voice, they rammed against each other as hard as they possibly could, it was Liz who finally shouted for him to stop, she had had enough but still she sank down on him keeping his still almost hard cock deep inside her body.

The lovers sat still both breathing hard, he was fucked totally, but he was a happy man and he knew that his young lover was very happy as well, she turned sideways so that when he pulled his cock out she didn't explode all over his clothing, she slid from his cock and lay out face down across the big seat, he searched for some tissues to clean himself up.

They were sat in the dark in the lay-by sorting out their clothing when he asked her. "What's with all this ass fucking then Liz?" she never answered him for a minute or so when she finally said. "I don't know Bobby it just feels better to me, more personal some-how, do you think that Susy will mind doing it to me with those strap on's?" He looked at her shadow in the darkness and said. "She loves you more than life itself Liz and if that is what you want then she will do anything to make you happy.

"He dropped her off at the school and headed for home, he was surprised to see Jill again walking her dog away from his estate, he looked at her in the mirror again and she was standing there watching him drive away, he would have to go and see Jill, to find out what was going on.

Chapter 11

Everywhere that Bobby seemed to go Jill would appear at some point, he was getting a little bit paranoid, even the night that he fetched Susy out of hospital he saw Jill standing by the main gates again, the next morning he booked a table at The Barn restaurant, which was Jill's place, he turned up on time and sat at his table, a waitress came and took his order, he had seen Jill going in and out of the kitchen.

Jill brought his meal, when she placed the meal down on the table he said. "Thank you Jill, will you join me for a drink later, I think we have something to discuss, don't you?" She gave a single nod and turned away from him and headed back to the kitchen, he watched her walk away and decided that she had a nice tight ass, she was maybe mid-forties, and as a younger woman must have been very beautiful, she had a fine firm body with a nice handful of firm tit.

His meal was first class and desert was even better, every part of the meal was home made by a first class chef, he sat drinking a large brandy when Jill came into the dining area, she looked around, there was him and one other elderly gentleman who was almost asleep, he caught her eye and held his hand out to the seat next to him, she looked a bit nervous but poured herself a glass of red wine and walked slowly over to him and sat down in the chair next to him, he looked at the stunning woman who avoided his glance and said. "Is there something wrong Jill, only where ever I go you seem to pop up and stare at me, if I have done something wrong then please tell me, and I will do my best to put everything right."

She looked at him for a long time, he held her gaze as she whispered "I saw you with those two young girls in the barn, I saw everything that you did to them, everything. I know how old they are and where they come from." He smiled and said "And?"

She blushed a deep crimson as she thought about her next sentence, she made up her mind and said. "I want you to meet me at the same place tomorrow afternoon at three and bring some blankets and pillows." With that she stood up and disappeared into the kitchen, he emptied his glass and sat there thinking, trying to decide if she had just made a threat or not, either way it looked like he was going to have to give her a fucking, ah well, there were worst ways to spend an afternoon.

Bobby drove his BMW down the bumpy lane to the straw barn, he couldn't see her so he laid out the blankets on the floor and tossed the cushions all over, he sat in the shade and drank a glass of red wine, sat and waited, he had removed his shirt and flip flops and sat there in his tight blue shorts, she turned up but stood looking at him before she approached, she stood maybe ten feet away from him in a thin flowered summer dress, with the sun behind her he could see the shape of her legs through the dress, he looked into her eyes and said.
"Well Jill, here we are then" she looked all around to make sure that they were on their own, she then looked at the blankets and cushions before saying. "It has been a long time for me Bobby, but when I watched you doing it to those young girls, I did things to myself, that I should have been embarrassed about, but it has been many lonely years since my husband sadly passed away, and I can honestly say that I haven't wanted any other man until I saw your size, and I have wanted you ever since and now here we are and I am like a school girl myself, soaking wet and as nervous as hell.

" It had taken a lot for her to say all that, he knew that, he poured her a glass of wine and patted the seat by his side, she walked over and sat by him, took the glass from his hand, drained it all in one go and passed him her glass, he placed both glasses on the floor and slipped his arm around her shoulders, she leaned against him as he reached to her face and turned her lips to his, he kissed her hard on the lips and when he pushed his tongue at her lips, she pulled away and looked puzzled, he smiled and said. "Trust me Jill, I will make it good for you, but only if you relax." This time when he pushed his tongue at her lips, she opened her lips and let him inside as soon as she felt his tongue in her mouth, she melted and came on the spot, he felt her tremble and then shudder, he pulled his mouth from hers and said. "That was the first one of many you will have today, she watched his hand as he placed it on her left braless breast as soon as he began fondling her breast, she pushed her lips to his again wanting to be kissed.

He rolled her hard nipple between his thumb and fore finger, a deep moan escaped from her throat, she reached into his lap and rested her hand on his thickening cock, he sat up and undid his shorts and pulled them open. He then turned to Jill and said.

"Why don't you take your dress off?" She looked into his eyes and then down to his hardening cock and said. "I want to see it first, I want to hold your big cock." She reached into his shorts and gripped his hard cock and pulled it out of his shorts and said "My god, I have never seen anything like that before." He put his hand around hers and gripped hard and pulled the skin down to expose his big blood filled knob, her eyes went big as he pushed her mouth towards his cock, she held back and looked up at him and said "I have never done that even though my husband wanted me to, when I saw the girls doing it to you I wandered what I had been missing, and what pleasure I had denied my husband."

He held her head and said. "You won't know unless you try it, will you?" He pushed her head again and she lowered her head towards his exposed knob, she opened her mouth and put it over his knob, but just held her mouth there, he said.

"Close your lips around it Jill. [when she had done what he asked, he then said] now lick all around the head [she did as he had been told]now when you grip it move your head back and forth and suck at the same time", [she did exactly as he asked] now he closed her hand around his shaft and began moving it up and down in time with her mouth, she looked up at him and smiled with her eyes, he reached under her dress and moved his hand up towards her fanny, she had on a thong that he pulled out of the way and began rubbing her fanny lips, when he went in search of her opening she opened her legs for him, when he pushed two fingers into her and began frigging her, her eyes went big again and she immediately lifted her mouth from his cock and held her breath, she lifted her hips up in the air and he could now get even deeper, he frigged her through her second orgasm, she looked up at him and said. "What have I been missing all these years Bobby?"

He smiled at her and asked her. "Have you ever tasted yourself?" She shook her head and grimaced, he did no more than pull his sticky fingers out of her fanny and hold them by her mouth; she looked at the sticky fingers, when she was with her husband he would never have offered such a thing. Now this handsome young man who had already got her to suck her first ever cock, was now offering a second new experience, she opened her mouth and he touched the tip of her tongue with his sticky fingers, she withdrew her tongue and tasted herself for the first time and had to admit it was quite nice, she opened her mouth and took both of his fingers into her mouth and licked them clean. When she had finished she let his finger slip from her mouth, he looked into her eyes and said. "Take all of your clothes of Jill and I will give you the fucking of your life." She hesitated for maybe half a second before she stood up and looked all around and then pulled the dress over her head, he looked at her firm body and she blushed deeply, he looked into her eyes and reached out and pulled the thong down her legs, she had shaved her fanny especially for today and he wasn't going to waste it, he reached out and gripped her buttocks and pulled her to him.

Her fanny was just the right height for his mouth, which he placed onto her fanny lips, she gripped his head with both hands and spread her thighs as wide as she could, he licked her slowly all over her fanny lips, and when he pushed his tongue between her swollen lips and touched her clit, he heard her gasp out loud, he could feel her holding her breath as he began sucking on the tiny button, she shuddered, trembled and called out in absolute delight, he then gripped her bum cheeks and pushed her hips forward where he could reach her opening, he pushed his tongue deep into her and immediately found her salty cum, he took his fill and then held some on his tongue for her to find.

He pulled his mouth away from her fanny and pulled her down to his height, he placed his lips onto hers and opened his mouth, it took her a few seconds to realise that he was waiting for her to go in search of her own taste again, she pushed her tongue into his mouth and he transferred her offering onto her own tongue, she licked it all from his tongue and took it back into her mouth and then used her tongue to spread it all around her gums, she then returned her tongue back into his mouth in search of any more that she may have missed. She finally pulled her mouth from his. He looked at her and stood up, he pulled her up and took her a few steps to where the pile of pillows were, he stacked one large pillow on top of the other and then used his hand to indicate for her to lean over them, she went down to her knees and moved her body so that she was leaning over the two thick cushions, she watched him as he removed his shorts, his big cock stuck out in front of him, he went down to his knees behind her, he looked at her big ass and thought about the smaller ones that had been bent over if front of him, the last time he had been in this barn, he saw her swallow deeply as he placed his knob at her entrance, he pushed forward and his knob slid inside her body, making her gasp out loud and grip the cushions with both hands, he pushed forward again, she was almost as tight as Liz's ass. Jill groaned out loud as he stretched her middle aged body for the very first time in her life, he had about two thirds of his big cock inside her, when he gripped her hips and began riding her with long slow strokes.

After only a few strokes she began to relax slightly, ever so slowly he went deeper and deeper until he had all of his big cock inside her, now that she was relaxed he picked up his rate and took her to her first ever orgasm with a real cock, she screamed out and began thrusting back at him, shouting. "My god, my god, did I just cum on your cock?" He slowed down and fucked her deep with long strokes, she began grunting out loud each time he reached full depth, her fingers were now scratching at the cushions again, when she came for the second time she was very disorientated, and in her erratic efforts at thrusting back at him, he shouted. "Let me do it Jill." She instantly held herself still and let him take her through her orgasm. When she was over the climax, he stopped and pulled his sticky cock out of her, she looked back at him and he just made a signal with his finger for her to turn over.

In a nanosecond she turned over, but she was too high for him, so he had to pull one of the cushions out from underneath her, she lay back down and he opened her legs wide and pushed his big cock back into her, he held his cock still while he lifted her legs onto his shoulders and gripped her inner thighs and began fucking her hard, her head was moving from side to side, he shouted. "Play with your tits Jill." Her hands went to her tits and she pulled them in all directions as he continued to ride her perfectly, she hadn't thought about him coming inside her until now, there was a slight chance that she could get pregnant, but if that happened she would take care of it, it was so easy these days. She was getting close again and looking forward to it, she closed her eyes in anticipation, when it came this time she was more controlled, the orgasm was the strongest yet and shook her to the very core. Bobby stopped again and she opened her eyes to look at him, he pulled his big sticky cock out of her and pulled her to him, he turned her around and placed her onto her hands and knees, he pushed his cock back into her and said. "Now it is my turn." He gripped her hips and began fucking her hard, she had gripped the blankets in both hands as he rammed his mighty cock back and forth, she was groaning all the time now, she could never remember feeling like this with her husband, this beautiful man had given her more orgasms in one afternoon than her husband had ever given her in all of their married life, in fact she couldn't remember one time that her husband had ever fucked her this hard, or for so long.

Bobby grunted out loud and exploded inside her supple body, Jill screamed out loud at every spurt that burned her insides, again and again he shot even more hot spunk into her, and when he pulled her back and pushed his big hard cock forward, she thought that he would choke her. He moved her fanny up and down against the base of his cock and when he let her go she continued doing it on her own, groaning all the time. He stopped her, moved her hips around and around a few times, as soon as he let go she again did it on her own. They came to a halt at more or less the same time, he had his head back and was taking deep breaths, she had her head hung down and he could see her back heaving as she took deep breaths, she jumped when his cock finally slipped out of her and their combined juices ran from her. She lowered herself down to the blanket and lay still, he looked at her gaping fanny and pale fluids bubbled out of her. He sat on his haunches with a huge smile on his face, he had done what he said he would do and gave her the fucking of her life.

Jill finally stirred and turned to look at him, she tried to smile but didn't quite manage it, he reached out and pulled her around and held her as she trembled in his arms, he asked her if she was ok, she looked up into his eyes and said. "What do you think, that was the best fuck ever, I have never experienced anything like that before, but I want to do it some more, I have a lot of time to make up for and a few more things to learn by the looks of it?" He smiled and said. "I will help you learn Jill, by the way here is another lesson [he lifted his limp cock and held it upwards] you have to clean up after a good fuck." She looked at his sticky limp cock, she began licking at the base and slowly worked her way upwards, he sat and watched this woman who had never sucked a cock before in her life giving him so much pleasure, when she reached his exposed knob she closed her mouth over the top and he closed his eyes as he felt her tongue licking all around the rim of his knob, she licked his knob all over and when she pushed the tip of her tongue into his piss-hole, he groaned out loud and almost shot his load again. Her job now done she lay with her head lovingly in his lap, they sat quiet and he could tell that she was deep in thought, he said. "A penny for them, Jill?" She shrugged and said. "If I hadn't seen you with those young girls the other day, I would still be an old maid with hardly any sexual experience, thinking that the sex that my husband I had indulged in was the best ever, but I now sadly realise that he never ever made me cum once in all off our married life, and I had denied him the pleasure of my mouth and the pleasure of his mouth on me.

I can remember when we first became married that he did try to use his mouth on me, but I pushed him away saying that it was disgusting, but now that you have done it to me and I have done it to you, I realise how selfish and wrong I have been and as for the act itself, well what can I say, only that you are an exceptional lover and I have been privileged to have spent an afternoon with you, and if you want to do it again anytime in the future you only have to let me know, and I will come to you or you can come to me, the choice is yours?" He thought about what she had said and replied. "Why are you talking about the future when there is still time this sunny afternoon, for some more fun and games." She lifted her head and looked at him and asked. "What are you thinking of then Bobby Francis?" he shrugged and said.
"If you can get some life into my friend down there, I'm sure that I will think of something."

She looked at his limp cock and lifted it up and shook it back and forth a few times, before she began moving her hand up and down his long thick shaft, seeing that she wasn't getting much response she lowered her head back down onto his big knob, and began letting him know what she had learned, as soon as he began growing she increased her efforts, her head was bobbing up and down on his now hard cock.

He stopped her and she looked disappointed and said. "I was enjoying that, I don't mind doing it all the way if you want, providing you agree to fuck me some other time?" He pushed her head back down, she changed her position so that she was now on all fours and carried on from where she had left off, her head was bouncing up and down, he watched her giving him a lot of pleasure, he reached out and pulled her bottom towards him, he reached under her ass and pushed two fingers into her fanny, she parted her knees and let him carry on, he soon had her on the verge of another orgasm and she gripped his fingers with her newly discovered fanny muscles as she came.

Jill didn't break stride as she climaxed on his fingers, she was thrilled when he kept his fingers inside her fanny, but was disappointed when he pulled his fingers out, she jumped a few seconds later when he was rubbing his fingers around her other hole making it all wet, he was obviously rubbing spit around her bum hole, she had never thought about her other hole for sex. Jill resisted slightly when he tried pushing his finger inside her crinkly button, but once it was inside she quite liked it, when he began frigging her bum hole she lifted her head from his cock and said. "Oooohhhh, I like that a lot." She then smiled at him and he moved around and got behind her and with plenty of spit dribbled around her brown hole he managed to get another finger inside her, now Jill was really into it in a big way and began moaning out loud and pushing her ass back at him.

He thought to himself *fuck it* and gripped his cock just below the head and readied it by her bum hole, he pulled his fingers out and pushed his big hard cock at her other entrance, she knew what he was trying to do and held herself dead still while he pushed his hard cock up her ass, she groaned out loud and let him take hold on her hips, he then gently began fucking her ass, she closed her eyes and lost herself in the experience. She had dreamt about this ever since she had seen him fucking the young girl's ass not so long ago, she had screamed out when he had cum up her ass and that was what she was looking forward to. Jill would never admit it to anyone, but after she had seen that young girl getting ass fucked she had gone home and taken her longest vibrator and with it well lubricated, she had managed to fuck her own ass and given herself the best orgasm that she had ever had, that was until today. Jill closed her eyes as she could tell that he was getting close, she relaxed as he pulled her backwards to meet his forward thrusts, he was a lot deeper than she had managed the other night and with his superior girth it felt even much better. Bobby grunted out loud and shot his cum a long way up her ass, bringing a blood curdling scream from her, scream after scream filled the clear blue sky, he pulled back slightly thinking that he was hurting her but she shouted for him to push it back in harder.

Jill washed his dirty cock with red wine and dried it with the edge of one of the blankets, she dressed and he watched her take a sanitary towel out of her dress pocket and position it in her thong somehow, she finished dressing and sat by his side and said.
"You are welcome to come around for dinner tonight if you want to and maybe even stay for a late drink?" He put his arm around her shoulder and said
"Can I have the same table as last night?" She nodded and said.
"Yes you can, nine o'clock then?" He nodded, they kissed long and hard before she walked away and he happily fell asleep in the late warm summer sunshine.

Bobby turned up at the restaurant, his table had been reserved. Jill served him with a smile on her face and the odd touch that spoke volumes. When the last customer had left she locked the door behind them and turned the lights down low, she walked towards him and took his hand and led him to a door marked *private* she turned the lights off and led him up the wooden stairs. The flat above the restaurant was very well furnished, he sat down on the settee and she poured them both a glass of red wine.

She sat down beside him and rested her hand in his lap and asked. "Will you stay with me tonight Bobby?" He answered. "If that is what you want then yes, I will stay, but only if you stand in front of me and do exactly as I say." She stood up and walked in front of him and stood there with her hands behind her back swaying, he said.
"Take all of your clothes off." She didn't hesitate as she began undoing the buttons on her blouse and removed it, she folded it neatly and dropped it on a nearby chair, she undid her bra and dropped that on top of the blouse, she undid her skirt and took it off, again she folded it neatly and placed it on the chair, she placed her fingers into the side of her white pants and pushed them down her legs and took them off and tossed them into his lap, he looked at her naked body and could feel his

cock growing, he looked into her eyes and said. "Now open your legs wide and play with yourself" she blushed and hesitated, but she opened her legs and he could see her already swollen fanny lips. She stared at him as she rubbed the fingers of her left hand along her fanny lips, her right hand squeezed her tits together, he watched her slide her fingers to her clit and begin rubbing from side to side, this is when she closed her eyes and lost herself in a special moment.

He was undoing his trousers when she opened her eyes and stopped masturbating, she took a step closer to him and lifted her right foot onto his knee, now her fanny was very close to his face, she closed her eyes again and lowered her fingers to her clit again, he watched her closely as her fingers moved faster and faster across her tiny button. Jill stiffened when she came but her fingers continued their journey, she eventually slid her fingers into her fanny and frigged herself for a few seconds and then lifted her fingers out of her sex and pushed them into her mouth, she sucked them clean and then pushed them back into her fanny and frigged herself some more, when she pulled her fingers out this time she pushed them to his mouth. Bobby opened his mouth and she rubbed her fingers all around the insides of his mouth, he ended up sucking her fingers clean, he then reached forwards and pulled her up onto the settee, her legs were either side of him as she pushed her fanny to his mouth, she closed her eyes and gripped his head again, as he pleasured her with his mouth.

Jill called out noisily in her orgasm and as she came with a shudder, she then rubbed her fanny all over his face moaning out loud, all the time; he pushed his chin out as hard as he could and when she found it with her clit, she used his chin to take her to another orgasm. Now satisfied for the moment, she lowered herself down into his lap and then reaching under herself she used her hand to guide his hard cock inside herself, she sank down his length and placed her arms around his neck and licked her cum from his face. When she was happy that he was clean, she began riding his hard cock, moving slowly up and down her eyes never leaving his, he reached behind her and gripped her ass cheeks, she sank down on his hard cock and said.
"Will you do something for me without question?" He nodded and she then said

"Reach behind that cushion and take out the vibrator and push it up my other hole." He reached and found the long black vibrator, she lubricated it with her mouth and he reached behind her and between them they managed to get it all the way up her bum, Jill groaned out loud as the black rubber cock slid easily up her ass, she gripped it tight while he turned the vibrator on, her eyes instantly closed and her nipples grew as hard and long as they could get, her whole body was covered in goose bumps as she began riding him again, he lifted his hands and twisted her hard nipples bringing even more moans from her.

Jill picked up her speed and her moans grew quicker as she took herself to her another orgasm, at the vital moment she opened her eyes and stared at him but he could tell that she could not see him, when she slowly rode herself through it she settled down to a much more normal pace, he suddenly wanted to punish her, hurt her, at that moment in time he hated her for whatever reason. Bobby looked around the flat for something, anything, his eyes settled on a long thin handled wooden spoon standing in the corner, he would wait his time, but he was going to punish her and he just knew that she would enjoy it. Jill picked up her speed again and he helped her through her orgasm by gripping her hips and helping her bounce up and down.

This time when she was done he stopped her and lifted her from his cock and made her stand up, she looked at him quizzically, he took her hand and led her to a deep leather chair and bent her over the arm of the chair and told her to stay there, he walked over and fetched the spoon, holding it by the round spoon end he swished it through the air. Jill knew what was coming and closed her eyes and looked forward to another new experience, he stood to the side and told her to open her legs wide, she did as he asked and he hit her across the ass cheeks with the thin handle of the spoon, when she did not object he hit her harder the next time, which had the desired effect as she yelped out loud, but still she did not object. He hit her six times across the same place, now she had red lines all over her ass and she was openly crying, he dropped the spoon and moved behind her and pushed his rock hard cock into her and gripped her hips, he could have been raping her he fucked her so viciously.

Jill was almost screaming at the top of her voice as he rammed his big hard cock into her fine body, when he shot his hot cum into her she was almost relieved, but still she called out at each spurt. They used each other's bodies as they ground against one-another, it was their final act together, because he knew that he would never fuck this woman again.

When he left the flat she was still bent over the arm of the chair crying out loud, his lasting memory of her was the red lines across her buttocks and the flat end of the buzzing vibrator sticking out of her ass.

Chapter 12

Bobby was feeling depressed, he could not understand why he had re-acted the way that he had with Jill, yes she was a bit strange, but then aren't we all. He had not left the house for three days, he spent his time sprawled out on the big leather settee in the living room, Helen had cooked and cleaned for him as usual, she had even sat down by him and asked him what was wrong, all he would say is "I don't want to talk about it" she left him to his thoughts and carried on working around him, when she left him that day he was still in the same position, she needed a plan to bring him out of it.

The next day when she went to the big house Bobby was still in the same position, she stood in front of him and removed her coat, she had on a tiny leather skirt, under which she was naked, she had on a tight white crop top underneath she was also naked, when he looked at her she did a little twirl in front of him making him smile for the first time in days, she began her work making sure that she bent over in front of him at every opportunity, when she caught him looking she would de-liberately open her legs so that he had a good view of her fanny, she went over to dust the settee on which he was lay, as she leaned over him she pulled up her crop top and dangled her firm tits all over him, she could see by the lump in his shorts that she was having the desired effect in him, Helen put her tits away and said. "I'm going up stairs now to make your bed, if you want me, you know where I am."

She walked slowly up the wooden staircase ever so seductively, when she looked back he was sat upright watching here every move, she reached the top of the stairs and turned and stared at him, he was star-ing back at her so she opened her legs wide and pulled the crop top over her head, she then lifted each breast to her mouth and licked each nipple, she then turned and walked away. When he walked into the bedroom she was naked and bent over the bed folding the sheets, she looked back at him and smiled, she sensed him walk up behind her, she stopped what she was doing, gripped the side of the bed, spread her feet wide and waited for him to mount her. She felt his big knob at her entrance and closed her eyes, she knew that this would be a fuck of re-leased tension, he pushed his cock into her willing body and gripped her hips, as expected there was no finesse in this fuck, this was just the means to an end, but that was ok with her as any fuck with Bobby Francis was better than sex with any other man that she had ever had, he rammed his hard cock into her for all he was worth, her orgasms came and went one after the other, where he would normally slow down after her orgasm and then build her up slowly to the next, he just fucked her hard and fast. He grunted and shot his hot seed into her more than willing body; he pulled her back hard and was stamping his feet as if he was trying to push his cock out of the top of her head.

When he let his cock slip out of her he flopped down onto the bed, their mixed fluids ran down both of her legs, she reached to a box of tissues kept by his bed and stuffed a handful against her tingling fanny, she then climbed on to the bed and knelt by his side, she then lifted his sticky cock and began slowly licking his manhood all over, she knew that he particularly liked this, she looked into his face and he had his eyes closed, when she closed her mouth over his tender, sensitive knob he jumped slightly, this made her smile to herself. Helen was rewarded for her efforts by a dribble of his cum as she managed to suck if from him, she carried on until her jaw ached; laying his slightly hard cock onto his thigh she crawled up his body and folded herself around him, he put his arm around her shoulder and stroked her lazily. They had been lay like this for a while until she said.
"Are you going to tell me what's wrong now?" So he told her all about Jill, he told her everything, even about hitting her with the spoon. Helen lifted herself up onto one elbow and looked down at him and said. "Are you telling me that you didn't know about mad Jill, rumour has it that she murdered her husband after driving him mad with her sexual and financial demands, that was how she got the money to open the restaurant and buy the flat above.

You will have to be very careful there Bobby you don't know what she might do." He nodded, realising that he had made a huge mistake.
He returned back to work at the school. He had almost finished the rest area, he just had to build a small ornate fence around the whole area and there were a few jobs left to do inside the school itself and then he could maybe take a holiday, somewhere hot with white sands. Two days later he was knelt down fixing the gate into position when a tall young woman walked up to him and coughed and said. "Please ex-

cuse me sir are you Bobby Francis?" He turned and looked the young woman up and down making her blush when he looked at her tits. He said. "Yes, that is I and who might you be?" She blushed even deeper and said. " My name is Philameena, but people call me Phil"; The Matron would like to see you at once Mr Francis." He looked her deep in her eyes and said "Call me Bobby like everyone else." She blushed again and said. "Shall I show you the way then, aye Bobby?" He nodded and stood up and followed Phil down the garden, he said. "You are a fine-looking woman Phil, if ever you need anything, anything at all just ask.

" She turned and smiled at him and said. "I don't know you Bobby, but there may be something that you can do for me, how can I contact you?" He took out one of his business cards and said. "Call me anytime." They arrived at the Matrons office and Phil knocked on the door, the thin voice told them to enter, Phil opened the door and let him walk in and then closed the door behind him, he walked to the old woman's desk and she stared up at him and said. "I just knew that you were going to be trouble, I tried to take precautions, but I just knew it, and now we have a problem only I don't know what to do about it?" He stood there thoughts flashing through his mind wondering if one of his young conquests were pregnant or had Susy told the Matron what had really happened to her, for her to get her injury. The thin old woman passed him a letter, it read.

Dear Matron,

      I have to tell you that one Bobby Francis is ravishing some of your young women, if you need proof I have the photos on my phone.

Mrs Jill Pouch

He passed the letter back to her and smiled and said.
"So you have received one as well, well I have about six of these and my friend at the police station has some as well, apparently Mrs Pouch was the local screw ball, you do know that he was accused of murdering her husband for his money, but there was never enough proof to convict her, look her up on the computer and you will see for yourself." The Matron looked deflated and said that she would indeed look into

Mrs Pouch, but if he was lying she would call the police herself. He left the Matron's office and swore to himself, that mad bloody bitch, he left the garden and climbed into his car and headed for the restaurant, it was only mid-morning but he guessed that she would be there. He went into the kitchen by the back door, his luck was in as she was standing with her back to him on her mobile phone, he stood back and watched her, she finished her call and placed the phone down on a work surface and went into the restaurant, he stepped forward and picked up the phone and walked out of the kitchen, he drove away from the restaurant and stopped up the road and looked through the phone, she had indeed photos of him with the two young girls, he got out of the car and placed the phone under the front wheel of the big car and drove over it, he got out just to check that the phone was destroyed, he kicked the bits all over the lay-by and drove away a lot happier.

Bobby returned back to work at the school, his head full of the thoughts about Jill, wondering if the photos were on her computer, maybe he should do a bit of flat burglary when she takes her dog for a walk. Bobby made plans and then stood up and smiled to himself as a new much cleverer plan formed in his head. That night he scanned the local news-paper to see who had been up to what, he soon found who he wanted to see, a young lad named Billy Bomford. He was the local tear away, he would be easy to track down and decided that he would start at lunch time the next day.

He was sat in his work van in Bewds Drive, on the local council estate, a young lad on a bike rode past Bobby whistled him over and said. "Do you want to earn a fiver?" the blond haired youth said.
"You ain't fucking queer are you mate?" Bobby smiled and said .
"No, I ain't queer, do you know Billy Bomford?" The youth smiled and said "Yea, I know Billy he's me cousin, what do you want with Billy?"

Bobby smiled and said "That's my business, can you go get him for me?" The youth held out his hand for the five pounds, when Bobby paid him the youth rode down the road about fifty yards dropped his bike in the road and ran up a garden path. A few minutes later a tall spotty youth with unwashed long blond hair ambled up the road, he stood and looked at Bobby and uttered. "Who the fuck are you?"

Bobby gave him his best smile and said. "I have a job for you, there is a ton in it for you, if you pull it off." "What do you want then mate?" Bobby said. "Get in and I will show you." The youth stood there and looked at Bobby and said. "You aint filth are you?" Bobby gave him his best smile again and shook his head, the youth climbed into the passenger seat and looked all around the van reassuring himself that Bobby was not the police.

Bobby drove down the road that passed the restaurant and pointed it out to the youth and said.
"See that place, there's a flat upstairs where a woman lives on her own, she walks her dog four times a day and all I want was her computer, anything else that you find in there was yours, ok?" Billy looked at the flat and said. "How soon do you want it done?" Bobby told him it was urgent and Billy nodded and said.
"Let's have the money up front?" Bobby looked at the youth and shook his head and said.
"After" he drove the youth back to his road and said. "I will be here tomorrow lunch time, don't let me down, ok?" Billy nodded and said. "Just make sure you have the money" and that was that, Billy ambled back to his council house, without looking back at him.

Bobby was sat in Bewds drive, at lunch time, dressed in the same clothes as the day before, Billy walked towards him with a carrier bag in his hand, he climbed into the van and gave him the computer, Bobby passed him a brown envelope, Billy checked the money before he got out of the van, neither of them had said a word. Bobby could not get into the computer, because of the password, but that was ok, he knew what he was going to do with it anyway, he drove down a dirt track to his private fishing pool, he looked all around and tossed the computer as far as he could into the deep water, end of problem. Bobby just happened to be looking through the local paper the next week when a headline caught his attention.*Restaurant burgled, takings stolen* it looked like Billy Bomford had had a good day, the day he robbed Jill Pouch.

Not much was happening in his life at the moment, he had almost forgotten Jill and was thinking about his holiday, his phone rang and when he answered it his face broke into a smile as a small voice said. "Is that

Bobby?" He said that it was and asked who this was, she said. "This is me Philameena, do you remember me?" he smiled and said.
"How could I ever forget your beauty Phil, what can I do for you?" She seemed to hesitate before answering. "You know that you said if ever there was anything that you could do for me, just ask?" He said.
"Yes, and I meant what I said, what can I do for you Phil?" She answered.

"Well, some of the girls and I are going camping one night soon, and we were hoping that you might buy us some drink and some cigarettes?" He asked her where they intended to go camping? She told him that they hadn't got that far yet, but it was going to be somewhere local, he smiled and said. "I know just the place and I can guarantee your safety." She asked him where this place was, he smiled when he told her that they could camp on his front lawn, that way they could use the loos in his house, and if it rained there was enough rooms in the house for them all. She became quite excited and asked if she and some of her friends could have a look at the intended sight, he said that he would pick them up the next evening at six by the front gates, she agreed and he couldn't wait.

He waited at the appointed time and four young women came running around the corner and climbed into his car, they were typical young women all excited and giggles, they were all a little bit nervous, but at the same time each one of them kept glancing at him, they all began whispering to each other and then giggling some more. He turned into the drive and when they caught site of his house they all went quiet, he pulled up by the steps at the front of the house and they all got out of the car, he walked onto the front lawn and stopped, and said. "There is all this grass to pitch your tents on and if you walk this way I will show you where the loos are." He showed them into the house and the young women were suddenly struck dumb as they looked around his home, he gave them a quick tour of the downstairs before leading them outside again, they all sat on the steps and made plans for the big night, Phil was sat close to him and asked him about the drink and stuff.
He told her not to worry about it as they were camping on his private land, he could class it as a private party. The girls all chatted excitedly at the prospects of a night away from the boring school, he took them all back to the school, they left him with the promise to give him plenty of

notice about the date of the big adventure. Bobby was sat watching the TV later that night when his phone buzzed, he looked at the message which read

Thanks for today Bobby, it was really exciting to see your beautiful home and thanks for all of your help, Phil XXX he smiled at the kisses and wondered what they really meant.

The day finally arrived and the young women at least twenty of them turned up with enough camping stuff to kit out a small army, he smiled as he watched them laughing as they struggled to erect their tents, he had used some of his vast wealth to make the event a bit special for them, he had arranged for afternoon teas on the lawn with waitress service, signs had been erected showing the ways to the loos, he had even erected the large family marquee in which he had tables laid out fully laden with all sorts of chilled drinks and wrapped goodies, electricity had been run into the marquee ready for the female run disco that he had arranged for later as a surprise, another surprise that he had not told them about was a burger van that would be parked up for three hours, all of which was free to the girls, well you only live once and if it helped to get into Phil's pants, then it will all be worth it.

He was sat on the steps watching the young women enjoying the afternoon teas, every-time he looked at Phil she seemed to be smiling at him, he waved her over and she walked up to him and sat by his side, she was so close that their thighs were touching, he said. "Is everything ok, so far?" She smiled and said. "Just perfect, only what about the drink you said that you would get?" He stood up and asked her to follow him, while they walked along towards the Marquee he asked her. "Can you keep a secret, Phil?" She said that she hoped so, he took her into the back of the large Marquee, she gasped when she went inside and walked along the side tables full of goodies, she turned to him and said. "But we can't afford all of this Bobby." He shrugged and said, my treat, he swore her to secrecy, as he told her of the rest of the surprises that he had laid on for them later, her eyes grew bigger the more he told her, she said.

"But how ever will we repay you for all this?" She blushed deep scarlet when he said

"I'm sure that you will think of something." He placed his hand in the centre of her back as he led her out of the Marquee as they reached the flap in the outside wall she leaned against him and reached up and kissed him on the cheek and whispered. "Thank you Bobby." He pulled her to him and kissed her full on the mouth, she hung onto him like a limpet as he pushed his tongue into her mouth, he put his hands on her ass cheeks and pulled her fanny against his hardening cock, she pushed herself even harder against him, groaned out loud and came on the spot, she pulled away from him and ran towards the house. Bobby had to stay where he was for a few minutes until his hard cock had returned to normal, he finally went outside and sat on the house steps, Phil walked out of the house and as she passed him she said.

 "Sorry about that" and returned to her friends, but she kept glancing his way, because she knew that he knew that he had made her cum in her pants.

When the burger van turned up the girls all began cheering out loud and formed a queue, the two men were kept very busy all of the time they were there, Bobby had watched the little darlings and couldn't fig-ure out where they were putting all of the food, the disco woman turned up and he helped her carry all her equipment into the marquee, he watched her set her kit up which did not take long, when she was ready he went and undid the flap at the front of the marquee, she turned on the flashing lights and put on her first song, Phil and her friends all walked nervously into the marquee, they gasped and clapped their hands when they saw all the drink, some of the young women be-gan dancing, Bobby went into his house and left them to it. The music grew louder and louder, but there was no-one living near to complain so it did not really matter, the girls made good use of the loos, but why do women always go in pairs?

Phil came into the house to find him she grabbed his hand and said.
"Please come and dance with us Bobby, everybody wants you to" he let her pull him up to his feet, he pretended to fall against her and pulled her into his arms again and pushed her against the door so that it closed, he kissed her hungrily and she kissed him back just as urgently, he pushed himself against her making her groan out loud, he pulled his body away from her and slid his hand up her skirt to her wet pants he did not hesitate and pushed his hand down inside her pants to her fanny, she had already opened her legs in expectation, so he slid his fin-gers along her fanny lips and pushed two fingers deep inside her, he

lowered his arm so that he could get even deeper and began frigging her, she clung onto him and groaned out her orgasm, he felt her anoint his finger with her virgin cum, he pulled his fingers out of her fanny and pushed her pants down her legs, he leaned back and opened his trousers and pulled his big cock out she reached forward and gripped his hard manhood, he lifted her skirt just as there was a knocking on the door, three or four voices were shouting for Phil; she pulled her pants off and gave them to him, she then adjusted her clothes and when he had sat back down, she opened the door and was gone with her friends, he lifted the wet pants to his nose and took a deep breath of her fanny juices and thought *third time lucky* but at least he now knew that she was game and wanted it just as much as he did.

The disco ended at one am, he helped the woman pack her kit up and put it in her van, he paid her and she was gone, some of the young women had moved into the tents and some still stayed in the marquee talking, none of them seemed to be overly drunk, he could not see Phil and couldn't very well go looking for her could he, he walked out of the marquee and was heading towards the house when he saw two of the young women walking hand in hand towards the gardens, not being slow in coming forward he decided to take a stroll himself, he kept in the shadows and followed them, they sat down on one of the benches and instantly began kissing, hands were up each other's tops, the taller of the two girls lifted her friends top up to show him a fine pair of tits, the tall girls began sucking her partners tits, the tall girl then knelt in front of her friend and reached under her skirt and pulled her pants down and off, she then held them to her face and said something to her lover, both young women laughed, the tall girl opened her friends leg and pulled her bottom forwards on the bench and then buried her face between her friends legs.

He had not realised that he had his cock in his hand and was slowly wanking, he put his cock away and watched the girl on her knees give her lover a fierce orgasm and left them to it. He went in search of his own young woman, he looked in the Marquee to no avail, there were a group of the young women sat in a circle talking, but he could not find her, he gave up and went into the house, he went into his sitting room, the door closed behind him and when he looked back Phil was leaning against the door smiling, she said.

"Now, where were we?" Bobby walked back to the young girl and took her in his arms and kissed her long and hard, she was rubbing her mound against his growing cock, he pulled away from her and asked. "Shall we go upstairs where I can strip you naked and make love to you?" She shook her head and said. "My friends might see us go up the stairs?"

He smiled and took her hand and led her out of the door at the other end of the room, he then took her through another door to the back stairs, they ran giggling up the staircase, he took her into the master bedroom and then locked the door, he turned around and she was sat bouncing on the bed, he pulled his shirt over his head, undid his trousers, pushed them down his legs and stepped out of them leaving his sandals there as well, now dressed only in his boxers he went to her she let him pull her top over her head, he looked down at her small put perfectly formed tits, she stood up and let him undo her skirt and drop it to the floor, she was now naked, her pubic hair was a thin line maybe half an inch wide, trimmed short in line with her fanny lips, he sat her back down on the bed and opened her legs, he was about to drop to his knees when she reached out and pulled his boxers down, he let them fall to the floor, she reached out and gripped his thick cock and slowly moved her hand back and forth, she looked into his eyes and said. "Now you can do what you were going to do."

She moved her bum to the edge of the bed and resting herself on her elbow she watched him as he placed his mouth onto her fanny, she closed her eyes and let him pleasure her, she lifted her feet onto the bed and shivered when he touched her clit, he sucked her clit until she or-gasmed, he then went in search of her beautiful cum, he took his fill and then holding some on his tongue, he stood up and transferred it into her mouth. Phil smiled and thanked him, he placed his knob at her entrance and pushed forward, Phil was no virgin, she arched her back and took every inch he had to give her, he lifted her legs and put his arms underneath and gripped her inner thighs and began riding her, she closed her eyes and lifted her hands to her small tits and pulled her thin nipples, she met every stroke that he made by matching him with her rising hips, for first time lovers they seemed to be perfectly matched. When she came she lifted her head and snarled at him, lying back down on the bed she closed her eyes again and resumed the nipple pulling thing, Phil came time and time again and each time she bared her teeth and snarled at him, she knew when he was about to cum and lifted herself to her elbows and watched him as he shot his hot spunk deep into her young body, she cried out and encouraged him to fill her up with his seed, she helped him by thrusting her hips at him, when he pulled her back and pushed forward she bared her teeth again and ground her hips against him until she took herself to yet another glorious orgasm.

Phil fell back on the bed and let him do his thing, when he pulled out of her and fell down onto the bed by her side, he gripped her hand as they both breathed heavily. After a while she sat up and looked down at him and said. "The rumours are true then, you really can fuck and the size of your cock. Fuck me you filled me to the maximum".
He smiled at her and said. "You were not so bad yourself, for someone so young you met me stroke for stroke, and when you pulled your nipples, fuck that was sexy."

She reached out and lifted his sticky cock, his big knob was fully on view, she squeezed it from the bottom to the top and when a drop of his cum appeared on the tip, she bent over and licked it off , tasting him she said. "Hhmmm, you taste nice." She lowered her head and took him into her mouth, she had definitely sucked a cock before and had been taught well, when she sucked on his knob he thought that she was trying to suck the very soul out of him, he began to react to her ministrations as his cock began to thicken, she looked up at him and smiled with her eyes, she gripped his shaft and holding him just below her lips she wanked him in perfect time with her mouth movements.

Phil got him hard and crawled up his body and straddled him, she then lifted herself up onto her knees and reached underneath herself she gripped his thick cock and put it to her entrance, she swallowed as she slid down his length, she brought her knees in tight to his body and leaned forward she rested her hands on his chest and the began riding him, he reached out to fondle her tits but she slapped his hands away, he found out why when as she neared her orgasm, as she sat bolt upright and closed her eyes and grabbed her tits, she squeezed them so hard it must have been hurting her, she called out loud in her orgasm which went on and on, she stayed sat up straight and used her strong thighs to ride him, her hands were now wrapped in her hair and she had a look of concentration on her face as she took herself to yet another orgasm, at which time she went through the tit pulling thing again, she slowed down and looked down at him and said. "Bend your knees up and when I stop, I want you to fuck me hard."

He nodded and wondered where she had learned her tricks, she placed her hands flat on his chest and bounced up and down on his giant cock, she stopped suddenly, lifted her bum, stared at him and stopped dead, he was true to his word and began ramming his big cock into her young body, she did not move but closed her eyes and let him make her cum, she began moaning out loud but still she did not move, she came hard and long eventually sinking down on his mighty cock, she instantly sat up and used her hips to prolong her orgasm.

When she had finished her orgasm she sat still with his giant cock still buried deep inside her and looked down at him and said. "I have dreamt of doing all these things Bobby, but I have never had the opportunity until now, the bloke who took me the first time lasted about thirty seconds and was fucking useless, I could tell that you were wondering where I learned all the things I know, I will tell you, but you must never repeat what I am about to tell you, my parents live in a house just like yours, and like you my father was never there, I was 14 at the time and just happened to be walking down one of the upper corridors when I heard what sounded like my mother in a lot of pain.

I listened at the door for a while and realised that she was in fact enjoying herself, and wondered what she was up to, so I hid around the corner and waited for her to come out of the room, she looked very flushed and checked her face in a long mirror, I saw where she hid the key to the room and bided my time, the next weekend she was going to meet my father someplace leaving me on my own in that big house, as soon as she was gone I ran up the stairs as fast as I could, my pants were already soaking wet as I searched for the hidden key.

I opened the door and switched the lights on, there were no windows in the room but lots of strange wooden objects and on the facing wall was a large screen, I sat on a wooden horse and put my feet in the stirrups and leaned forward as if I was riding a horse, I looked under where my fanny was and there was this hole in the wood, well I dismounted and looked at this hole which had a thread inside It, so I started to look for whatever screwed into the hole. When I looked underneath the horse there was a slot and hidden in this slot was a big thick wooden cock, maybe eight inches long and quite shiny, well I screwed this wooden cock into the hole, stood back and looked at my handy-work and could immediately see the reason for it, well I moved onto the next thing which was a wooden box with a cushioned seat on it, so I sat down, when I looked down there was a remote so I picked it up and pressed number 1 and almost shit myself as this thing hit me straight in the fanny, I jumped up and this thick rubber cock was moving up and down, I stood and watched it and pressed number 2 the rubber cock began to go faster, I pressed number 3 and the rubber cock came out of the hole even further, number 4 and the cock came out to its fullest which would resemble your big cock.

I placed the remote back down and continued walking around the room, there stood a single bed in the middle of the room, so I climbed onto the bed and looked around, I found 2 remotes on a bedside cabinet, the first one controlled the bed which did all sorts of weird and wonderful things, the second remote turned on a hidden camera, on the screen in front of me came a list of names, some were in French, I chose one at random and this film started playing, well it was the strongest porn that I have ever seen and these blokes all had big cocks like yours, as I flicked through the films I realised that some of them were films about rape and some of the rapes must have been real, I left the film running and explored the bedside cabinet, each draw was full of vibrators, there were all different sizes and shapes, there was all different sorts of lubricants.

I climbed off the bed and there was this rail sticking out of the wall, I gripped the rail and wondered what it could be used for, on the end of the rail was a button so I pressed it, this buzzing sound made me look up and this arm was lowering down, I stood fascinated as another arm came out of the first arm and a thin plastic rod extended out of the arm and then stopped, I stood and looked at the strange machine, I pressed the button again and had to jump out of the way, I can only call it a whipping machine.

I carried on looking around the wall and there was another rail, but this one stuck straight out of the wall, well I looked at it and held onto the rail and soon realised that I was facing the wrong way, so I went to the other side of the rail, I was now almost trapped between the wall and the rail, I looked behind me and yet again there was a piece of flat wood fixed to the wall in which was another hole with a thread in it, I looked around and found a wooden box which was full of rubber cocks of all shapes and sizes, I took out one of the biggest and screwed it into place and then took up position and could see how it would work, on the screen a young blond girl was getting fucked by two men and she was sucking another one and wanking another, in the corner of the room was another strange object. I stood and looked at it for ages trying to work out what it could be used for and as we are now with your hard cock inside me [she held her hands out in front of her and continued] imagine a rail at this height and my mother bouncing up and down on this big thick rubber cock.

On the screen now another young girl looked like she was in pain as this coloured bloke with a very big cock was fucking her ass, I went and made sure the door was locked and stripped myself naked, I was a virgin at the time and the only thing that had been inside me was my thin finger, so I lay on the bed and chose a selection of vibrators and some lubricant, I chose a white one about six inches long and as thick a broom handle, I tried pushing it inside me and had to change positions loads of time until I managed to get some of it inside, I realise now that I must have been against my barrier well cutting a long story short I made myself cum and from that moment on I was hooked, I lost my virginity on that wooden horse, I don't mind telling you I fucked that horse so many times.

On the screen now another young woman was sucking a great big cock and when he came he shot his cum all over her smiling face, that was how I learned to suck a cock, I practised for hours with different sized vibrators watching other women on that big screen, I particularly liked the thing in the corner that was where I learned to ride cocks, If the truth be told, I spent hours in that room fucking myself stupid, but one thing that I did learn and that was not to fear the size of any man's cock, but to embrace his size and when I heard about your size I wanted you to fuck me, and now that you have and I have fucked you and now when I lift myself off your mighty cock, I want you to fuck me from behind and shoot some more of your wonderful seed into me". With that she lifted herself off his magnificent cock and climbed from the bed and took up position on the thick carpet.

Bobby took up position behind her and pushed his hard cock back into her young body, he gripped her hips and fucked her to a standstill, just as he shot his hot load into her she began to scream out loud, each spurt making her scream louder, they stayed locked together until she made herself cum again, as soon as he slipped out of her she turned and licked him clean, happy with her work she stood up and stuffed some tissues into her fanny and dressed, she kissed him hard on the mouth and pressed a piece of paper into his hand and was gone, he looked at the paper and on it was written.

"Bobby, if I have given you this note it means that I have told you all about my mother's secret room, well I will be returning to my parent 's house in four weeks-time for two weeks, the second week I will be on my own, I will tell my parents that friends from school will be coming to stay, that way they will arrange food and things, if you would like to come and stay with me, I will make you more than welcome. Phil and underneath was her mobile number. He took out his mobile and sent a text saying.

Please forward address and date of arrival followed by a smiley face.

Chapter 13

Bobby was in love with Phil, they had not been together since that first night, but he was doing his best to get her back to his house, they texted each other all of the time and when she was free to talk she would send him a pre-arranged word and he would ring her, he had tried to meet her in his car, but she would not do it in his car saying that she wanted freedom to move around. Out of the blue he received the text that he had been waiting for, it said.

"Bobby please arrive at the address above on the 24th. Can't wait. Phil." He smiled and punched the air and made his plans. He packed enough clothes for a week which included a dress suit, just in case there was something on that they could attend, he had put a case of nice champagne in the car and a giant box of chocolates, he locked the car and went to bed early, so that he could get up early and begin his long journey to his young sexy lover.

He arrived at her big house and she ran down the stone steps to meet him, they kissed briefly and then ran back up the steps into the house, once inside she turned and wrapped herself around him pressing her mouth onto his, their tongues doing a lovers dance in each other's mouths, she was rubbing her mound against his hard cock, she pulled away from him and grabbed his hand and pulled him along after her, she burst through two big doors into what turned out to be the pool room she began removing her clothes saying.

"I have always wanted to do it in the pool, get your kit off quick" she ran and jumped into the pool naked and stood there watching him remove his clothes he could see that she was frigging herself, he landed in the water next to her, she moved through the water to the steps and turning around she sat down and opened her legs wide for him, he moved between her legs, she reached down to guide his huge cock into her hot willing fanny, once he was inside her she wrapped her legs around his back and held him firmly in place, the sex was full of urgency to full pent up desires.

She opened her legs and gripped the side bars and urged him to fuck her, ripples covered the whole surface of the pool and moans and groans filled the air of the big pool room , she placed her hand flat on his chest and pushed him out of her, she turned around and placed her feet on the second step and bending forward she gripped the side bars again, he moved up behind her and pushed big cock back into her, he then gripped the side bars just below her hands and began ramming his cock into her again.

Phil liked this a lot as he was now deeper inside her than he had ever been before, she knew that she was making a lot of noise, but she did not care, she had fallen in love with this beautiful man with his big hard cock that can last for hours, just what she needed. Bobby called out and shot his hot spunk into her, forcing her to scream out at the top of her voice, to any passer-by they would think murder was being committed, they pushed towards each other with Phil making a lot of noise as she as always did with him as she ground against him, giving herself to another glorious orgasm

Phil wore a pair of white pants and a panty liner as they walked around the big house hand in hand, she pointed out everything as they walked, she showed him briefly into her bedroom and then continued the tour of the upstairs, they came to one door and she leaned against it smiling and said "I will have to know you better, before I can take you into this particular room" he smiled and said "is that the room, you know, your mothers special room?"

She nodded and smiled and said "and when you can't fuck me anymore, I will take you in there and give you a show that you will never forget" he made her promise by crossing her heart, they walked to the end of the corridor where a thick door marked private stood in front of them, he looked at her and asked "well, what's behind that?" she looked down at his hanging cock and said "I was saving that for when our friend down there had a bit more life in him, maybe if you could encourage him to show some interest, then just maybe I will show you a surprise that I had planned for us"

He placed his hands on her shoulders and pushed her down to her knees and said "Phil is it your job to encourage our friend down there to show some interest in proceedings" she smiled up at him and said "I will do my best Sir" she lifted his cock and licked all along his shaft to his knob, she pulled the loose skin down and exposed his purple knob, she dribbled some warm spit onto the tip before closing her mouth over the top, she began sucking from the off and as she wanked him with her right hand she managed to twist her hand at the same time increasing the stimulation, when she looked up into his face he had his eyes closed and his teeth bared, he looked down at his young lover and gripped the hair either side of her head and bean fucking her mouth, she placed her hands on his pubic hair and held him back so that he did not choke her, he continued to fuck her mouth even though he was now hard, she pushed him back and when he opened his eyes and looked down she whispered

"you can carry on if you like and finish, we can save the surprise until another time", she lowered her mouth back to his cock and began bouncing her head back and forth, he reached down and pulled her up and said

"Go on Phil ,please show me your surprise" she reached into a deco-rated pot and took out a big iron key and unlocked the big door, she took his hand and led him up a wooden staircase to a small door at the top, she opened the door and pulled him out onto the roof of the house.

He stood and looked at the stunning views, everywhere he looked rolling countryside filled his brain, they could have been the only two people left on the earth, the silence was deafening, when he looked at her he said.

"Almost as beautiful as you." She took his hand and led him across the roof, behind a false wall lay on the floor were several laid out blankets, on top of which were piled cushions of various sizes, a drinks cabinet stood of to one side, she removed a bottle of champagne from the cab-inet and poured them both a glass of the amber liquid, they stood arm in arm and sipped at the sparkling wine, she glanced down and his cock had begun to wilt, she said. "Our friend needs reviving again." She tut-ted and went down to her knees again, she dipped his knob into her champagne flute and sucked the liquid from his knob making him take a deep breath.

She did it again and again until he was rock hard and desperate, she moved away from him and gripped a rung on a ladder that was fixed to the false wall, he pulled her shorts down and she leaned forwards and opened her legs, he mounted her and gripped her thighs and began ramming his cock into her, in her position she was able to push back at him and matched him stroke for stroke, as lovers they were perfectly matched and proved it to one another over and over again. Bobby was sweating in the hot summer sun, but he felt like he could fuck this beautiful woman forever.

Bobby had a wicked grin on his face as he thought of a change of position, he would wait for her to cum again and then he would put his plan into operation, she began moaning out loud and suddenly stopped moving, held herself dead still and let him ram his big cock into her as hard as he wanted to, Phil screamed out her orgasm and began thrusting back at him, he slowed down and stopped, she looked back at him as he stopped, he leaned over and put his mouth by her ear and whispered.
"Come with me and live dangerously." He pulled out of her and bent down and picked up one of the larger cushions and walked to the edge of the roof and placed the cushion near the edge and told her to kneel down on the cushion facing the edge of the building, she nervously did as he asked, he then went down to his knees behind her and mounted her but held himself still, he moved her closer to the edge and when her head was almost over the edge, he stopped her and gripping her hips again he began ramming his cock into her, Phil was not happy and began screaming as his rammed his big cock into her, her head would go over the edge of the roof, she was pushing back trying to get away from the edge which excited Bobby no end and made him ram his cock into her harder, but what he hadn't realised was that all of the time she was moving ever nearer the edge.

The more that she was screaming the more he was enjoying it, he had lost it and was shooting his cum into her, but all she was doing was screaming for him to pull her back from the edge. He had his eyes closed and was pushing hard into her, she started slapping him with her right hand and screaming at the top of her voice. He suddenly stopped and realised that she was actually terrified as her top half of her body was hanging over the edge of the roof, he pulled out of her and pulled her back, he tried to hold her but she pulled away from him and ran from the roof screaming, he heard her screaming as she ran along the corridors, the screaming stopped when he heard a door slam.

Bobby held his head in his hands and realised what he had done, she had been really terrified and he had only made it worse, he went searching for her, he ran from room to room calling out her name, he came to her bedroom and the door was locked, he could hear her sobbing on the bed, he tried talking softly to her but she would not answer him. He sat back against her door and wondered if he had gone too far, he tapped the door and said. "Come on Phil, I am truly sorry it was a stupid thing to do and I will never do anything like it ever again, please let me in.

" He heard her sobbing on the other side of the door, he had to listen hard as she whispered. "You have ruined everything Bobby, I had such plans for us, all I wanted to do was have as much sex as we could manage, I loved you Bobby Francis, I would have married you if you had asked me, I know that you love me, but I could never ever trust you again, now I want you to go and never contact me again." With that she burst into tears, he went to speak but she said.

"If you are still here in ten minutes I will call the police and tell them that you broke in here and raped me, I have the evidence inside me so you had better go." That was their last ever contact, he did see her around the school, but every time she saw him she burst into tears. Bobby heard that she left the school two weeks later after trying to harm her-self.

Chapter 14

Bobby was sat in an empty car-park overlooking the wide empty grey looking sea, where he was he did not know, all he knew that he had to get away from the school, he had done wrong and he knew it, every pair of eyes that had looked at him in the school seemed to be accusing him. He had sent Phil flowers and texts but she would not speak to him. Susy and Liz were ignoring him, maybe he needed help.

Bobby started the car and drove out of the car-park and turned left, he didn't know where he was heading, and it did not matter, he came to a large industrial estate, he saw a large black car standing in pride of place on the fore-court of an Audi show room, he pulled into the car park and thought *fuck it, I will treat myself*, he walked to the car and looked through the windows, it was a nice car and he wanted it, a young woman of maybe late twenties came out a smiles and asked if she could help him, he asked her. "Now, how soon can you get this car ready for me to drive away." she smiled and answered. "Well, we can get it fully fuelled and ready in three hours" he looked at her name badge and said. "If you will come and have lunch with me now Sally, I will have it." She smiled and said. "Just give me ten minutes and I will be ready, oh by the way are you trading the Bm?" He nodded and she walked towards the showroom.

He watched her walk away, she was fit, slim and beautiful and he wanted to fuck her, he stopped and slapped himself in the side of the head and thought *I'm at it again, whatever is the matter with me.* She came back smiling and said. "Everything is underway, I have put you down for top book price for the Bm, shall we go?" She directed him to an isolated riverside restaurant that had 4stars over the door, they walked in and there was one other couple in the restaurant, but he told himself that it was still early. She asked him what his name was, he told her and she said that Bobby was a nice name, they ordered their meals and a bottle of nice red wine. She was sat opposite him leaning on the table, her nipples were rock hard, she knew it and so did he, she tried to cover them up, but decided to let him get a good look at them.

Sally excused herself and went to the loo, he watched her walk back to the table and her nipples grew even bigger, when she sat down she sat next to him and asked.

"What is it that you do Bobby?" He shrugged and said.
"I don't need to do anything if I don't want to, just have a nice time with nice people." She blushed at this, he was about to speak again, but their meals were placed in front of them, the food was very good and worth of all its 4 stars. The meal over they drained the bottle of red and he asked if she wanted another, she looked coy and said.
"Are you trying to get me drunk Bobby?" He leaned forwards and made a point of looking at her hard nipples and said.
"Do I need to get you drunk Sally?" She blushed and shook her head then said.

"No Bobby, I don't suppose you do, shall we go?" He paid the bill and they walked to the car, as he drove away from the restaurant he asked her to lead the way, she directed him away from the showroom and when they had been on the road for ten minutes she told him to take a left turn, they turned into a static home park, she directed him to the end home, they climbed out of the car and she took some keys out of her bag and opened the door, he followed her inside and as soon as she had placed her bag down, she took his hand and led him into the bed-room, she closed the door and turned and looked at him and said.

"I have always wanted to fuck one of my customers, and you are the best looking one that I have ever had, I am married and on the pill." She began undoing the buttons on her blouse, she removed the blouse and reached behind her back and undid her bra and pulled it down her arms and dropped it on top of the blouse, her nipples really were huge, she reached behind her to the button on her skirt, as she did this he reached forward and twisted her nipples, she dropped the skirt to the floor and stood there in a tiny white thong, her fanny hair was neatly trimmed, while he played with her tits she reached out and undid his trousers and reached in and gripped his huge cock and pulled it out, ex-citedly she said."Fuck me, my dreams have all come true at the same time." He pushed her down to her knees, she looked up at him and smiled and said.

"My pleasure, but don't you cum, I want you inside me." He closed his eyes as she exposed his big knob and did something that he had never experienced before, she closed her lips around the rim of his knob and just gave him a blow job, but only on his knob, it was the sexiest thing that he had ever had done to him. He felt his cock growing at her ministrations, he would have quite happily let her take him all the way, she stopped after a few minutes and lifted her mouth from his knob and stood up, she pushed her thong down her legs and turned away from him and bent over and gripped the bed, when she opened her legs she was the perfect height, she groaned out loud when he pushed his big cock into her, stretching her to her limit for the very first time in her life.

Bobby gripped her hips and gave her the fucking of her life, she came and came as he went on and on, they fucked for an age and she eventually had to tell him to stop, he stopped but held his cock deep inside her, Sally was panting hard, she turned to him and said. "I'm too sore Bobby to carry on, where ever did you learn to fuck like that, if you pull it out, I will suck you off."

He looked down and dribbled some spit onto her brown hole, she looked back and asked what he was doing, he did not answer her he dribbled some more spit onto her brown hole, he reached forward and rubbed it all around, he slowly pulled his rock hard cock out and placed the tip of his cock to her brown hole she was not sure about this, but it was too late as he pushed forward and his knob slipped up her bum, she groaned out loud and went to say something, but he pulled her back and pushed forward, his cock slipped up her ass making her scream, but he was in to the hilt and he began fucking her ass, it took maybe twenty strokes and her still screaming before she began to relax a bit, she bent lower and gave a little push back, she went mad then and began groaning out loud, as she rammed her body back at him, she began calling him all of the names under the sun, as he shot his spunk up her ass bringing forth her loudest scream yet, she continually screamed at the top of her voice as he pushed his huge cock hard up her ass.

He eventually pulled his half hard cock out of her and let her go, she flopped forward and curled up on the bed holding her stomach, he walked out of the bedroom and found the bathroom, he washed his dirty, bloody cock in cold water and cleaned himself up, he went back into the bed room and she was now sat on the edge of the bed, she had placed a sanitary towel around her ass and fanny, she looked up at him and said.

"Where ever did you learn to do all that, I have had a few men but you are the biggest and the best ever and when you fucked my ass, fuck me, I have wondered about that but never had the nerve to do it, now that I have I will definitely be doing it again.

Sally looked at the clock and said. "We should be getting back, they will wonder where I have been?" They drove back to the showroom and his new car was standing on the forecourt almost ready, he sat in the car and she went into the showroom, she came back a few minutes later and said we are just waiting for the road tax, it will be maybe 15 minutes, I will get the trade plates and take you for a test drive." She was definitely walking differently than she was earlier, he smiled to himself as he remembered her screaming as he fucked her ass, she came back smiling all the way, she attached the plates to the car and climbed into the passenger seat, they drove out of the forecourt and down the road, she absently reached into his lap and rubbed his cock.

Bobby looked down at her hand as it rubbed his cock. He looked at her and said "I thought that you were to sore for any more sex?" She smiled and said. "You have changed me Bobby, and for that I want to reward you by sucking you off." He stopped at some traffic lights and she tried to open his trousers unsuccessfully, so he did it for her, she reached into his trousers and pulled his big cock out and began wanking it, she tried to get her mouth to it, but the steering wheel was in the way, she said.

"I love your big cock Bobby, I wish you lived near here, I would let you fuck me whenever you wanted."

His cock began to show some interest, so he pulled his lovely new car into a secluded lay-by, she leaned over him and pressed some buttons on the door panel, his seat moved back to its limit and stopped, when she pressed another button, the back of his seat began to lower down, she gripped his cock with her right hand and lowered her mouth to his knob, he had his left hand on her back and pulled her blouse up and undid her bra, he turned slightly sideways in the big car and reached under her and fondled her tits, he reached down her back and pulled her skirt up, he slid his fingers down underneath her and rubbed her fanny through the thin sanitary towel.

Sally opened her legs wide and began moaning, he pushed his fingers under the towel and pushed them into her soaking wet fanny and began frigging her, her hips began bouncing as his fingers pleasured her, she lifted her mouth and looked at him. She reached back and pulled his finger out of her fanny and turned sideways so that she was facing him and removed her thong and pad, she lifted her right foot onto her left knee and said. "Make me cum Bobby." He reached down and pushed his fingers back into her fanny and she lowered her mouth back onto his cock, her right hand went to her fanny and she began rubbing her clit from side to side, she lifted her mouth and stared at him as she climaxed, he felt her hot cum on his long thin fingers, she let his fingers carry on for another minute or so before snatching them away.

Sally sat up and looked around, seeing no-one close by, she crawled into his lap and reaching underneath herself she guided his huge cock into her hot wet fanny, she clung to him and fucked him hard using her hips and thighs, her fanny was squelching as she fucked him, she gripped his hard cock with her fanny lips and it was like a small hand gripping his cock, she looked into his eyes and said
"C'mon Bobby shoot it into me, all the way Bobby shoot it deep inside me." He grunted and shot his seed deep inside her, Sally closed her eyes and smiled as she felt his warm seed flooding her insides, he shot spurt after spurt into her, all the time she smiled gratefully into his eyes.

As soon as he had stopped coming, she lifted herself from him to avoid his clothes getting too wet, she lowered her mouth to his cock and sucked a few drops of cum out of him, she licked his cock clean and everywhere else that she could reach. Sally sat up and looked at this beautiful man and said. "Look what have you done to me Bobby, you have turned me into a desperate woman, why don't you stay locally tonight and I will come and see you?" He smiled and said. "I might just do that, I have no plans to be anywhere." She adjusted her dress and cleaned herself up as best she could, she asked him to drive down the road to the supermarket and she would clean herself up in the toilets, he did the same and they headed back to the showroom, the tax was ready by now, he went into the showroom and filled out all of the relevant paperwork, he paid for the car and Sally walked him to his new car, she passed him her phone number and told him to let her know where he was staying and she would see him later.

Bobby drove out of the showroom and waved at Sally as he left, when he looked in the rear view mirror she was stood waving at him. Bobby drove down the road in his new car and opened the window, screwed her number up and tossed it out of the window and drove on to who knows where.

Chapter 15

Bobby was laughing out over his last conquest and the way that he had dismissed her, tossed her out of his life, as if she was nothing but he thought to himself "She was a bloody good fuck." He still had no plan as to where he was going, he thought about his distant aunt in Scotland, but that was a very long drive, but then he had all the time in the world, so what did it matter either way. Bobby saw a sign for a country hotel and spa, he took the turning and headed there, it was still early evening, but he was not yet hungry, but he could have a swim and use the spa. He walked into the Blue-springs Spa and booked a room and a massage, he was shown around the hotel and the spa.

Everywhere he looked the place was full of pretty young things, he changed into his swimming trunks and put on a spa dressing gown, he walked down to the pool and sat on a lounger, he ordered a whiskey and soda and sat and watched two delightful young ladies swimming length after length, one had blond hair and the other wore a swimming hat, the one with the hat had glanced at him every time that she swam past, so he made a point of watching her as she swam by and smiling at her, the next time she swam past she stared at him longer, so he smiled longer at her, this went on for another ten minutes until the two women climbed out of the water, the one with the hat looked back at him, but her friend grabbed her arm and dragged her into the changing room. Bobby closed his eyes and dozed, he was woken by a Chinese woman stroking his hand, he opened his eyes and she said. "Mr Francis it is time for your massage, please follow me."

He stood up and followed her, she was tiny and very doll like, she took him into the massage room and he removed his dressing gown and laid down on the massage table, when she began the massage she seemed to be the perfect height, he looked down and along one side of the table where a step had been erected, he smiled and let her carry on, as she was very good with her hands.

He asked her what her name was and she told him*Tan Lee* he tried to get her to talk, but she wasn't getting involved, she had finished his back and legs and asked him to turn onto his back, he turned over and she looked at the bulge in his swimming shorts, he watched her swallow deeply, when she leaned over him, he could see down her shirt to her tiny tits, but her tiny nipples looked rock hard. She had finished on his chest and stomach but her eyes seemed to be locked onto his cock, she swallowed again and moved down to his legs, she was rubbing his thigh muscles upwards from his knees to just below his balls, the more she did it the harder she pressed, his cock began to grow slightly the more she massaged his legs, not long after his giant cock was straining at the thin material of his swimming trunks.

Tan Lee was getting very hot as she worked away, she was trying her hardest not to look at his growing manhood, but was struggling. She stood up and looked all over his body and said. "I think that is every-thing" and went to step down from the step so Bobby said. "Excuse me Tan but do you think you could lean over and massage this shoul-der for me only it feels a bit stiff."

The shoulder he pointed to at was the one opposite her step, so she had to lean right over him to reach the spot, she looked at him doubt-fully, but put some oil on her hands and leaned over him, as soon as she had, he placed his hand on her hard little ass, he rubbed her ass and she didn't seem to mind, it was when he pushed his fingers under her ass to her fanny, she looked at him and hesitated, as he pushed his fin-gers along her swollen fanny, she opened her legs slightly and let him carry on.

He tried to get his other hand down her shirt, she lifted her tiny body and let him slide his hand down her shirt to her naked tits, her tits were so small, he could quite easily get them both in one hand, she moaned out loud so he pulled his hand up and slid it down inside her shorts, his finger slipped into her fanny easily, she reached behind herself and pushed her shorts down so that he could now get a second finger inside her, she turned to the side and pushed her hand into his swimming shorts and gripped his hard cock, she turned to look at his giant cock as she pulled it out of his trunks, she gasped out loud and let go of it and jumped down from her step, she pulled her shorts up and pulled her shirt down she took another look at his mighty cock before she ran from the room shouting.

"Too big, too big, too big." He burst out laughing and smelt his fingers, he had never smelt Chinese cum before, unsurprisingly it smelt the same as every other woman's.

Bobby waited until his cock had shrunk back to normal and walked into reception to have a look round and book his evening meal, Paul the receptionist called over. "Mr Francis, I have a note for you" he passed him the note which he opened, it read. "Hi Bobby, this is me from the pool, I will be back later for aerobics between 8and9. If you fancy a drink I will meet you in the bar. Sandy." He smiled and put the note into his dressing gown and went up to his room to shower and change. Bobby ate a hearty meal and relaxed, from a viewing station he watched a group of very fit women doing aerobics, he tried to figure out which was the woman from the pool, but to be honest it could have been any one of them and did it matter anyway.

The women ended the session by applauding the instructor, he walked down the stairs and into the bar, he ordered a bottle of red wine and two glasses and waited, a young braless woman came smiling towards him, she had blond hair held up in a ponytail and was not only very beautiful, she was also very fit, she sat down next to him and said.
"Hi Bobby, I'm Sandy do you come here often?" She giggled to herself and said "I have spent the last hour thinking about what I would say to you, and all I could think of was, well you heard it?" He smiled his killer smile and said. "Hi sandy, I'm Bobby would you like a drink?" She nodded so he poured her a large glass of wine and asked her.
"What is it that you do Sandy?" She smiled and said. "Well, basically, I look after my husband and keep myself fit, as you can see." She pushed her tits out at him and by telling him she was married, it was obvious that she was on the pull, he looked at her tits and said.

"They are very nice, but they would look better if they were in my hands" she glanced around the bar and said. "Then tell me what room are you in?" he told her and she said. "See you in a minute then, oh and take the wine up with you." She left the bar as if she was leaving the spa, he walked up the stairs to his room and sat down at a table that had two chairs by it, he poured two more glasses of wine and waited, he had left the door slightly ajar and she was not shy in walking in, she closed the door behind her and locked it, she smiled as she walked over to the chair and sat down, she picked up her glass and drank half of her wine, all the time they looked at one another, he reached out and stroked her left breast, she looked down at the big hand on her tit and said. "You were right, it does look better in your hand, shall we go to bed?" He stood up and held his hand out to her, she took it and let him take her into the bedroom, she was not slow in coming forward, she stood by the bed and pulled her top over her head to show him a most beautiful pair of tits, he reached out and fondled them, she pushed her shorts down her legs and kicked her gym shoes off, she stood there in a red thong.

He undid the buttons on his shirt and took it off, she looked at his hard body and rubbed her hands over his hard chest, he undid his belt and his trousers and let them fall to the floor, he put his hands in the side of his boxers and pushed them down as well, she reached out and lifted his heavy cock and said.
"Fucking hell, that is what I call a cock, I have never had anything that big before" she began wanking his cock and watched it as it grew in her hand, and said. "Fuck me, when does it stop growing?" He reached out and pushed her thong down to reveal a hairless fanny, her fanny lips were well swollen, he rubbed his finger along her slit and she opened her legs for him, he slid his finger into her wet fanny, she turned and looked him in the eyes, and said in a husky voice. "Make me cum Bobby and then fuck me with this monster cock."

He pushed another finger into her fanny and began finger fucking her, she pushed her hips forward and closed her eyes and let him take her to her orgasm, she soaked his fingers which she pulled out of her fanny and put them into her mouth, she quite happily sucked her own fanny juices from them, he turned her to the bed and sat her down, she lay back and opened her legs wide and then lifted them up, he placed his big knob to her entrance and pushed forwards, she arched her back and growled as he stretched her to her full limit, when he was deep inside her she lifted her legs and he took their weight on his arms, he gripped the inside of her thighs and begun fucking her ass off, she had been fucked before, many times but never like this.

This Bobby was huge and he was still stretching her every thrust he gave her, she could tell already that he was a well-practised lover and would give her the best fuck of her life, why hadn't she found someone like this instead of the workaholic bastard that she had married, that fucked her once a fortnight if she was lucky, and he had never made her cum with his little cock, she always had to do it to herself when he was asleep, she had told him what she did, but he just shrugged and said. "It's the best I can do, if you don't like it go somewhere else, just don't tell me about it." But she would tell him about Bobby and his giant cock, she would count how many times he makes her cum and she will tell the useless bastard that as well, and fuck him, if he didn't like it he could fuck off.

She concentrated on this man who was looking down at her, watching her closely, ready to fuck her harder when the time was right, and that time was fast approaching, she closed her eyes and waited for him to begin ramming his big cock into her. Bobby was the perfect lover, he took her slowly to her orgasm, and as soon as she was through it, he built her up to the next one and the next one, time and time again he made her cum without much sign of his own release, he eventually slowed down and stopped, he looked down at her and told her to turn over, she did not need telling twice, she took up her position and spread her knees until she was in the right position for him, she knew that he would cum in this position, she wanted to feel him shoot his cum into her, she wanted to become pregnant by this man, this beautiful, wonderful man, and it would serve her old man right.

He pushed his big cock back into her, he was even deeper inside her now, he gripped her hips and then spread his feet and then began his own journey, she began to scream quietly as he plundered her depths like never before, she thought that she was choking from the inside and when he shot his burning hot seed into her, it was like no other feeling that she had ever felt, spurt after wonderful spurt erupted deep inside her young fit body, her screams filled the room, each spurt brought forth another ear piercing scream. When he pulled her back he made her cough, as he pushed his huge cock hard inside her, he was hurting her, but she did not care, she closed her eyes and ground herself against the base of his thick cock and took herself to yet another orgasm, which number it was, she did not know and to be honest she did not care.

Bobby let her slip down on the bed, she groaned out loud when he pulled his wilting cock out of her, he pulled her around so that her head was now near the edge of the bed, he gripped her hair and turned her face towards him, when he pushed his giant cock at her mouth, she opened her mouth and let him push his cock deep inside, she gave him a very good blow job, using all the skills that she had learned over the years of shagging behind her old man's back, she licked his whole length clean, when she was done, she sucked his knob again, just to say thank-you.

Bobby woke early and had breakfast in his room, he had showered and was stood looking out of the large window at the rolling countryside, all he had on was a towel wrapped around his waist. A knock came on the door, he called for whoever it was to come in, a dark haired woman of somewhere in her mid-thirties, wearing a grey business suit and a blue shirt, entered the room. She looked at him and then at his big cock that was out lined by the tightly wrapped towel, within ten-seconds she looked at his cock 5 times. She shook her head and said. "Good morning Mr Francis, my name is Ruth Chard and I am the manager of the Hotel and spa, I have come to see you this morning, because we have received a number of complaints about a woman screaming last night on numerous occasions, and I have come to check on the woman's health and to see if everything was ok?"

She was standing just inside the door holding a clip board and a mobile phone, he walked over and stood in front of her and said. "Hi Ruth, please call me Bobby as for the screaming, well it was one of your female clients enjoying proper sex, for the very first time in her life, she made a few sounds in her most intense moments in a show of appreciation for my efforts."

She blushed slightly and said. "And was this client gone now,[he nodded] do you always talk down about women like that, we are not all like that you know, having sex with complete strangers. You wouldn't catch me doing anything like that ever, I am a very happily married woman thank you." He took a step closer and said.

"If you are so happily married, why have you looked at my big cock 11 times since you have been in my room?" She started to stutter a response when he reached out and grabbed her wrist and placed her hand on his cock, her hand folded around his thick shaft, he moved closer and said. "And if I put my hand up your skirt and slipped my hand down into your pants, your fanny won't be wet then?"

He leaned against her and slid his hand up her skirt and pushed his hand down into her pants, and as he ran his fingers along her slit she opened her legs to allow him access to her most private place, showing no finesse he pushed two fingers deep into her wet fanny, she instantly began bucking against his fingers, he reached down and snatched his towel away, her slim hand automatically gripped his big cock and began moving her hand up and down, she closed her eyes and soaked his finger with her cum, he took a step back and looked at her dishevelled state, her hand was still moving up and down his thick cock, he looked into her eyes and said. "If you want me to fuck you with my big cock, take all of your clothes off."

She chewed her top lip for maybe thirty seconds, all the time she looked him straight in the eyes, she slipped her jacket off and dropped it on the floor she slowly undid her buttons on her shirt and removed it, she dropped it onto the floor, she took her bra off and dropped that on the floor, she reached for the back of her skirt but he stopped her, he looked at her thick nipples and taking one in each hand, twisted them until she winced, he then lowered his hands and let her finish removing her clothes, standing naked in front of him she looked up into his eyes, he took her hand and led her into the bedroom, he sat her down in a soft leather chair and reached out and gripped the back of her head he pulled her head to his hard cock, she had never sucked a cock before, because he had to talk her through it, he let her carry on for a few minutes before pulling her up to her feet by her hair, he looked deep into her blue eyes, all over her pretty face and then back to her eyes.

Bobby asked her. "Tell me the truth Ruth, have you ever been properly fucked?" She did not hesitate in shaking her head. He smiled and said. "So this will be the best fuck of your life?" she chewed her top lip, but did not answer him, he turned her around and bent her over the arm of the chair, he gripped his cock and placed his knob at her entrance and pushed forward, she groaned out loud as he stretched her insides, he pulled back to the edge of her fanny and pushed forward again bringing forth another deep moan from her, he gripped her hips and slowly began fucking her.

Ruth did not have much experience for a woman of her age, she grunted every-time he reached full depth, he watched her closely and when he thought that the time was right, he began ramming his cock into her, she began screaming as her orgasm built, and when she came a low long scream escaped from her as she scratched the arm of the leather chair, as soon as she was past her orgasm he slowed down again and built her up slowly to another strong climax, as soon as she was past her orgasm he stopped fucking her and pulled his cock out making her jump, she turned to look at him as he gripped her hand and pulled her up, he took her to the front of the leather chair and sat her down, he lifted her legs and pulled her bottom to the edge of the chair, he put his cock just back inside her fanny and looked at her and said. "Now you can watch me fuck you, and I want to see you play with your tits."

He pushed his cock all the way into her body and the manageress gritted her teeth and arched her back, she gripped the arms of the chair as he began riding her again, he took her to the edge of her orgasm and he made her jump again when he shouted for her to play wither tits, she did not hesitate as her hands went to both breasts, she had never done this in front of a man before, either. A scream began to rise in her throat as her orgasm built, her climax when it came exploded through her body, making her pull her tits so hard it must have hurt her. Bobby watched the woman that was now in a place where she had never been before, he decided to give her another experience that she would never have dared to do before with her husband, he pushed her legs higher, and waited until she looked at him and he said. "Ruth listen, when you start to cum next time I want you to play with your clit, I want to watch you doing it, ok?"

She nodded her head, but he was not sure whether she would do it or not. She began moaning so he picked up his pace, she slowly slid her hand down to her mound and placed her two fingers on her clit and began rubbing slowly, but she soon saw the benefits and her fingers were suddenly moving very fast, she screamed out her orgasm and looked him hard in the eyes, as she began using her hips to meet every-one of his long thrusts, her fingers never left her clit from that point on.

He began to fuck her hard and shouted. "Get ready, I am going to fill you to the brim with my spunk." She nodded and began looking forward to the feeling deep inside her, one that she had never felt before, he grunted and she began screaming as the first spurt hit her deep inside, she felt his warm cum spread through her body, each spurt brought another scream from the manageress as she continued to rub her clit, each long spurt of his seed brought a new reaction from Ruth, he finally stopped coming and pushed his still hard cock hard into her, she moaned continually and screwed her face up as if in pain, but infact she was in heaven, finally she had been well and truly fucked.

The manageress suddenly realised that her fingers were still rubbing her sensitive clit, but lowly now, she was way past the point of any embarrassment, this wonderful man had released the woman in her, she had wondered about such things a long time ago, but now that she has actually done them, she would definitely be doing them again, if not with her husband then she would choose carefully, and fuck as many men as she could, she had never cheated on her husband before, but she was so glad that she had with this fine specimen of a man. Bobby pulled his cock from her and gripped her head as he leaned forward, she did not hesitate in taking his cock into her mouth and sucking it, she received a few drops of his cum, the first man spunk that she had ever tasted and was surprised at the saltiness, but it wasn't unpleasant, and she decided there and then that she would be tasting man cum again, very soon.

He pulled his cock from her mouth and said. "Now lick it clean from the bottom up" she gripped his cock and did what he demanded, finally he was happy and stepped back and sat down in a chair opposite her. They sat and looked at each other for long minutes until he asked her. "Are you happy?" She smiled and said. "More than you will ever know, I have done things today that I thought about long ago, but had also forgot about, because as I accepted my husband's lovemaking for what it was, his release.

Fuck me, well I can tell you Bobby you have changed my life, in the past I have turned down offers and passes from really good looking men like you, but never again, I want to fuck, I want to suck cocks, I want to rub my clit when I am being fucked, I want to try other things like sex with a woman or a threesome, I wish you were staying for a while Bobby I feel that there are more things that you could teach me"

He nodded and said. "Unfortunately, I have to be somewhere, but if I pass this way on my return journey, I will call in and rape you, how does that sound?"

She smiled and said. "Just let me know and I'll have everything ready."

That was how they left it, he took her number with a promise to ring her, if he was passing.

Chapter 16

Back on the road again Bobby laughed out loud again at his luck, everywhere he went women wanted him to fuck them, and he was not going to say no, was he? He was back on the motorway heading north when his phone rang, he pressed the hands free button and Helen said. "Hello Bobby is that you?" he answered. "Hi Helen, is everything ok?" She sounded pissed, when she said. "Well, it would have been if we had known where you were and what your plans are, your grand-father is worried to death, you could have rung him Bobby and what about me, you could have rung me at least, I thought that I meant something to you?"

He suddenly felt like a selfish bastard and apologised to her, and said that he would ring his grandfather straight away. He turned off the motorway and headed down a main road towards another anonymous town, he stopped at the first parking space that he found and called his grandfather, who called him a selfish bastard and asked him when he was coming home, he told the truth and said that he would be home soon, but that he would keep in touch in the meantime.

He bought a sandwich and a coffee and was sat in the local park minding his own business watching families doing what families do on a nice hot summer's day, when a black Labrador came up to him with its tail wagging, so Bobby gave him the last of his sandwich, making him sit first.

A young woman came running up and put a lead around the dog's neck, she said how sorry she was for interrupting his lunch but how did he make Toby sit first saying. "I have been trying to get him to do that for weeks but the useless dog won't do anything for me." He looked at her, she looked about eighteen with long blond hair and nice tits, she was slim and blushed when she saw that he was checking her out. She wore a white tee shirt and a short white skirt.

He said quickly.
"Have you got any doggy treats?" When she said that she had, he said.

"Well then, it should be easy, c'mon I will show you." She said that she did not want to take up his time, he shrugged and said. "I have plenty of time for someone as beautiful as you, lets walk over there where it is quiet, there will be less distractions for Toby, what's your name?" She seemed a bit concerned so he said. "My name is Bobby Francis, I am twenty years old, single and have that much money, that I do not have to work, ok?"

She smiled and said. "My name is Molly and you can't be too careful these days, I mean you might be a rapist or a murderer?" He smiled and said. "No, you are safe in that regard, don't get me wrong I like sex and I am very good at it, but a rapist, no." They turned to walk together towards a quiet corner of the park where he spent the best part of two hours teaching them both doggy tricks, he went and bought them both an ice cream, they lay on the grass together and ate them. They chatted about their lives, he didn't exactly tell her the truth, but he would never see her again after today, so it didn't really matter what he said, did it?"

Molly said that she had better be going as her friend was waiting for her, he put his arm around her shoulder and asked her.
"Can I ask you, you're not gay are you Molly?" she blushed and said
"No, I am not, what a strange thing to say?" He shrugged and said.
"Like you said Molly you never know these days do you, you may be a murderer or even a rapist?" She laughed at this and said that he was being silly, he still had his arm around her shoulders, as she didn't seem to mind, he kept his arm there, he asked her if she would like to go out for a meal later, as he was on his own and new in town." She looked up at him and smiled, but shook her head and said. "I can't, I promised Tracy that I would cook for her tonight and I would hate to let her down as she does not have many friends."

He smiled down at her and said "Then bring Tracy along, we can all go out to eat, you choose where we go and I will take us in my new car?" Molly smiled up at him and said. "You're quite a nice person really, aren't you?" He hugged her closer and kissed her on top of the forehead and said. "I try to be a nice person, that way you get to meet nice people, just like you."
When she smiled up at him he knew that he almost had her eating out of his hand, they were passing a line of trees, he stopped and turned her

and eased her back against a tree and kissed her on the lips, she kissed him back and when he touched her lips with his tongue she opened her mouth and melted into him and placed her arms around his neck, he had made the first move the second was up to her, she touched her mound to his growing cock so he began rubbing against her, she moaned into his mouth, he put his hand under her tee shirt at the back and undid her bra, she did not object so he glanced around and seeing no-one close, he put his hand up the front of her tee shirt to her naked breast, she let him feel her tit for a few seconds, then pulled away from him and whispered. "Not here Bobby, take me somewhere in your car."

She reached behind her and did her bra up and then took his hand, he led her to his car and she climbed into the back seat with her dog, he said. "You will have to tell me where to go as I am new to the town." She thought about it for a few seconds and told him which way to go, he wanted to test her to see how far she would go so he said. "Show me your beautiful tits Molly." She smiled into the rear-view mirror and lifted her tee shirt and bra to show him a fine pair of firm tits but put them away again.

She told him to turn down a side road, at her instructions they turned into what looked like a deserted farm yard, she told him to drive to the far corner, when he stopped the car she forced Toby the dog into the front passenger seat and tied his lead to the armrest, Bobby lowered the back of his seat all the way down and crawled into the back seat, as he neared her she lay back on the long wide seat, he pushed her shirt and bra up and began sucking her tits, he eased her legs open and lowered his hardening cock onto her mound, she was trying to lift his shirt off his back, so he sat up and pulled his shirt over his head, he then lifted her tee shirt over her head and pulled her bra off.

He could see up her short skirt and she had on a small pair of white pants that were very wet, he put his thumb onto her fanny where her clit should be, as he began rubbing she closed her eyes and opened her legs as wide as she could, he reached forward and pulled her pants to the side, now he pushed two fingers into her very wet fanny, he moved around so that he could finger fuck her properly, she lifted her head as he gave her a most beautiful orgasm, he pulled his wet sticky fingers out of her fanny and put his fingers by her mouth, she opened her mouth so he rubbed the sticky fingers all around her gums, she made sure that she had sucked them clean before he could pull them out.

Bobby then put her legs together and reached under her short skirt and pulled her pants down and took them off, he opened his trousers and pushed them down his legs, he did the same with his boxers, he turned to her and went to open her legs but she said. "Take my skirt off, I want to be naked with you." So he pulled her skirt down and pulled it off, she had all of her pubic hair, he thought about going down on her, but he only really likes going down on shaved fannies.

Bobby turned to her and opened her legs and lifted them up, he then knelt up on the seat and held his big cock in his right hand and placed it at her entrance, he pushed forwards and she screamed out in the big car, he pushed forwards again and most of his big thick cock slipped inside her, she put her hand on his chest to stop him and looked down to where they were joined together and said. "You could have warned me you were hung like a fucking donkey"

he said he was sorry and asked her if she wanted him to stop, she said. "Don't you fucking dare, this is the biggest cock that I have ever had and I want to enjoy it so carry on and fuck my ass off." He did his best to oblige the young woman, he rode her and rode her and she had orgasm after orgasm, he stopped and turned her over, now on their hands and knees he could really ram his cock into her. Molly made a lot of noise for one so young, in this position when he took skilfully her through her orgasm, she was hitting the top of her head on the window but it did not deter her one bit and she did not complain either when he shot his cum into her.

She screamed out loud but began to really thrust back at him, and when he pushed hard into her he pushed her face flat against the window of the car making her moan out loud, but again she did not complain. When Bobby finally pulled his cock out of her he turned and sat down on the back seat, as for Molly she sort of slumped into a heap on the back seat and stayed there for a good few minutes until she asked him to pass her pants, he found them on the floor and passed them to her, she did not put them on she pushed them against her fanny and turned around and lay with her head in his lap and said. "Fuck me Bobby that was good, can we do it again later?" He said. "I was thinking of spending the night here so yes you can come to my hotel to eat if you want to?"

She was deep in thought when she asked him. "Can I bring Tracy with me, she would love your big cock?", he lifted her head so that she was looking at him and asked her. "You and Tracy, have you two ever messed around, like with each other?" She blushed so he knew that they had done something, she said. "Well, we have kissed a few times and we did feel each other's tits the once, but that is basically it". So he asked her. "So if I managed to get you both naked on or in the same bed do you think that you would go further with each other, and if I was to offered to teach both of you how to love each other properly, do you think that Tracy would be up for it?" She lay there looking at him and answered.

"When I tell her about your big cock, she will want you to fuck her, and if I were to say but we may have to do some things to each other first, that way I am sure that she will be up for it." She sat up and looked at him and asked. "Where are you staying then Bobby?" He shrugged and asked. "Tell me which is the best hotel in town, and I will stay there?" She nodded and bent down to pick her bra up, he said.
"Ah, what are you doing Molly, we are not quite finished yet are we?" She looked at him doubtfully, so he lifted his sticky cock and said.
"You have some cleaning up to do first.

" She smiled and licked her lips, before placing her mouth over his limp cock, Molly had sucked a cock before and had been well taught by someone, she exposed his knob licked all around the rim before sucking him dry, she was not a bit scared when she took most of his cock down her throat, she cleaned his cock and asked him, can I get dressed now or do you want me to do something else for you?" He sat and looked at the young girl and said. "Show me how you rub your clit?" She blushed a deep red and shook her head and said "Not now, but I promise to do it later for you, when Tracy is there and we can do it together." He nodded in agreement and they both got dressed, he looked at the young girl and asked her. "Have you got something nice to wear tonight?" She shrugged and said, "No doubt we will find something

that we can wear." He put his hand in his back pocket and pulled out a wad of cash, he pulled off four fifty pound notes and said.
"Now both of you go out and buy yourselves a nice dress each, and have your hair done, let's make the evening special" he pushed the money into her hand and her eyes lit up but she said. "If I take your money I will feel like a prostitute, and I don't want to feel like that." She held the money out to him, he smiled and closed her hand around the money and smiling said. "Look Molly, I have more money than I know what to do with, and if I can make you happy by buying you a new dress then that is what I want to do, and if I want to buy you both a nice meal tonight, then that is also what I will do, ok?" She smiled and stuffed the money into her skirt pocket and said.

"Put like that I will happily take your money and look forward to tonight. Molly showed him to the Riverside Hotel and said that she would walk from there and that she would see him later at 8pm, she leaned over and they kissed deeply, she said. "I can't wait to get your big cock back inside me Bobby" he looked deep into her eyes and asked her. "If I asked you and Tracy to do something to make this night special for us all, would you do it?" She kissed him again and said. "Just name it Bobby and if we can do it, then we will." He smiled and said. "I want you both to shave your fanny's clean." She smiled and said "We would be only too happy to shave for you, consider it done." On that note she left him at the hotel, they had arranged to meet in the reception area at 8 and that is how they left it, she waved as she walked away, he smiled and walked into the hotel and booked a double room and a table for three at 8.15.

Bobby sat on the bed and thought about the last threesome that he had had with Susy and Liz, and the way that they had enjoyed the strap on cocks that he had bought them, he decided to take a walk around the town and see what he could buy. Bobby found what he was looking for at the Pleasure Parlour, he placed the bag in his room, showered and dressed smart but casual, it was early yet, but he decided to go down to the reception and read the papers and wait for his dates. He was sat thinking about nothing really when a smartly dressed woman came and stood in front of him and asked if there was anything she could do for him while he waited, he looked at the beautiful woman and wished that he had not agreed to tonight's entertainment, he asked her if she would please get him a glass of red wine, she said that she would be pleased to and if he needed anything else to just let her know at reception, and that her name was Shelly Preston.

"I will be working all night if you need anything else, sir." She said to him with the widest smile that he had ever seen, he nodded and said that he would remember that, he thought that it may be worth staying another night if he could get the beautiful Shelly into bed.

Bobby thought about Shelly and just happened to look at her and she smiled back at him, he smiled back and waved her over, she carried a pen and a pad and asked if she could do anything for him? He looked at her and she was fit, she obviously worked out, he asked her to sit down for a minute or two, when she was sat opposite him and he said.

"Tell me if I misread the situation but are you working tomorrow night as well, because I have company for tonight but tomorrow night, well I will be on my own." She smiled and wrote something on her pad and passed him the folded note and said. "Tomorrow night is my night off, but if you ring me at say lunch time and you want to do something in the afternoon, well my husband is away for a few days so that leaves me at a loose end and I could use some company."

She smiled and went back to her desk. The two well-dressed young women walked into the hotel and they had really made an effort, both of them were smiling at him as they approached his table, he stood and greeted them both, he asked if they wanted to go straight through to the restaurant and they said that they did, sat at the table he ordered champagne.

He turned to Tracy and looked her over, like Molly she was braless and her hard nipples were jutting out against the thin material of her new dress, he said that she looked beautiful tonight and he was looking forward to getting to know her better, he turned to Molly and told her that she looked good enough to eat, she leaned close to him and said "I have done what you asked, so if you do want to eat me, I can't wait" he turned to the other young woman and asked her "Have you done as I requested?" She smiled and said.

"Yes, I have done as you asked, but can I ask you something [he nodded and told her to ask away] are you as big as Molly says you are?" He glanced around the restaurant and no-one was paying them any attention so he reached out and took her hand and placed it on his thick long limp cock, she rubbed her hand along his length and looked into his face and smiled. "That will do nicely for me, thank you." They ordered their meals and drank some more champagne and chatted about their lives, he told them a complete load of lies, he would not be seeing them again so did it matter?. They had finished their main meals and they were waiting for their deserts, Tracy was messing with her napkin in her lap, she reached out for his hand and pulled it into her lap, she then leaned in close to him and said.

"Bobby, feel just how naked I am under this dress." She opened her legs wide and placed his hand onto her naked fanny, he smiled at her and ran his finger along her slit to her fanny opening, he pushed his finger as deep as he could inside her, she moved her bottom forward on her chair so that he could push another finger inside her and begin frigging her, it took less than a minute to make her close her eyes and shudder, she pulled his hand from her fanny and smiled at him, Bobby looked at Molly and said "Open your mouth Molly, I have something for you." She opened her mouth and he pushed the sticky fingers into her mouth, Molly closed her lips over his fingers and looked at her friend and sucked her sweet cum from his fingers and from her facial expression, she really enjoyed the taste, as for Tracy she looked at her friend with a broad smile all over her face.

They had finished their meals and drank a whole bottle of champagne, he ordered another bottle, and when it came to the table he said.
"Shall we, then ladies?" both young women stood and followed him to the lift, once in the lift and the doors were closed, he turned to look at the young ladies and said "Kiss each other." They did not hesitate and were still kissing when the doors opened, they walked hand in hand behind him as he led them to his room, he locked the door behind them, he stood with his back to the door and the two women stood hand in hand looking at him, he looked from one to the other and said.

"Why don't you strip each other naked?" The women looked at one-another, before Molly lifted her friends dress over her head and draped it over a chair, she was a bit shy standing there naked in front of a stranger, but she played the game and stripped Molly naked, they turned and looked at him, he studded their naked bodies before walking to them and taking one in each hand he led them into the bedroom, he told them both to get onto the bed and to lay on their sides facing each other, he stood there looking down at them and told them to kiss each other, they sort of pecked each other's lips so he said "C'mon girls you can do better than that."

They began kissing and the kissing soon became more urgent, he said. "Play with each other's tits." They did not hesitate as they continued to use their tongues in each other's mouths, he moved to the bed and lifted Tracie's top leg and placed her foot flat onto her bottom leg, he them moved to Mollie's and lifted her top leg and placed it onto her bottom leg, he stood back and said. "Right, play with each other's clits."

Molly moved her hand straight to her friends fanny and began rubbing her friends clit, making her friend moan into her mouth, so Tracy lowered her hand and did the same to Molly, within seconds they were moaning into each other's mouths, as their hips had begun moving, he said. "Stop, now move your fingers to your friends fanny and finger fuck each other to orgasm.

He watched them finger fuck each other for the very first time, as he expected Tracy came first, but Molly was not too far behind, both young women were very vocal in their orgasms, they continued to kiss long after their orgasms were over, he told them to stop kissing and then asked. "Do you two want to go further with this, like I told Molly this afternoon, I don't mind teaching you what I know." The women looked at one another and they both nodded and looked up at him. Bobby stripped himself naked and both women stared at his giant cock, he then said. "Right who wants to go first."

Like at school Molly raised her hand, so he reached out and pulled Molly from the bed, she automatically gripped his big cock and began wanking him, he reached for Tracy and pulled her around and placed a pillow under her bum, he opened her legs wide and pushed them forward, he pulled Molly's head down so that she could watch him, he licked the naked fanny in front of him slowly, but deliberately with a flat tongue, he began down by her entrance and licked upwards, he did this maybe a dozen times, before he reached up and parted Tracy's fanny lips, he licked her again with a flat tongue, he then used a pointed tongue to titillate the tiny button in front of him, at his first touch of her button Tracy moaned out loud, she had been groaning up to now, but suddenly she was getting very vocal. He closed his lips over her clit and began sucking.

Tracy instantly lifted her head, hissed at them and began thrusting her hips up and down as her orgasm flooded through her loins, he continued to suck until the young woman calmed down, he lifted his head and Molly said. "Who would have thought so much pleasure could be gained from using a tongue?"

He stood up and told them to change places, they did this enthusiastically and he went through the whole thing again, only Tracy was into it in a big way which surprised him, because she was so quiet.

When they had finished pleasuring each other doing what he had just taught them, they lay on the bed holding hands whispering to each other, he stood there with his cock rock hard watching the two women and asked. "Do you want to learn some more?" They both looked at his hard cock and said yes, so he bent over the young women and pulled Tracy up simply because she was the nearest to him and turned her around, he leaned over and moved Molly onto her back and opened her legs wide, he ran a finger up her fanny lips making her jump slightly, he then moved Molly on top of her friend only her head was by her friends fanny, up the other end he opened Molly's legs and lifted Tracy's head and placed her mouth onto her friends fanny.

Molly instantly began moaning as her friend gave her new untold pleasure, he went to the other end and pushed Molly's face down to Tracy's fanny, he stood back and watched as first one woman would lift her head, moan out loud and then the other would do the same, the fanny kissing went on for an age as both young woman gave the other her orgasm, finally Molly growled out loud and pushed her fanny down hard onto her friends face and let out a low scream that was almost ghost like, she then rolled off her friend and lay there licking her lips with her eyes closed. Tracy lay where Molly had left her also licking her lips, she lay there with her legs wide open and her swollen fanny on full view, he so much wanted to crawl onto the bed and push his hard cock into her and fuck the living daylights out of her, but he had other plans first, he left the bedroom and fetched the brown paper bag, he walked back into the bedroom and neither young woman had moved a muscle, he said. "Look at me you two." Both women turned their heads and looked at him, he looked from one to the other and said. "I can see from your faces that you both enjoyed that, so would you like to try something else?" A slow nod came from both girls so he tossed the bag onto the bed and said "Let me see what you can do with those." They both sat up and Molly picked up the bag and looked inside, she shouted out loud. "Oh my fucking god, just look in here Trace." Trace looked in the bag and whooped out loud and told her friend to tip them out.

Molly tipped the contents onto the bed, there were two strap on cocks, one black and nine inches long with a wide girth, a pronounced knob and thick veins running the whole length, the second was also nine inches long, gold with a knob almost the size of a tennis ball, rows of pronounced nobbles ran from top to bottom, two black butt plugs and two different lubricants, they swopped rubber cocks excitedly, but they were confused with the butt plugs and looked at him, he sat on the bed and said. "C'mon girls, use a bit of imagination." Tracy had switched them all on and they began acting like small kids as they poked each other in the tit and fanny, he said. "Ok, enough, work out how to put them on and I will show you both what the small black ones are for." They helped each other put the rubber cocks on, Molly had the gold one strapped to her hips and Tracy had the black one strapped to her hips, they laughed as they had bit of a cock fight, using the cocks as swords, he held a bottle of lubricant out to Molly and said. "Rub some of this all over both cocks."

He lubricated the small black butt plugs and held them ready, Molly was still rubbing the lubricant up and down the rubber cock so he said "Right then. Tracy, get onto your hands and knees." She did as he asked and looked back at her friend who was moving up behind her, he said nothing as Molly pushed her rubber cock into her friend who arched her back, groaned out loud, looked back and her friend and growled.

Molly gripped her friends hips and was just about to begin fucking her friend when he moved up behind her and told her to bend forward, he dribbled some spit onto her brown hole and used the tip of the butt plug to lubricate her crinkly hole, he pushed the butt plug up her ass and she was quite relaxed about it and began laughing out loud. Tracy looked up to see what her friend was laughing at, he moved to kneel in front of Molly, he could see where the rubber cock was stuck deep inside Tracy, he put some spit on his finger and rubbed it around Tracy's brown hole, he used the tip as he had done before and tried to push the black vibrator inside her, but she was resisting him, so he slapped her ass and told her to relax, she did it instantly and allowed him to push the vibrator up her ass and she also began giggling.

Bobby sat back on his haunches and indicated for Molly to begin. Molly fucked her friend like she had been doing it for years, and to be honest Tracy loved every second of being fucked by her best friend and lover, he had no doubt that they would be using the rubber cocks long after he had gone and forgotten them. He watched Molly take her friend to two orgasms, before she asked Molly to stop, Molly pulled the cum covered cock out of her friend and looked down at the sticky rubber cock, Tracy sat up and licked some of the cum from the tip of the strap on, but she was so desperate to fuck her friend that she moved behind her lover and pushed her forwards onto her hands and knees, Molly spread her knees and Tracy moved up behind her best friend and pushed the big rubber cock into the young woman's body, Molly arched her back and instantly began thrusting back at her lover, they were soon in perfect harmony as Tracy fucked her best friend, he watched them as Molly came twice and she stopped her young lover as if by some hidden signal.

Bobby still sat on the bed looked at the young women and said.
"Right then girls, take those rubber cocks off, I am going to fuck you both, who wants to go first?" Molly said. "You came up me earlier, so fuck me first and cum up Tracy."

He nodded and pulled Molly to him, he pulled her off the bed and bent her over so that she had to grab the side of the bed, he pushed her feet apart and using his right hand and pushed his big hard cock all of the way into her young body, he gripped her hips and began fucking her, he used long slow strokes that made her grunt every time he reached his full depth, he looked at Tracy and said. "Open your legs facing me and play with yourself." She moved around so that both of them could watch her and she pulled her knees up and let her knees flop open, she stared at Bobby and placed her fingers onto her clit and began masturbating, as soon as she began her best friend began moaning as her orgasm neared, she came with a stifled scream as she met each of his hard strokes.

Bobby was trying to watch both women but he could not take his eyes from the young Tracy, she had had so many new experiences this night that she would never forget it, she had now moved her fingers from her clit and now had two fingers deep inside her fanny and was frigging herself stupid, he looked back at Molly and she was really into fucking in a big way, he did not know how much more she could take as she must have been sore from the afternoons session, her next orgasm began to build and she reached out to her friend and held her leg as she went through her fierce orgasm, she came down from it and waved for him to stop, he held his cock deep inside her as they both watched Tracy reach her climax, her fingers were still moving inside her fanny when he pulled his cock out of Molly, he stood where he was and Molly crawled onto the bed, he reached out and pulled Tracy to him, he placed her into the same position as her friend, when he pushed his sticky long hard cock into her she grabbed the bed and arched her back, she looked back at him and said. "Fuck Bobby, that was a tight fit."

He gripped her hips and began riding her, she was a lot tighter than her friend who was sat watching them fuck, he looked at Molly and then at her fanny, she did no more than pull up two pillows and lean against them, she them lifted her knees up as far as she could and spread them wide open, she reached down with her left hand and parted her fanny lips and held them wide open, with her other hand she placed a lot of spit onto her fingers and began rubbing her clit, she stared at him as her fingers moved ever faster, he looked back at Tracy and had not realised that she was going through her orgasm so quickly, he began ramming his cock into her and she screamed out loud, she had barely come down from her orgasm, when she began her next one, he was more or less ramming his cock into her all the time now which she seemed to like a lot, so he kept up the pace, but he knew with her tightness he would not last long at this rate.

Bobby was ramming his big cock into the young woman for all he was worth. Tracy was loving it and was making a lot of noise, he could not tell when she was coming as she seemed to be in a permanent state of orgasm, he felt his cum shoot up his cock and grunted when he exploded inside her, Tracy was screaming at the top of her voice as he filled her young body with his seed, when he pulled her back, and he pushed forward she thought that he was splitting her insides, but she could not help herself from grinding herself against him as another orgasm built inside her. Molly was making a lot of noise on the bed as her fingers were now moving deep inside her fanny as her own orgasm matched her best friends, the two young women stared at one-another as they shared a most intimate moment, he waited until Molly had finished before pulling her bodily towards him, she knew what was coming and lay on the bed waiting for him to pull his cock out of her best friend and push it into her mouth.

The two women had discussed this moment and decided that they would share their reward, Tracy turned around and helped her friend lick his cock clean, they took it in turns to suck his big knob, they managed to keep him hard for a good few minutes, but now his cock was finally shrinking, they were all relieved. The three of them lay flat out on the beds all totally fucked, all very happy and tingling where it mattered; the women crawled around the big bed and held each other tightly, the had already bought the morning after pills and were more than happy to use them, they had done so before and would probably use them again.

When Bobby woke in the morning, the young women were gone, so had all of the vibrators, so had the bottle of champagne all he had to remind him of the evening were the memories, he closed his eyes again and thought about his next sexual partner, Shelly the receptionist. Bobby finally made an effort and climbed out of bed, he showered and dressed in some nice summer clothes, he packed his suit case and walked down to reception, he ordered a sandwich and coffee. Bobby finished his breakfast and carried his suit case out to the car and stowed it in the boot, he then took his phone out and rang the number on the note, the phone was answered after the second ring, she said. "Hi Bobby, where are you?" He smiled that she knew whom it was and said

"I am actually leaning against my car outside the hotel, where are you?" She said "If you look at the right hand side of the hotel there is a sign that says *To the river* just follow that sign and you will find me on my boat."

She hung up and he followed the path down to the river, the path twisted and turned, but inevitably led downhill towards the river, he came to the green looking water, where a long wooden landing stage ran along the bank with a number of different sized boats moored there, he began walking along the mooring and found her stood on the end boat and the sheer sight of her almost made him cum on the spot. Shelly stood holding onto the steering wheel, her long blond hair hung freely down her back, and she wore the smallest white bikini that he had ever seen, her tanned body showed of the minute material perfectly, she smiled when she saw the effect that she had had on him, he walked up to the boat and asked for permission to come aboard.
 Shelly smiled and said. "Cast us off and then you will be welcome to come aboard."

He untied the ropes and stepped onto the large sea going boat, she took the ropes and rolled them up and put them in their place, she than went and started the powerful engines, Shelly handled the large boat with great skill as she headed slowly down-stream, he removed his shirt and sat and watched the world go by, but he could not keep his eyes from her perfect body, she would turn and smile at him occasionally.

He looked at the small gap at the top of her legs, and could see that her bikini bottoms were very wet, so he stood up and walked up behind her and pushed his naked chest against her back, she leaned back against him and purred like a kitten, he put his right hand around her and slipped it inside her bikini bottoms to her very wet clean shaved fanny, she opened her legs and his two fingers slipped easily into her swollen fanny.

Shelly turned her head so that they could kiss, as they kissed she rubbed her bottom against his hardening cock, she pulled her lips from his and whispered. "I'm coming Bobby, I'm coming on your wonderful fingers."

She closed her eyes and moved her bottom harder against him, she shuddered in his arms and slowly opened her eyes and looked deep into his eyes and whispered. "Thank you Bobby, I really needed that, you will be rewarded greatly for your efforts."

She put the boat into neutral and they drifted out of control as she turned and placed her arms around his neck and pushed her lips to his, within seconds they had their tongues in a wrestling match and she was really rubbing her mound against his hard cock, she began moaning into his mouth as she was coming again so he pushed his hard cock against her and let her take herself to another climax, she looked at the river and pulled away from him, she then put the boat into gear and looked for somewhere to moor up, they went slowly around a bend in the river and there were a line of metal posts sticking up out of the bank, she pulled alongside and he jumped off the boat and tied the ropes to the posts, he stepped back onto the now quiet boat and Shelly was no-where to be seen so he followed the sound of her voice and he descended a small flight of steps, she kneeled naked on what looked like two long seat cushions that fitted perfectly on the floor between two benches, one either side of the boat.

 He walked up to her, she reached up and undid his belt and then his trousers, she put her fingers onto his zipper and then looked up into his eye and said. "I hope that you are as big as you felt when you were rub- bing against me?" He smiled and said. "Why don't you find out?" she pulled his zipper down and gripped both sides of his trousers and slowly pulled them down, his half hard cock pushed against his boxers, she looked up at him again and said. "Hhhmmm, looks very promis- ing."

She pulled his boxers down and gasped out loud as he saw his huge cock, she pushed his clothing down to the floor and he stepped out of them.

Shelly did not hesitate when she lifted his cock, then licked her lips and closed her mouth over his big exposed knob, he stood there with his feet spread wide and his eyes closed, he couldn't help himself when he gripped her head either side and fucked her mouth, she pulled away from him and looked up into his eyes and said. "When you cum, I want

you to cum inside me." With that she turned around onto her hands and knees and waited for him to mount her. Shelly was not only beautiful in every way she was also very tight, when he tried to enter her it felt like he was too big for her, he tried but for the first time he could not get his big cock into her fanny, she turned around and said.
"Lay down and let me do it, you see I have never been really stretched before and if you saw my husband's cock you would piss yourself laughing it is so small."

She straddled him and gripped his big thick cock and held it to her entrance, she closed her eyes and very slowly sank down his length, she groaned and moaned and went very pale as she managed about half of his cock, she placed her hands onto his chest and looking down at him asked. "How am I doing?" He looked down to where they were joined and said "You are about half way, do you want me to push up as you push down, that way it should all go in?" she nodded and said. "Ready?" He nodded and she closed her eyes and gritted her teeth and screamed out loud as his cock finished its tight journey and she was now impaled on his monster cock, she smiled and said. "It feels like I have a fence post shoved up me, maybe I should have started with a lover with a smaller cock." He smiled and asked her. "Am I your first lover then Shelly?"

she nodded and said. "Yes, you are the chosen one and I want to get fucked as much as I can while we are together, I chose you because you are very good looking, and I also know that you will be gone by tonight, and if I become pregnant I will be very happy indeed, it may have looked like I knew what I was doing when I sucked your cock, but to be honest, that is the first cock that I have ever sucked, it is surprising what you can learn on the internet, I have seen all those big cocks on the porn films and dreamt of having a cock like that myself one day, but when I saw your monster cock I almost shit myself, because I knew that I was small down there, but look at me now sat here with your monster cock inside me, now that I have told you all about me, do you think we can fuck now because I really do want to get fucked properly before I die." He looked up at her and said.
"Well, Shelly you sure fooled me, I thought that with your beautiful body and looks, you would have had plenty of experience." She shook her head and said. "Look Bobby, will you do it to me please, I don't

care how just make me a real woman and then I can die happy, he took a quick look around and lifted her from his hard cock, he turned her around and knelt her on one of the side cushions, she was facing away from him and she was just about the right height he spread her knees and put his cock back to her entrance, she pushed her bum back and he pushed his cock back into her, this time although she was still very tight, his cock slipped to its full depth making her groan out loud, he waited until she was relaxed and began to ride her, slowly at first gradually increasing his speed.

Shelly began making squeaking noises from the start, but now she was getting what she wanted, her first ever orgasm with a cock frightened her at first with its intensity, she screamed out into the stillness of the boats interior, now she knew what to expect she became very involved and not only made a lot of noise she also pushed her ass back at his every thrust, her second orgasm was better than the first because she realised that he had a lot of control in making the orgasm better for her. She realised that at the build up to her climax he was ramming his giant cock into her and when she was through it, he would slow down and gently build her up to the next one.

Her husband pushes his little cock into her and goes like fuck until he shoots his load and within 30seconds he his asleep. Well, after today he had better change or I will kick the useless fucker out and go out shagging every-night, she thought. She began to get the tingling feeling again and closed her eyes and let him take her there. They were now fucking like real lovers she had learned a lot in a very short space of time and she hoped to learn some more before they had to part company, he slowed down and stopped, she turned her head and he said. "Time for a change of position[he kept his cock deep inside her and said] I will take your weight, then you lower your right foot down to the floor,[she did as he said]now lower your other foot down" now she was standing with her back to him, he lifted her hands and put them behind his head, she clasped her fingers together realising that she was totally at his mercy, he began moving his hips and therefore his big cock back and forth, she fell into time with him and they were soon fucking hard, Shelly like this and when he squeezed her tits hard, she almost came on the spot, she whispered.

"Do that harder Bobby, squeeze my tits hard." So he did as she asked which brought loud moans from her he felt her hard nipple were about to explode in his hands, the tit action took her to the edge of her orgasm so he lowered his hand and frigged her clit as hard as he could, she was really screaming now and her knees were shaking so much he thought that she may faint.

Bobby changed his tactics and slowed down again, he wanted to pull out but she wanted a long hard kissing session, his fingers of his right hand were still working on her clit and his left hand had both tits squeezed together, they were still fucking, but now it was long slow movements which were making her moan continuously. He reached up and took her hands and bent her forward so that she gripped the side of the boat, he pushed her feet wider apart and taking hold of her hips, he began to fuck her hard, he was really deep inside her now and she was letting him know it with her deep moans, he watched her body for signs of her nearing her orgasm, she was trying to squeeze her right tit but could not balance with just her left hand, he fucked her hard through her next orgasm and he sensed that she was flagging so he slowed down and asked her if she was ok, they were still moving together, but she turned sideways and said.
"You have given me more orgasms in twenty minutes than I have had in ten years of marriage, so this is all new to me." He pulled his cock out and turned her around and said.
"Do you want to carry on or do you want to stop?" She did not hesitate and said
"I really want to watch you cum inside me." He nodded and sat down he pulled her into his lap, he positioned her knees either side of him and held his sticky cock still while she used her body to guide him inside herself, he placed her knees in the right position and her hands behind his head and then used his hands to show what he wanted her to do with her hips, he leaned her top half back and nodded, she started slowly but was soon fucking him hard now that she was in control, he grabbed her tits and was pulling them in all different positions, she was taking herself to her orgasm for the first time and she loved it, being in control, her eyes were closed and she was blowing hot breath into his face, he began to get that old feeling and warned her, she stared into his eyes as she fucked him as hard as she could, he pulled a funny face and grunted, she sank down on him as he shot his first load of hot seed into

her bringing forth a scream like he had never heard before, he gripped her hips and encouraged her to start riding him again, she closed her eyes and put every fibre of her being into fucking him, she screamed out loud she had tears running down her face as she cried with sheer joy and happiness, she wanted this feeling to go on and on forever.

He finally stopped her and she fell against him still crying out loud as he rubbed her back trying to comfort her but she continued to cry, all he could do was wait for her to calm down, which she did eventually, she said. "You will never realise how happy you have made me Bobby, as I sit here full of your seed and a tingling in my fanny that I have never felt before, I feel so sore that it feels bloody marvellous, I have so many thoughts running through my mind that I am confused." With that she placed her lips onto his and wrapped herself around him, they stayed like this until he was about to slip out of her, he warned her and she lifted herself from him and stood amazed at the love juice running down both of her legs, she looked at her lover and he was holding his soaking wet cock in his hand, he looked from her to his cock and back again, she frowned and he said. "It is always polite to clean up after a good fucking."

He looked from her eyes to his cock again, she looked down at her legs again and a small pool of cum was pooled by each foot, she knelt down and took his cock from his hand and looked at his big cum covered knob that was oozing his pale cum, she closed her mouth over his knob and sucked the last of his cum from him, she obviously liked it because she sucked hard on his cock to see if there was any more to be had, he watched her as she held his shaft at the bottom and licked his cock clean, she examined his whole length to see if she had missed any, happy that she hadn't she closed her mouth over his cock and began to give him a proper blow job. He watched as her head bounced up and down as she gave him a lot of pleasure, she began to slow down and as she lifted her mouth from his cock she kissed the tip of his knob, she looked up at her lover and standing up she sat in his lap and wrapped her arms around his neck, all she wanted now was their closeness.

Shelly finally stood up and looked down at her legs, their love juices were still running down her legs, she disappeared into the toilet and after a few minutes she came back out, she opened a fridge and pulled out a bottle of good chilled champagne, she poured them both a full flute and they sat side by side and drank the fine wine, without looking at him she asked. "Are you in a hurry to leave, only we could spend the night on the boat naked and whenever you wanted to we could do it again, I could phone up to the hotel and order some food, anything you want and get it delivered to us?"

He looked at her and asked
"Do they deliver food then, I thought that the riverside was to upmarket for that? "She smiled and said. "When your father owns it, it is surprising what you can get if you want it, we would have to move back to the hotel moorings, but that was not a problem." He nodded and said that he would like that, so that was what happened, he smiled when three waiters walked down the steps carrying laden trays of hot food, she took delivery dressed in a blue silk dressing gown, she tipped them well and they ate well.

Shelly was very happy, sat naked and being held by him listening to the radio, he had his arm around her shoulder and was stroking her arm, both lost in their own thoughts, they had been sat like this when her phone rang, she picked it up and answered it, he could hear what was being said and her husband was not a happy chap, he had arrived home to find the house empty, she sat there and listened to him as he began to rant at her, accusing her of all sorts, she waited for him to finally finish and asked him. "Have you finished Brian[he grunted, and she continued] well you can fuck off if you don't fucking like it, see if some other soft woman will put up with your small cock and what you call sex, I have just been fucked properly for the very first time in my life and if you don't shape up in bed in the next month, then I want a divorce."

She cut the call off and tossed the phone onto the floor, he looked at her with a shocked expression on his face, she smiled and said. "What, I have been thinking of getting rid of the useless ponce for months now, you fucking me the way that you did, just made my mind up, so thank you for that. Now, talking about fucking, I'm just about ready for round two, so what have you in mind, I want to try everything." He sat and looked around the boat, seeing not much of interest, he pulled his boxers on and went out on deck, he looked around and a plan began formulating in his mind.

Bobby went and put his shoes on and climbed from the boat and broke a willow branch from a nearby tree he stood and pulled all of the nobbles off the branch and swishes it through the air, he walked back into the boat and placed the swish down on one of the benches and disappeared back on deck, he had been gone a few minutes when he returned below, Shelly was holding the swish in hand and asked.
"Bobby, you're not going to hurt me are you?" he shrugged and said "Not if you don't want me to, but whenever any woman that I have ever known has been asked what her fantasy is, it was to be raped.

If you are not comfortable with that then we will have to think of something else." She felt as though she was being put under unnecessary pressure to do something that she was not happy with, and yet she wanted to please this wonderful man, she chewed her top lip and didn't know what to say, so he took her silence as a rejection of his idea so he picked up the swish and went back on deck and dropped into the river, it was at that point that he began questioning his need to hurt such a beautiful woman, he dug his nails into his hands and his thoughts took him back to wondering if he did need help, she came up behind him and wrapped her naked body around him, they stood in the near darkness, the quiet and stillness all around them was deafening in its own way, they looked up at the star fill sky at the millions of bright shining stars.

He knew that this beauty that was wrapped around him had fallen in love with him, he had to admit that she was the most beautiful woman that he had ever met and fucked, but could he love her? He doubted it very much, it was then he realised that he did not know what he wanted out of life, he had all the money in the world, it looked like he could fuck any woman he wanted, he had the house and the grounds, he had everything and yet in his mind he had nothing. What worried him the most was the fact that he knew that all Shelly wanted was for him to fuck the ass off her, and yet he tried to get her to do something that she obviously didn't want to do, he knew that if he had pushed it, then she would have done anything to please him, maybe that was his problem straight sex was not enough for him anymore, maybe he was having too much sex and not respecting the women involved, abusing young women, spoiling them for married life because he and they all knew that to find and marry a man that has a cock like him and can fuck like him, would be almost impossible.

Did he really want to get married, just look at today, this beautiful woman was naked and wrapped around him, he had fucked her once and now he seemed almost bored with her. At that point she reached around and gripped his thick cock and began to slowly move her hand back and forth along his length trying to get him hard so that he would fuck her again, he looked at the tiny hand wrapped around his growing cock and made the decision that tomorrow he would get help, he would call Helen she would know what to do. He was brought out of his thoughts by noticing that Shelly was on her hands and knees in front of him sucking his big cock, he decided to give her what she wanted and then he would head for home and Helen.

He pulled her up and turned her away from him, she gripped the side rail of the boat, she was looking out over the river as he pushed his big cock into her, this time there was no problem as his cock easily slipped into her easily, he gripped her hips and began fucking her, Shelly was into it in a big way by all of the noise she was making lots of noise, and pushing back at him, yet he wasn't really interested at all, he closed his eyes and thought back to Phil on that roof and the terror in her screams as she looked certain death in the face as he fucked her, all of a sudden it was like his cock was a rod of iron and Shelly was hanging over that roof edge, he was fucking her hard now and she was appreciating it.

Bobby kept the sight of the terrified Phil in his mind and he managed to give Shelly the best fuck that she would ever have in her life, on and on he rode her and she was making every noise under the sun, he could well have been raping her at that point because in his mind he was raping Phil, he exploded inside her making her scream out loud, he was ignoring her as he thought only of his own pleasure.

He came out of his deep thoughts by her shouting his name, he shook his head and looked down at her, she was bent over the side of the boat, her top half were waving about as he held her bottom half in his arms, he pulled her back and she began crying against his chest as he held her tight, she was shaking in his arms so he took her down below, where he sat down and held her tight, it was a long time before she spoke, she said. "What happened Bobby, you scared me, it was like you were a man possessed, even though you gave me the fuck of my life, I know that you were not thinking of me while you were fucking me. You were thinking of someone called Phil, you were shouting out the name Phil. Was Phil a man Bobby, are you really gay?"

He was stunned that she even thought such a thing, he shook his head and said. "Phil is Philameena, she was 17 and went through a very bad time and I feel responsible sometimes, that's all, I am sorry if I fright-ened you Shelly." She nodded and went down to her knees and sucked him dry and licked him clean, but things had changed, she was not the same, he pulled her up to standing and he picked her up and sat down with her on his lap and pulled a blanket around them.

Not another word was spoken between them, he waited until she had fallen asleep and then he quietly dressed and he climbed the steps to his car. He set the sat-nav for home and began his long drive south.

Chapter 17

He arrived home just as dawn was breaking, he walked into his home and sat down in his favourite chair, and waited for Helen to arrive for work, when she arrived he was curled up in a ball with his eyes wide open. Helen knelt down and pulled him to her, and held him tight as he cried in her arms, they rocked back and forth until he had calmed down enough for her to persuade him to go up-stairs to bed, she undressed him and put him into bed, he pulled her down and she held him, she knew that there was no sex intended, he just wanted someone to hold him. Helen stayed with him for most of the day, she did her work and cooked for him and his grandfather, checking on him every half hour or so.

When he finally woke up she held him tight and talked to him softly, reassuring him, until   holding her hand he told her everything, he told her about every young woman and full grown woman that he had had sex with, when he got to Phil she had to coax the whole situation out of him, she tried not to look shocked when he finally told her everything. It had taken hours for everything to come out, and when she asked him if he would let her help him, he told her that was the reason that he had come home to her, because he knew that she would know what to do. She asked him if he trusted her to do what was best for him no matter what she did, he nodded and said that he trusted her with his life, she pulled the blankets up to his chin and kissed him on the mouth, and told him she would be back in a few minutes.

Helen went down stairs and phoned the family doctor who said that he would be there as soon as possible, she went back up to Bobby and he was sleeping restlessly, she sat with him until she heard the doctors car on the gravel drive, she went down stairs and told him some of the things that Bobby had told her, she told the doctor that in her opinion he was depressed and having some sort of breakdown, and he needed urgent help. Dr Hope sat and talked to Bobby and prescribed anti-de-pressants and said that he would contact a friend in Harley Street and come back as soon as he could, but he advised Helen not to leave him on his own, she phoned her husband and told him the outline of what was going on, with which he was quite happy to let her do whatever she had to do. When she went back upstairs Bobby asked her to hold him, she lay down on the bed and held him, but he wanted her to get into bed with him, she went and locked the door and pulled her dress over her head and got into bed with him, he immediately folded himself around her and held her tight. She knew that it was wrong but she was getting very turned on, because she could feel his big cock resting against her ass, she loved Bobby with all her heart, but she knew from what he had told her that he was ill.

Helen waited until he had finally fallen asleep which meant that the pills had finally taken effect, she climbed out of his bed and looked down at her wet pants, what-ever was wrong with her, she stood looking down at her sleeping patient and pushed her hand down inside her wet pants and rubbed her fingers back and forth over her clit, she pulled her hand away from her fanny and pushed her pants down to the floor and stepped out of them, she opened her legs and spread her knees and pushed two finger deep into her fanny, she stared at Bobby while finger fucked herself to an orgasm, she pulled her fingers out of her fanny and looked at the thick sticky cum all over her them, she put them into her mouth and sucked them clean, she had not had enough and slid her fingers back to her clit and closed her eyes as she took her time and made herself cum again, and just like always when she masturbated over Bobby she instantly felt guilty, but it won't ever stop her doing it.

Dr Hope came back and checked his patient, when he was happy he took Helen from the room and sat her down, he went through what he had been doing, and he had the name of a specialist in this particular field, her name was Dr Elaine Cartwright and Bobby had an appointment the next day at 4pm, and he would be happy if she went with him, she said that she would take him there herself. Bobby did not want to go to Harley Street, he wanted to stay in his room with her forever.

She finally persuaded him to shower and dress, she had to help him dress, because the pills were making him a bit dopy, she was pulling his socks on when he reached down and began fondling her tits, she did not object because she did not want to upset him, she was tying the laces on his shoes when he pushed his hand down inside her top and he began playing with her naked tits again, she thought that she was reasonably safe, because the doctor had told her that the pills would suppress his sexual urges. She pulled his hand out of her top and he looked disappointed and said. "Please show me your lovely tits Helen." She shook her head and said that they had to go down stairs and get into the car, because they had an appointment, he shook his head and said. "Not until you show me your tits, I will sit here until you show me." She stood in front of him and looked at his smiling face and relented, she lifted her top and pulled her bra up, he reached out and touched both firm tits.

She stepped away and pulled her clothes down and had to more or less drag him down the stairs to the car, she strapped him into the front seat and began the long journey south. He would drift in and out of sleep telling her that he loved her and always had, he would touch her tits as she drove, but she ignored it even though it was affecting her down below. He woke up the once and leaned against her and slid his hand up her skirt, and began rubbing his finger along her slit, she knew that he didn't know what he was doing, but she wanted him to carry on doing it until she came.

She opened her legs as wide as she could, whether he knew what he was doing or not he was trying to get his fingers into the side of her pants, she pulled into the inside lane and pulled her skirt up as far as she could, she reached down and pulled her pants to the side giving him access to her wet fanny, he pushed two fingers into her and began finger fucking her, she pushed her bottom to the front of the seat and allowed him to frigg her to orgasm, as soon as she has cum, she pulled his hand out and straightened her clothing, he looked at his sticky fingers and began laughing, he put the sticky fingers to her mouth and she sucked them clean, she was sure that this was not part of the treatment, she looked into his lap at his cock, if he had been hard she would have pulled of the road and fucked him there and then, but thankfully he was limp.

Sat in the plush waiting room, Bobby was leaning against her fast asleep, Helen had seen a woman of early thirties, she had long dark hair held in a ponytail, she wore a blue silk blouse with the top three buttons undone and black high heeled shoes, she was slim, fit and very pretty. Helen hoped that she was not the doctor, because she would have no chance with Bobby, she would bet her life that he would have bent over her couch in the first session. The pretty woman came out of her office and motioned for them to follow her, Helen pulled her charge to his feet and sort of dragged him into her office, they all sat down and he leaned against Helen again and closed his eyes, so Helen told the doctor everything that Bobby had told her, all the way through the relaying of the story, Elaine would glance at Bobby and then back to Helen.

With the story finally Elaine made a lot of notes while Helen looked at the doctor, and realised that she would have to say something to her, warn her so she coughed quietly and said. "Can I speak to you woman to woman [Elaine looked over her glasses at Helen and nodded] I have to warn you that Bobby was very easy to fall in love with and once you have had him, and you will, you will want more and more, but I must warn you that was part of his problem, it was that he soon gets bored with the woman involved, it as if it was the chase that excites him more than the act itself." The doctor put her pen down and crossed her arms under her tits and looked at them both before saying. "I can assure you that I will not be having him as you put it, because I am more likely to fancy you over him, so therefore I am will immune to any advances that he may make and secondly the drugs that I will prescribe will suppress any sexual urges that he may have.

Now I have a house nearby that I use as a private hospital, the house was fully staffed and a doctor was minutes away at all time, I will need to spend some time with Bobby and find out what this problem stems from, and therefore prescribe the right treatment." Helen asked how long he would be there and about visiting times. The doctor told Helen that there would be no visiting for quite a while, as she would be working one to one with Bobby, and she would call her and give her regular updates.

Helen reluctantly left her lover with the doctor and as she drove back home she was almost in tears, because she knew that her lover was quite ill, as for Bobby he was transferred to the Doctors house, he had his own room and was given some drugs to make him sleep until the next day, that was when his assessment would begin, two young nurses undressed Bobby for bed, they had his pyjamas ready, both nurses had seen a few cocks before, but when they saw Bobby's cock they stared in awe at his sheer size they then mouthed the words* fucking hell *to each other. Gwen the youngest nurse looked at her friend and mouthed the words*go on, I dare you." Julia the other nurse shook her head, but could not keep her eyes off his giant cock, Gwen looked at the patient and could see that he was out of it and reached forward and lifted his big cock up, she held it for a few seconds and slowly exposed the knob and then lowered it back down, both nurses stood looking at each other with their mouths hanging open.

They finally put him into his pyjamas and were about to cover him with the bed clothes when Gwen leaned over and kissed his exposed knob, Julia reached over and slapped her friend on the arm, both nurses giggled when they left the room. Bobby's treatment started the next day as soon as the drugs had worn off enough for him to become with it enough to talk to Elaine. She would sit and talk to him for hours on end, and he would stare at her legs or her tits, so the doctor began wearing trouser suits when she was with Bobby, it was on the fourth day that the first incident happened, Elaine was talking to him and out of the blue he said. "I love you doc and I think you have nice tits." He reached out and felt her right breast, this had never happened to her, before but she had been warned that it might happen, she had been told to ignore it, but she looked at Bobby and said. "I don't think you should be doing that, do you Mr Francis."

He smiled at her, she looked down and he had his thumb in between the buttons of her blouse and was rubbing her rock hard nipple, she let him carry on for a few seconds and pulled his hand away, but he was smiling at the sight of her hard nipple as it pushed at the thin material of her blouse, the Doctor looked at his smile and felt herself blush deeply, she had to uncross her legs and cross them the other way, she had become very wet over a man and this was a new feeling for her and, one that had her very confused.

The next day the Doctor wore a light sweater over her blouse to prevent a repeat of the previous days event, she had on a pair of light green trousers, they were sat opposite each other on two chairs as usual. She was asking him questions about his childhood, and he was staring at her tits trying to get a reaction, this went on for the best part of the session, and towards the end her nipples reacted to his constant stare and they both grew rock hard, a broad smile broke out on his face as he lifted his eyes to hers, he said. "You like me don't you Doc, I can tell [he lowered his eyes to her hard nipples and then back to her eyes] have the nurses told you about my big cock, because I know that they sometimes touch me at night." She looked into his eyes and did not know what to say, he stared into her eyes and reached out and with his thumb he touched her fanny just about where her clit was, he pressed hard with his thumb and rubbed the area where her clit should be.

She swallowed hard as no man had ever touched her there before, they stared into each other's eyes, she could not help herself as she opened her legs, he smiled as he rubbed his thumb up and down her fanny lips, he could tell that she was close so he stood up and pulled her up and pushed her back against the door and pushed his right hand between her open legs and rubbed her fanny hard, his other hand was finding its way inside her clothing to her perfect firm tits.

She was moaning and moving her hips against his fingers, so he did no more than undid the button on her trousers and pulled the zipper down within seconds his fingers were deep inside her fanny and she was loving every second of his ministrations, he pushed his lips onto hers and she instantly pushed her tongue into his mouth, she moaned out loud, pushed her hips forwards and soaked his fingers. He stopped when she had cum and looked deep into her eyes, he took her hand and placed it onto his limp cock, but she still gasped at his sheer size, he stood there and let her feel him, he reached down and undid his zipper and reached in and pulled his big thick cock out. The beautiful Doctor folded her hand around his massive cock and rubbed it up and down but nothing happened, he looked down at her hand as she moved it up and down his shaft and said "If you want me to fuck you Doc, you will have to change my drugs."She closed her eyes as he began frigging her again, she was moaning out loud as his fingers were taking her to another hard climax, her right hand was now flying up and down his mighty cock, there was some growth, but not enough for him to be able to fuck her, he pulled his fingers out of her fanny and pushed them into her mouth, she stared at him the whole time because for the first time in her life she wanted a man to fuck her, not any man, this man. He took her hand and took her to the leather settee, he laid her down and he gripped her trousers and pulled them off, he gripped her pants, but she told him to lock the door first, he did as she asked, he went back to her and pulled her pants off, she opened her legs and let him see her shaved fanny, the first man to ever look at her down there, he went to his knees and was about to lowered his mouth to her wet fanny, when she stopped him and whispered,

"I know it is not hard but please try and put it into me, as I have never felt a real one before." He looked down at his banana shaped cock and lifted her up and placed a cushion under her bum, he moved between her legs and gripped his half hard cock and pushed it at her opening, he managed to get some of his cock into her, he kept trying and got maybe three quarters into her, he tried fucking her but he wasn't hard enough, but he gripped the base of his cock and that just about enabled him to fuck her, Elaine smiled as he began fucking her, it was better than she expected, but soon realised how good it could be if he was really hard, she stopped him and lifted her knees up to her tits, opening herself up to him totally, he was fucking her at a fair rate and he was getting harder all the time because this cock virgin was really enjoying the real thing by the look on her face, he said.

"Let me see your tits, she lifted her top clothing to reveal her perfect tits, she moved her knees sideways and her tits began to bounce as he fucked her, he was close to fully hard now and he was really fucking her, she had cum a few times, but now he could take charge and fuck her properly, when he took her through her next orgasm she began to call out, but she covered her mouth with her hands.

He took her through another orgasm and stopped he pulled his cock out of her, and standing up he pulled her up, she looked down at his now hard cock and asked him.

"Did you have all of that inside of me?" He nodded and moved her to the end of the settee and bent her forward she instinctively gripped the arm of the furniture and he pushed his hard cock back into her, she had to spread her legs wide to try and relieve the discomfort of him stretch-ing her in this position. Bobby had gripped her hips now and was ram-ming his cock into her for all he was worth, and she was really loving every second of having a man inside her body for the very first time, he grunted and exploded inside her, she grabbed a cushion and screamed into it, she met each spurt with a stifled scream. The joy that she felt when he pulled her back and he filled her full of real cock as something that she would remember for the rest of her life, she ground herself against him, closed her eyes and came again, he eventually pulled out of her and she fell forward, her world had just been changed forever, he gripped her hair and pulled her around and pushed her to her knees, he gripped his massive cock and held it at her mouth, she had sucked a rubber cock, before but this was different, but she would do her best.

Elaine closed her lips around his big knob and licked it all over first tasting herself she then sucked hard and a few drops of his cum landed on her tongue, oh the sheer joy of tasting him, she began bouncing her head up and down, she did this for a few minutes and then lifted her head from his knob and holding his shaft she began cleaning his shaft with her tongue. The doctor looked up at him and he was smiling down at her, she stood up and kissed him hard on the mouth, when she pulled away she looked down at her legs and she had another first experience, pale warm cum was running freely down both of her legs, she seemed spellbound at the sight as if she could not believe what was happening. Bobby went and fetched a box of tissues and he held it out to her, she took three or four without looking, her eyes were still watching as droplet after droplet still ran down her legs, he left her there and got dressed and sat back down on his chair.

The phone on her desk began ringing which broke the spell, she stuffed the tissues against her fanny and went and answered the phone, she said yes a few times and then she said five minutes. She put the phone down and broke into a panic as she tried to wipe the cum from her legs and get dressed, in the end she just grabbed everything and disappeared into another room which he took to be a bathroom, she came out of the room looking all professional and took a spray can and walked around the room spraying air freshener, she unlocked the door and stood with her hand on the door knob as they kissed, she finally said. "Same time tomorrow, Mr Francis" and let him walk out of the room.

Bobby had not had any medication since the night before and he could tell that he was back in the land of the living, not only did he feel better he had had bit of a hard on earlier when he was thinking about the doctor, which took his thoughts to two young nurses that had been taking advantage of him while he had been slightly out of it. He knew that they had been playing with his cock, getting more and more adventurous as the nights had gone on, knowing that he could do nothing about it, well they were in for a shock tonight because he felt as randy as hell. Bobby had a plan for later, he would lay down on the bed and play dead and when they started on him, we will see how brave they were then.

He was lay on the bed fully dressed waiting for the two young nurses, he had requested a bed bath and was looking forward to it, he heard a trolley being pushed towards his room so he closed his eyes and waited, they came in and stood either side of the bed and began undressing him, he made it hard for them by making himself stiff, they had taken all of his top clothes off and were starting on his bottom clothes, they took his shoes and socks off and began on his trousers, they pulled them down his legs and then pulled his boxers down, he sensed them stop and look at his cock, he heard them whisper something to each other, but could not make out what they had said, they began washing his top half first, they missed his midriff and washed his legs and dried them, he waited with baited breath as one of the nurses lifted his cock and began washing it, he heard her gasp when it began growing in her hand, she said.

"Fuck me Julia, look at this fucker growing." Everything went quiet and Gwen the other nurse said. "Go on Ju give it a wank he won't know, just look at him he is dead to the world." He felt the small hand moving up and down his now fully hard cock, Gwen said. Stop it Ju, look at the size of that fucker, just imagine that inside you, fuck I bet it would feel good." He knew that Gwen was on his left so he let his hand fall off the bed and lifted it slowly making sure that his hand went up her uniform, he half opened his left eye and watched her looking down at his hand, he touched her somewhere between her legs and he heard her gasp, he rubbed her fanny lips through her wet pants, she opened her legs and said. "Look Ju, he has got his hand up my uni, he's touching my fanny, what shall I do?" He heard the other nurse walk around the bed, he saw Julia lift her friends uniform and watch as his fingers as they rubbed along her friends fanny. Julia said.
"Shall I pull your pants down and see what happens?" Gwen had obviously agreed but she whispered. "Lock the door first, just in case." He heard the lock on the door, he waited and felt hands pulling her pants down, he carried on doing what he was doing and she opened her legs a

bit more, it was just enough to allow him to get his fingers into her fanny, he heard Gwen gasp and say.

"Look Ju he's fingering me, tell me what to do?" He saw Ju shrug and say

"Just enjoy it and when he has done it to you, I want my turn." Gwen turned slightly towards him to make it easier for him, he was really finger fucking her when she groaned and anointed his fingers with her cum, she snatched his fingers out of her fanny and said

"Fuck, that was good, quick let him do it to you." He felt a different fanny move onto his hand, this one had less fanny hair around it, she was very wet and his fingers slipped easily into her, she reacted differently to Gwen.

Julia moved her fanny over his fingers, she was also more vocal than Gwen, as she neared her orgasm, she closed her eyes and began squeezing her tits, she groaned out loud and soaked his fingers, but he kept his fingers moving inside her fanny and her cum had pooled in the palm of his hand, she lifted herself from his hand and the nurses stood next to each other and held hands and looking at his hard cock, Gwen said. "Go on Ju, I dare you, get on that big cock and help yourself, he won't know will he, if you do it then I will do it after." He felt the bed move and her move into position, she stabbed at getting it inside her when she asked her friend for help, he felt a tiny hand around his thick cock and then a tight warm fanny sinking down his length, she stopped after a bit and said. "Fuck me that is a tight fit, it is stretching me to fuck, how much more is there to go in?" Gwen said I can't see properly. Let me lift your uni off."

He watched as Gwen pulled her friends uniform over her head, Julia was naked apart from her bra, so he slowly lifted his hand to her tits and rubbed them Gwen said

"He must be fucking dreaming, let me take your bra off." Within seconds she was naked and riding his big cock, the longer she rode him the deeper she sank down on his shaft, she was getting close and said to Gwen. "Pull my tits Gwen, go on pull em hard." He watched through half closed eyes as Gwen began pulling her friends tits, he lowered his hand and rested it on her leg, she had her hands on his chest now and was really riding his big cock for all she was worth, he felt her begin to shudder and groan out loud and say. "I'm coming on his big cock

Gwen, it feels fucking great, uuurrrrgggg." She sank down on his cock and began grinding herself against him.

He could see Gwen removing her uniform and bra, she stood naked waiting to get on his hard cock, she had to encourage Julia to get off his cock, they were both on the bed at the same time, no sooner had one nurse got off him the other was trying to get his big cock into her, she was almost crying in her frustration, when he felt a hand fold around his cock and a warm fanny slowly sinking down his length, Gwen took most of his cock in one go, she moved her knees in close and began riding him hard and fast, she was groaning as she enjoyed his size inside her fanny, he saw her friend playing with her tits and Gwen lifting herself so that she was sat upright riding him, she lifted her right hand into her hair and with her left hand she pulled her friends mouth to her tits, Julia sucked both of her friends tits and this helped Gwen to reach her orgasm, which hit her hard, she placed her hands on his chest and began riding the end few inches, so he began thrusting upwards.

Gwen shouted "Fuck, fuck, he's fucking me, look Jools he is actually fucking me." Gwen was having the time of her life as he fucked her, he took her to another orgasm and slowed down and stopped, Gwen lifted herself from his cock and Julia remounted him, she sank down and began fucking herself, when he began thrusting upwards, Julia began shouting. "Look Gwen, just fucking look, he's doing it to me now."

He reached out and held her hips and really began ramming his giant cock into her, he grunted and she tried to get off quick, but he held her in place and filled her full of burning hot spunk, she began screaming at the top of her voice, Gwen had to pull her face to her body so that her screams were somewhat stifled, she began moving her fanny back and forth over the base of his cock taking herself to yet another orgasm, he held her in place while she still moved her fanny over him, when she stopped he dropped his hands to the bed and let her get off. Gwen got off the bed and began crying saying. "He cum up me Jool's, what am I going to do now, I can't be pregnant, I will lose my job." Gwen was the voice of reason and said "Don't worry mate we will go and get some of them pills tomorrow, that will sort you out, but fucking hell did it feel fucking good or what, pity he missed it all really I think he would have enjoyed having two fit young nurses naked in his room, just look at all that cum all over his big cock, I'm going to taste it to see what it tastes like." She lowered her head and licked his naked knob, deciding that she liked it she closed her mouth over his knob, she sucked hard and was rewarded by a spurt of his cum which she swallowed down, she licked all around his knob and lifted her head, he then felt two tongues licking him clean.

When they had finished, one of them washed his cock and the tucked him into bed, he sort of watched them washing themselves and getting dressed, he could see them standing looking at him when Gwen said. "No-one would believe us if ever we told anyone what has just happened, we must never tell anybody, do you agree Jools?" Jools shrugged and said. "What about him?. Surely he should know what has happened and could we be done for rape?" Gwen said. "No, I don't think so, I mean he got involved didn't he, I mean he fucked us both at the end of the day, didn't he?" Gwen sort of agreed but pointed out the fact that he was still unconscious, so how could he possibly have done what he did, they left it at that, he felt both young women kiss his cheek and Gwen said. "I can't wait until tomorrow night and I can ride that big cock again." With that they left him to his dreams, he went to sleep with a smile on his face.

Bobby was sat outside Elaine's office waiting for his appointment when she came out of her office carrying her bag, she smiled and said.
"C'mon Bobby, we are going on a field trip today to see how you react amongst other women." He smiled and stood up and then followed her out to her car, she drove confidently through the London traffic, she pulled into a small courtyard called Gloucester Terrace, which was neat and tidy and very secluded, she stopped the car outside number 4, she unlocked the door and walked into the town house, he followed her inside and closed the door behind them, she took him into the kitchen and took two beers out of the fridge, they stood and drank the cool beers just looking at one-another when she said. "I have brought you here to my home to apologise for what happened yesterday, I have told my long term partner what has happened and we agree that if I am pregnant we will keep the baby and bring it up together, you realise that you could get me struck off for what happened, it was very unprofessional of me and I will regret it for the rest of my life."

He looked at her and her nipples became hard again, he said. "So if I were to get my big cock out her and now, you would not want to take me upstairs and fuck my brains out then?" She watched him as he pulled his zipper down and reached inside his clothing and pull his big cock out, she was staring at his cock when he exposed his big purple knob, he moved his hand back and forth a few times when she walked towards him and took his hand and led him upstairs, she took him into the spare room where there was only a mattress on the bed, she closed the door and drew the curtains and went down to her knees and lifting his big cock, she closed her warm mouth over his knob.

Bobby looked down at this confirmed lesbian sucking his cock and it proved to him that he could have any woman he wanted, he began undoing his shirt and taking it off and dropped it onto the end of the mattress, she had got him rock hard and stood up and began removing her clothes and watched every move he made as he stripped himself naked, he pulled her onto the mattress and knelt her down in front of him, he mounted her in one thrust that almost pushed her off the bed, he gripped her hips and gave her the best ever fuck that she would ever have, he rode her hard, on and on and she came and came until she begged him to stop, he knelt there still buried deep inside her and she hung her head down and said. "I'm sorry Bobby but I am too sore to do it anymore you will have to take it out and I will use my mouth on you"

He looked down at her brown hole and dribbled some spit onto the crinkly button, he dribbled some more spit down there and rubbed it all around her other hole she turned and looked at him quizzically, he slowly pulled his hard cock out of her and place it at her bum hole he pushed forward and she half screamed and half groaned, half of his cock was up her bum, she was moaning out loud as he pushed again and the rest of his cock disappeared up her ass, he gripped her hips and began fucking her ass, she was not happy about what he was doing to her and wanted him to stop, but she would let him carry on now that he was inside her, he grunted and came deep inside her, she screamed out loud as he pushed hard up her ass, she knew that he had split her, but could do nothing about it, but it did give her an insight as to his problem, he pulled his cock out of her bottom, and she got up and ran crying into the toilet.

Elaine had been gone for a long time, she came out wearing a dressing gown, she picked up her clothes and went silently into her bedroom, she appeared dressed and her make-up had been repaired, she stood waiting for him to come out of the bedroom, he was dressed and he followed her down to the car. Elaine drove to a café where she bought two coffees and sat opposite him, she questioned him about what had just happened and said that she felt violated, even raped and that he would never touch her again.

 She then sat for two hours asking him questions about his child hood, and who lived with them at home throughout his childhood, he told her everything that he could remember, but he was holding something back but what, that was what she wanted to know. She left Bobby at his room and said. "One of your problems was that you think you can do no wrong and when you do do wrong, you do-not have the balls to apologise." With that she turned and walked away leaving him with his dark thoughts.

He sat on his bed and thought about all of the women that he had abused sexually over the last few years, and the recollections made him hang his head in shame, he wondered if he should ring Helen and ask her to fetch him, but then if he did that not only would he miss out on the two young nurses tonight, he may never find out what was wrong with him, because he knew that he had a problem and needed help.

Bobby had slept the sleep of the dead for five hours, he had showered and dressed in just a pair of shorts and nothing else, he sat in a chair facing the door waiting for the arrival of his two favourite nurses, the door opened quietly and Julia was first to enter followed by her friend Gwen who said. "Oh, hello Mr Francis are you feeling better today, you do look well?" They both stood looking at him he said. "Close the door and lock it." Gwen did as he asked, they then stood there like naughty school children, he then said "I know what you both did to me last night and what you were planning to do to me tonight, well plans have changed, I want you both to remove all your clothes." They looked at on-another and began undoing their uniforms, he watched them strip naked, they both stood there with their hands over their fanny's, he waved at them to move their hands which they did, he then said. "Tell me girls, do you think that you need to pay a forfeit for what you did or would you prefer to be punished?" The girls looked at one another and Julia said "We will do a forfeit, whatever you want."

He looked from one to the other and pointed at Gwen and said. " Lay down on the bed and open your legs." She did as he asked and he pointed to Julia and said ."Lay down on top of her but facing the opposite way and open your legs." She did as he said but he had to move her slightly, he stood by the bed and both girls were looking at him, so he said, "I want to watch you both kiss each other's fannies until you both cum and then I intend to fuck you both, now get on with it." He sat on a chair and watched them both. He gave them certain instructions like when to use their fingers and when to rub the others clits, he watched Gwen cum first, she lifted her head for a second and growled out loud and then shuddered, she then lowered her head back to her task, Julia lifted her head and looked at him and came on the mouth of her best friend, he said that they could get off the bed, they stood in front of him like naughty children, he stood up and pushed his shorts down to the floor and stood there with his hard cock sticking out.

He took hold of Julia and turned her around and bent her forward, she gripped the bed and opened her legs. He moved up behind her and pushed his hard cock into her young body. He stepped forward and gripped her hips and made her groan out loud when he began fucking her, he looked at the other younger nurse and said, "Get underneath her and suck her tits and when she is about to cum, rub her clit."

He enjoyed being in charge like this and that was one of his main problems, but she did exactly as he asked, he made her cum twice before he pulled out of her, she stood up and smiled at him, he then pulled Gwen into place and mounted her making her scream out, he told Julia to do exactly the same to Gwen as she had done to her, he began fucking the young nurse, riding her hard, she turned and said.
"Please don't cum up me Bobby." He had made her cum three times and was close, he pulled Julia out from underneath her friend and held her by his side, he said. "I am going to shoot my cum into your mouth, get ready" she looked up at him and opened her mouth, he held onto her hair to stop her pulling away, he grunted and pulled his cock out and pushed it at her mouth, she reached forward and wanked his cock

as hard as she could, her mouth and all around her chin was covered
with his cum, Gwen had turned around and was licking his cum from
her friends face while she sucked his cock as hard as she could.

Gwen was pushing her mouth at her friends' mouth because she
wanted a go at sucking his cock. The young women had licked his cock
clean and they were all lay naked on the bed holding each other, he
asked. "So will you to be doing things to each other in the future when
I am gone?" The young women smiled at one-another and linked fingers over his waist, it was Julia that spoke for them when she said.
"Well, we have snogged a bit in the past and I have felt her tits but that
is as far as we have got until today, you have taken us to where we both
wanted to be but were always much too embarrassed to say so to each
other, but now I will want to kiss her fanny all the time and if she wants
she can kiss my fanny, she can do it whenever she wants to." He smiled
and said, "You are welcome my young lovers, and if you come back
tonight I will have a surprise for you both." It was left at that, all three
of them looking forward to the next nights adventure.

Bobby was sat outside Elaine's office, his appointment time had come
and gone, he wondered what was keeping her, surely she still wasn't still
pissed off at him, it was a good hour later when she opened the door
and nodded at him, she sat at her desk and he sat on the opposite side
to her, she sorted some papers that were in front of her and then
looked up and with a voice full of hostility said. "Well Mr Francis I
would like you to know that I have been talking to your father
overnight, and he passed on some very important information about
your aunt Matilda that now lives in Scotland, apparently she was asked
to leave your home when she was found with you in her bed, when you
were a very young age and she had been doing certain things to you, because apparently you were very well advanced in your body develop-
ment, I was also informed that the subject has never been brought up
again, by any member of your family members.

Now Mr Francis I have spoken to a colleague of mine a Doctor David
Sterling and he has agreed to see you because having heard all the facts,
he thinks that he can help you, therefore you will be transferred to his
unit today, just as soon as it can be arranged, my bill will be sent to your
home within thirty days.

I think that is everything, I wish you well in the future, goodbye Mr Francis." That was that, she never looked at him again and she obviously hated him, and that made him feel much worse about himself. When he returned to reception, his cases had been packed and a driver was waiting to whisk him away, he felt like he had been thrown out and maybe he deserved to be for what he had done to Elaine.

Chapter 18

Bobby had spent a good six months with David Sterling and apart from a fumble with one of the cleaners he had had no sexual contact at all, all he wanted to do was go home and sleep in his own bed and see Helen, Dr Sterling had totally changed Bobby's way of thinking about women, he no longer saw them as sexual objects that were only there for his pleasure and gratification alone.

He sat in reception with his case by his side waiting for Helen to collect him, he was going home and couldn't wait, he looked at the reception- ist and she gave him a wide smile, he smiled back and turned his head back to the front door, gone were the days when he would have gone behind the desk and tried to fuck her there and then. His face broke into a smile when Helen walked into the clinic reception, he stood to meet her and they hugged like long lost lovers, he carried his case to the car, once under way she asked him how he was, he looked at her and said "I have changed Helen, I feel different in myself as in I can now look at any beautiful woman and not have strange sexual thoughts about them, Dr Sterling has put me on a new drug that will control my urges to dominate women and as long as I take the drugs, I will be a normal lover." She gripped his hand and said. "I am pleased for you Bobby, because I have heard some of the things that you have done to different women of all ages, from the police.

You were being investigated a few months back, because of complaints made by women from all over the country, you were being classed as a sexual predator but luckily for you your father has used up a lot of favours, and it has all now gone away, except your children that you have all over, but your father has his lawyers working on that as we speak, and I have to tell you that a young lady named Philameena called me. We have chatted on quite a few occasions and it was on one of these later chats that she told me what you did to her and to be honest Bobby, I would have told you to fuck off as well, but she wants me to keep in touch with her, and if in the future I can see that you have changed then I am to pass on her new number, but I will only give you her number if I am sure." He nodded his agreement and thanked her for what she has done for him.

She looked at him and chewed her top lip as she asked. "What about us Bobby, will you still want to see me?" He placed his hand on her leg and said. "You will always be my first love Darling Helen, and yes I have been dreaming of the day that I can come and see you again. Will everything be the same; well I hope so, because I can honestly say that you are the only person that I have missed in all of this." She smiled her happiness and drove him home.

They arrived home and he almost burst into tears at the sheer sight of the old place, she held his hand as he walked up the steps, he entered his home and went and sat in his favourite chair. Helen carried his suit case up to his room and put his clothes away, she went back down to the kitchen and made him a cup of tea, she took him a plate of sand-wiches that she had made in preparation for his return, she sat at his feet and just looked at him, she had really missed him more than he would ever know and she wanted him inside her as soon as possible. He finished his food and she took his plate from him and set it down on the floor, she then stood up and curled herself into his lap, she reached her arm around his shoulder and said. "Welcome home Bobby, the house and I have missed you so much." He kissed her on the cheek and thanked her again for everything that she had done for him, espe-cially standing by him and protecting him when he was in a very bad place.

She was so wet between her legs, she could feel his limp cock under her leg, she wanted him to fuck her but she did not know how fragile he was, and if he rejected her, well she could not live with that. Bobby looked at his first love and said. "I have missed you so much Helen, it was the thought of coming home to you that got me through a lot of bad things, but now I am home with you here in my arms and knowing that we will soon be making love, that was if you want to, [she nodded like a little school girl] then let us please go up to my room." She climbed from his lap and her fanny was already well ahead of her, she could cum now just from holding his hand, they headed up stairs to his room, where he would fuck her and make her happy, very happy.

Once inside he locked the door and asked her to stand in the middle of the room, because he wanted to remove all her clothes, she had goose bumps all over at the thought of him undressing her, he walked slowly around her lightly running his finger-tips all over her, he stopped in front of her and tweaked both of her hard nipples, they smiled at each other as he moved about behind her, she felt him reach for the zip on her dress, it took him an age to undo the zip all the way down to the top of her bum, he held her dress open and kissed her all over her back and shoulders, he eased the dress over her shoulders and let it fall to the floor, she stood there in matching white bra and pants, he un-clipped her bra before moving back to stand in front of her, he looked into her eyes and could tell that he was driving her mad with desire, he kissed her lightly on the lips making her groan out loud, he reached to her shoulders and pulled her bra straps slowly down her arms, when her beautiful breasts came into view he gasped at their forgotten beauty, he dropped the bra to the floor and leaned over and sucked both nipples making her purr like a kitten, he looked her in the eye again and lowered himself down to his knees, slowly kissing her all the way, she closed her eyes when she felt his fingers in the sides of her wet pants, he pulled them down to the floor and held them for her to step out of them, he kissed her slowly up her legs to her fanny, he kissed her at the top of her slit, he then kissed her all of the way down to her opening, her legs were wide open and her hips were moving back and forth, he reached up and parted her fanny lips and flicked her clit with the tip of his tongue.

That was a step too far as she shuddered and moaned out her long awaited orgasm, she moved for the first time and gripped the back of his head and pushed her fanny onto his mouth, he used all his skill to kiss her clit and search out his reward, he held some of her cum on his tongue and stood up, he held his tongue for her to see what he was of-fering, she closed her lips over his tongue and sucked his tongue into her mouth, she sucked her cum from his tongue and opened her eyes and smiled her thanks.

Bobby took her to the bed and sat her down, he stood in front of her and removed all his clothes, when he stood there naked in front of her, his monster cock rock hard she fell in love with him all over again, she reached out and gripped his hard cock and moved her hand back and forth, she looked up into his eyes as he lovingly smiled down at her, she asked him. "Would you like me to suck it for you Bobby?" He shrugged his shoulders and she bent forward and exposed his huge knob and closed her lips around his rim, she had been sucking his cock for a good five minutes when he lifted her head and said. "Lay back my love and let me make love to you." She lay back on the bed and he lifted her legs and pulled her to the edge of the bed, he put his knob to her entrance and pushed forwards, she arched her back as though he was stretching her for the very first time, she let out a huge moan as he began to move slowly back and forth, he was really deep inside her as he made love to her slowly, he only increased his speed when she was going through her orgasm.

Bobby lasted for an eternity, long gone were the times when he rammed his huge cock into her from the off, the only time he rammed his cock into her now, was when she was coming and when he was coming, he finally shot his cum into her and she was relieved, all her pent up sexual tension had now been released. Bobby finally pulled out of her and lay down on the bed by her side and held her hand, she eased herself up and kissed him hard on the mouth, he kissed her back and her fanny was off again, she leaned over and sucked a few drops of cum out of his sensitive knob, she used her mouth to return the pleasure that he had given her, she gave him perfect mouth sex, when she was finished they lay silently side by side like life-long lovers.

They made love every afternoon for six days, Helen began her periods on the last day but she offered to give him mouth sex everyday, if he wanted her to, all he had to do was ask. Bobby drove his car down to the school to have a look around, he sat and proudly watched some of the young women using his relaxation area, he saw Susy and Liz, they had spotted him and were sat watching him, wondering what he was doing there.

 He smiled and drove away to where he did not know, he stopped the car in a familiar place and walked down a familiar lane he stood looking at the back of rose cottage, he could see Sylvia Tombs working in the garden and his child Roberta in a pushchair sleeping, he smiled as he noticed that the hanging basket was still hanging on the left telling him that the coast was clear and that he was welcome. He tossed a stone into the garden and she looked up, she had to shade her eyes to see who it was, realising who it was she waved and smiled at him, she took the pushchair and went indoors leaving the backdoor wide open in invitation, so he walked down and tapped on the back door, she stood there with her arms wide open in deep affection, he went to her and they hugged, he held her at arms-length and asked how she was, she told him all about his daughter and how much she would like another child, and how him turning up was a well-timed godsend. Sylvia turned him to her and wrapped her arms around his neck and began rubbing her mound against his hardening cock, she looked into his eyes and said. "Make love to me Bobby, lay me back on the table and make love to me, he turned her to the table and lifted her light summer dress over her head, she stood in a pair of white pants which she pushed down and let them fall to the floor, she then sat back on the table and reached down for his belt, he stepped back and stripped himself naked, he pushed his hard cock into her and lifting her legs onto his arms he gripped the insides of her thighs.

Bobby made love to her just as she had wanted him to, it was the longest most intense session of love making that either of them would ever experience. She kissed him hard on the mouth as he was about to leave, she had a premonition that she would never see him again, so she hung onto him for as long as she could, she put her lips to his ear and whispered. "Please make me cum one last time Bobby, use your fingers and make me happy forever." He did as she asked and used his fingers to give her orgasm, tears ran freely down her cheeks as she kissed him on the cheek and said. "Goodbye my love, thank you for my children, may god go with you." She turned and ran from the room crying her heart out.

Bobby returned home and sat in the darkness of his old home, he listened to the old house creek as the old wood cooled down, he was sat in his favourite chair and thinking about Sylvia, and the way that she had acted as though she would never see him again. His mobile phone buzzed in his pocket telling him that he had a message, the message read "What are you doing back here, why don't you fuck off forever and I warn you don't ever come near my wife again, or I will kill you !" He read the message over and over again, he looked and the number was blocked so he did not who the text was from, but it was definitely an angry husband. Bobby kept himself to himself, he rarely left the house anymore, taking his pleasure from a willing Helen, he told her about the text and she assured him that he was safe as far as her old man was concerned, it had to be someone else's husband.

Weeks had gone by since he had returned home and he was turning into a recluse in his mid-twenties, Helen came to work the next morning and passed him a piece of paper on which was a mobile phone number with the name Philameena above it, Helen said. "I have told her that it was ok for you to ring her, but please be careful Bobby, she was still very nervous of you." He took out his phone and rang her number, she answered on the first ring, neither of them spoke at first, it was her that said. "Hello Bobby, how are you?" He could feel his heart thumping at hearing her voice, he said. "I am so sorry Phil for what I did, I know now how terrified you must have been, and I have regretted it every day, I know that you will never forgive me, believe me when I say that I have changed, I have had treatment because I know that I had a problem." he waited for her to speak, to say anything, she finally said.

"I believe you Bobby, but only because Helen has reassured me that you have indeed changed, on that basis I am prepared to meet you at somewhere busy, somewhere where we can talk." She chose the time and place and he agreed to be there, he even offered to take Helen along if she wanted, she told him that that would not be necessary and that she would see him then. Bobby disconnected the call and stood up and hugged Helen and thanked her for her help, she hugged him back and said. "Then how about taking me upstairs and rewarding me?" He grabbed her hand and they ran up the stairs like first time lovers, he stripped her naked slowly, just how she liked it, he laid her on the bed and kissed her fanny, just how she liked it and then he made love to her, just how she liked it.

Sated he was back down stairs and she was doing her work, he saw something move on the tree line and a man was standing there watching him, or at least watching the house. Bobby went to the gun cabinet and took out a shot gun and put a hand-full of cartridges in his pocket. He started off across the lawn to the place where the man had been standing, when he arrived at the place the man had gone, but there were some cigarette stubs laying on the ground, someone had definitely been watching him. From that day on Bobby had become paranoid, he spent hours standing looking out of the window a loaded shotgun always leaning against the wall, every time that he went out in the car he was constantly looking in the rear-view mirror, just to see if he was being followed.

Helen had told him to go to the police if he was that worried, but he said that he could handle it. The evening finally came for his date with Phil, he was sat in the crowded restaurant waiting for her, when she walked into the restaurant, he felt a smile break out on his face, she smiled and sat down opposite him, they chatted and she asked him about his treatment and how he had been lately, he answered each of her questions truthfully, he asked her how she was doing, she said that as he had been so truthful she would tell him the truth. Philameena told him how much he had terrified her and broken her heart, she told him about all of the plans that she had made for them when he had come to stay with her, she spoke quietly when she told him of her list as to where she wanted to have sex with him, and in what position and how he had ruined everything by one selfish act, he reached across the table and took her hands and said that he was so very sorry and that was the day that he realised that he had a serious problem, but being a typical bloke he thought that he could handle it his own way.

He admitted to her that it took another similar incident to finally make him realise that he seriously needed help, and that he then went home and asked Helen to help him, which she did, and since his treatment his life has been perfect except that he was missing her, he walked her to her car and asked her if he could see her again? She said that she would think about it and let him know in a few days, she let him kiss her on the cheek before she drove away. He took out his phone and thanked her for seeing him and hoped that she would see him again.

Her text came a few days later, it simple said. "Same place, same time, Friday." Bobby was so excited he didn't know what to do, he decided to go for a drive, he went out to his new Audi and stopped dead in his tracks, someone had scratched his car bonnet, when he stood in front of the car, he could see what had been scratched on the car, the words said *you were warned* he stepped back and carefully looked everywhere to see if he was being watched, seeing no-one he retreated into the house and called Helen, who said she would be there straight away, she turned up and looked at the car before entering the house, she could see the state that he was in and hugged him, she whispered to him. "It is time to call the police Bobby." She felt him nod his head so she pulled away from him and took her phone out of her pocket and called the police who said for them not to touch the car. It was later that morning that an unmarked police car turned up, the tall police man looked at the car before standing in one place and scanning the whole grounds before entering the house, he shook their hands and introduced himself as Inspector Ian Davis.

He asked a lot of questions and listened carefully to their answers, he looked at the warning message on Bobby's phone and asked if he could take the phone as the police have ways and means of retrieving certain information. Ian Davis took out his phone and spoke to someone in his office, he then told them that the finger print team will be there soon and asked them not to touch the car, at that he left saying that they would be in touch and warned them to be extra vigilant at all times. Bobby took up his position standing by the window, constantly scanning the tree line watching for any movement.

A white van pulled up next to his car and two women climbed out of the van and donned blue paper overalls, they looked at the car from all different angles before one of the women took out a large camera on a tripod and took a lot of photographs also from every angle, they then began doing things with brushes, constantly twisting them, it took them a fair while to cover the large bonnet of the big car, when they were done with the brushes, the two women walked all around the front end of the car, pointing at different places, they stood these little markers on the car and took more photographs, they then took out these clear plastic sheets and pressed them down on the cars bonnet, removing the finger prints. It took them a very long time to complete their work, they made a final check of the car before loading their equipment into their van and driving away, Bobby began his watching again, and began feeling very isolated and scared.

Friday came and it was time to go and meet Phil, she entered the restaurant smiling and this time she sat next to him, they chatted like old friends and nothing was mentioned about the incident on the roof the whole evening, when it was time for her to leave he walked her to her car, and this time she allowed him to kiss her on the lips before saying that she would call him, she waved as she drove away smiling, he stood there watching her car driving away, his heart thumping in his chest.

Bobby was driving back home when he noticed a car following him, he tried speeding up and he tried slowing down, but the car stayed with him, he thought about what inspector Ian Davies had said and did as he was told, he drove to the police station and calmly walked inside, not looking at the following car that drove slowly past, he stayed in the police station until a car could escort him home, two policemen walked all around his house making sure that everything was locked before they left, they told him that he may see torch lights in the woods, but take no notice as dog handlers will be making regular visits throughout the night and patrol cars will be making regular checks around the surrounding area, so he should be quite safe, but he didn't feel safe. He stood looking out of the window all night with the shotgun leaning against the wall, loaded and within easy reach.

When Helen arrived at the house he was still standing at the window watching, she could tell just by looking at him that he had not slept at all, she took his hand and took him upstairs to his bedroom. She undressed him to his boxers and got him into bed with the promise that she would not leave him, he was asleep within seconds, she sat watching him and as soon as he began gently snoring she went downstairs and unloaded the shotgun and put it back in the gun cabinet, she checked on Bobby every half hour or so but he slept soundly for six hours, She finally had to wake him because the inspector was back and wanted to speak to him. Helen made coffee while Bobby sorted himself out, he finally came down stairs looking like death warmed up, he sat down opposite the inspector who passed him his phone and said. "We have traced the number to a Mr Brian Tombs and the hand prints on the car confirm that it was in fact Mr Tombs that damaged your car, we are trying to locate this gentleman, we have been to his house and his wife has said that she has not seen him for four days.

I have to tell you that Mrs Tombs has been badly beaten by our Mr Tombs, because according to Mrs Tombs unbeknown to her, her husband had installed hidden cameras around his house and has seen you with his wife, and has vowed to kill you and as yet we cannot find him, but we will find him have no fear about that. Until we do the police presence will continue for as long as it takes." With that he was gone, Bobby went to the window to watch the inspector drive away, without removing his eyes from the window he asked Helen where his car was, she told him that she had arranged for the garage to pick it up and re-pair the damage and it should be back within the hour. He nodded but still did not look at her, because he knew she wanted to know about Mrs Tombs, but he also knew that she would not ask him about her, because she knew it could lead to trouble between them, and that was the last thing that she wanted.

Because Helen's husband was away driving somewhere on the conti-nent, Helen thought it best if she stayed at the big house with Bobby just in case, plus with her staying it meant that she could get him to go to bed, this suited her because secretly she had always wanted to spend the night in bed with him after a good sex session, where they could hold each other and fall asleep like that.

Mr Tombs was being very hard to track down and Bobby swore blind that he had seen him in the woods watching him several times, but when the police had arrived there was no sign of him, this went on for weeks and the only time that he left the house was to go out on a date with Phil, and even she said he looked awful and she was worried about him. She even offered to have him at her house to stay, at least until the police had caught this man, but he refused saying that he did not want to place her in any danger, as he had lost her once and he did not want to lose her again ever.

On their last date when he had walked her to her car they had kissed for a long time and when he tried to take things further she pulled away from him, but she had held his face in her hands and whispered.

"Very soon my love, soon everything will be forgotten." He drove home with a heart full of joy, he was in love with Phil and he knew that he wanted to spend that rest of his life with her.

It had been weeks since there had been and sign of Mr tombs and the police presence around his house and estate had dwindled to maybe once a night. Helen's husband had been home for a week's holiday so he had not seen much of her, he had fallen into the habit of taking the loaded shotgun to bed with him, that was the only way that he could sleep. Things with Phil had moved forward slightly, they spoke on the phone every day now and she has asked him if they can go away on holiday together, just as soon as this matter with Mr Tombs has been sorted out, one way or the other, he readily agreed saying that he would take her somewhere very hot, with hot white sands and clear blue skies, to which she replied that she could not wait.

Helen was in bed with Bobby, they had just had a marathon sex session, she was very sore but also tingling all over, as for Bobby he was fast asleep by her side, she lay awake wondering how much longer she would be having sex with the love of her life, because she knew that he was deeply in love with Philameena.

She had been lay awake when she heard a sound down stairs, she nudged Bobby and made him wake up, she jumped out of bed and grabbed his dressing gown and ran out of the room, she ran down the stairs and looked around, she heard a sound in the kitchen and walked that way, she slowly pushed the door open a man dressed all in black stood there pointing a menacing looking shot-gun at her, he growled. "Where is he bitch?" She stepped to the side and asked. "Who are you and what do you want?" He stared at her with blank eyes and growled "You know who I am and what I want, now tell me where he is, I don't want to hurt you but I will if I have to, now tell me where he is?" She reached out and grabbed a long carving knife and ran at him.

He did not hesitate and shot her in the stomach, throwing her backwards, she was dead before she hit the floor, Brian Tombs stepped over her dead body and reloaded his shotgun as he walked towards the stairs, he stood and looked up the long wooden staircase, he took the first step and then walked slowly but deliberately upwards. When he reached the top landing he went from door to door, he finally opened a door where there was a human looking shape in the bed, he did not hesitate and lifted the gun and shot twice into the bed, feathers exploded in all directions, realising that he had made a mistake, he tried to reload his gun, but Bobby stepped out from behind the wardrobe and shot Brian Tombs twice in the chest, a look of surprise was on his face as he flew backwards only to land dead on the floor.

Bobby dropped his gun and ran out of the room and down the stairs, he saw Helen lay on the floor surrounded by a large pool of blood, he heard cars pulling up outside his house, he lowered his head onto his arms and cried, armed police raced through the house, he felt a gun at the back of his head, strong arms reached around him and grabbed his wrists and pulled them tight behind his back, he then felt the handcuffs being clipped into place, he was lifted up and placed face down on the cold stone floor. Bobby could see feet and legs running all over the house, he could hear police men shouting clear as they went from room to room, men were talking into radios and alien sounding voices came back in answer.

He was suddenly lifted up by two big men and carried out of the front door and forced into the back of a van, he lay face down on the floor as the door was slammed behind him. After a noisy journey the van stopped and he was dragged out of the van and carried bodily into a room, he was forcefully pushed into a hard chair and left on his own for an age, tears ran freely down his face at the loss of his first love and best friend.

A man dressed in white came into the room and wiped something all over his hands and left the room. Bobby had been left on his own for a long time, when Inspector Ian Davis entered the room, he unlocked Bobby's hand cuffs and then sat down opposite him, he asked Bobby if he wanted anything, he shook his head, the inspector then asked Bobby to tell him exactly what had happened. Bobby told him everything that had happened from start to finish, finally when he had shot Brian Tombs. The inspector nodded and said he would be back in a few min-utes, that few minutes turned into two hours, his only company was a bored looking policeman who leaned against the wall watching him.

The inspector and another big man named inspector Matt Woods sat opposite him, Ian Davis began talking, he said.
"Scenes of crime officers have agreed with what you have told us, we are forced to hold you, until we are told that you are free to go." They

read him his rights and he was allowed to call his solicitor, he used the phone again to call his father who said that he was on the way.

Bobby was placed into a cell on his own where he cried like a baby, he finally lay on the hard bed and closed his eyes, he was woken sometime later when the cell door was opened and his father and the family solicitor walked into the cell, his father hugged him and said. "Come on son, let's get out of here." He had been released into his father's care, his passport had been seized and his house was under armed guard.

They went to a local 5 star hotel where he was sat at a table and his father and solicitor listened to him tell the complete series of events from start to finish, the solicitor wrote notes throughout the telling of his grim story, when he had finished talking his father turned to his solicitor and said. "Well?" The solicitor looked quickly through his notes before saying. "I don't think we have much to worry about, I will start sorting things out first thing in the morning." He bid them goodnight and his father sat by his only son and heir, and said all the right things to try and reassure him, they eventually retired to bed.
Things moved very quickly in the next few weeks, Bobby had been interviewed many, many times, his father and Bobby had been back to the house to find it covered in all sorts of police tape and finger print dust, and secured front and back by police officers. His father told him not to worry, he would have the house cleaned professionally from top to bottom.

The day came for Helen's funeral, his mother arrived two hours before the service smartly dressed all in black, the whole private service was a very sombre affair, Bobby watched Helens' husband Charles as his shoulders heaved as he openly cried in the 14th century church, The wake was also very sombre affair, Bobby sat with his parents throughout the sad proceedings, eventually people began to leave, Charles shook lots of hands and nodded his thanks, he suddenly broke away and walked over to Bobby and his family, he asked if he could borrow Bobby for a few minutes and led him outside, they sat on a bench side by side, Charles finally said. "I know that she loved you Bobby, she told me often enough, that was one of the reasons that I do the job that I do, she wanted to spend more and more time with you, I know that you were sleeping together, she told me that as well, you see Bobby, I loved her more than life itself and when she had been with you she always came home happy, and for that I thank you from the bottom of my heart. They have told me that she died trying to protect you, for that we must all be very proud of her.

I will miss her Bobby as I know that you will miss her to and as soon as is decent I will move away, because I don't think I could live near you anymore, simply because when they told me she had died trying to protect you, I wondered why you didn't die trying to protect her, I would like you to answer that Bobby, are you a coward? Was she braver than you? What was it Bobby? Please tell me, make me understand."

Bobby could not look at the man, all he could do was tell the truth, he said. "The truth of the matter is she was a lot braver than me, with the drugs that I take now, I have difficulty in waking up. Helen shook me hard and before my brain reacted, she was running out of the bedroom and down the stairs, I heard the shots and knew that he was coming for me and when I heard his footsteps getting closer, I stuffed the pillows under the bed cloths and stood by the side of the wardrobe, he shot at the bed thinking that it was me, and before he could reload his gun I stepped out and shot him.

I ran down stairs and that was when I found her." The older man had watched Bobby throughout the telling of his story, he had seen the real tears streaming down his cheeks, he put his arm around the young man's shoulders and said that he believed him, and after hugging him he said. "Thank you for making her happy for me Bobby."

He then stood up and walked away, leaving Bobby to his own sad thoughts.

Chapter 19

The court case into the two violent deaths at Daleridge House lasted ten days, the outcome was a foregone conclusion according to the CPS, but Philameena had still been in court every day, and sat as close to Bobby as she could to support him, even when the truth about his affairs with Sylvia Tombs and Helen were told, she did not lower her head once, instead she would lean forwards and touch him reassuringly. The summing up took most of the tenth day, the outcome being that Bobby was to face no charges.

Outside the crown court Bobby, Phil and his parents and even his grandfather were congratulating each other when Bobby caught sight of a very pregnant Sylvia Tombs, he left his family and walked over to her, the past lovers hugged briefly and walked a short way together while his family and Phil looked on, the conversation between then was difficult but Sylvia said. "Don't blame yourself Bobby, I knew what I was doing, I knew that Brian would have great difficulty in fathering children, that was one of the reasons that I did what I did, if it had not been you it would have been someone else, you see I so desperately wanted children and would have done anything to get them but then I heard stories about your size and staying power, so I thought why not as I had never had any half decent sex. You may think that you chased me and won me over, but trust me Bobby I set you up easily by playing hard to get, and I do mean that it was dead easy really but I did not expect or want to fall in love with you like I did.

I knew about the hidden cameras Bobby, but by then my marriage was already over and I wanted him to see us making love, I wanted him to see that I was a real woman and that I really could love a man. I don't want you to worry about me Bobby, I will be moving back home with my parents, they have agreed to take us all in, if you want to be involved in the children's lives, then you will be welcome and if you want to provide for them, well then that will be welcome as well but then if you don't, well then I will manage somehow. Brian was a good man really Bobby I just didn't realise that he loved me as much as he did, but when he beat me after seeing us doing it in the kitchen and me not only reacting to you, but also showing that I was capable of enjoying sex as well, that was something that I had never done with him, I could tell by the look in his eyes that at that precise moment in time he really hated me, I really thought that he was going to kill me, [Sylvia looked back at Philameena and carried on] she looks like a nice person Bobby and I can tell that she really loves you, I hope that you will be happy together, but should you need a bolt hole or just good old sex, then you have my number and don't worry, I will meet you anywhere you want, goodbye for now Bobby Francis, I will always love you, please don't be a stranger." With that she walked away from him and never looked back.

Bobby walked back to Phil and took her hand and they all walked away from the court together to have a celebratory drink, and talk about their future's together, just before his parents left to resume their hunt for properties with land, his father passed him a large brown envelope and told him not to open it until he had returned to Daleridge house. Bobby watched his parents and his grandfather walk away towards their car. They stood hand in hand and watched them drive away, to where only they knew that. Bobby and Phil had decided to stay at a hotel rather than drive home, just so that they could sit quiet and discuss their futures together, Bobby did not really want to return to the house at all, even though it had been cleaned from top to bottom. The pair sat on a soft leather sofa in a very expensive 5 star hotel out of earshot of everyone else, there was a lot to talk about because even though they had been seeing a lot of each other lately, they still had not made love since that awful day on the roof of her house.

Bobby turned slightly and took her hands in his, he looked into her eyes and said. "Look Phil, I have been fretting about this for days now, only I only know one way of asking the next question and that was head on, so here goes, Look Phil you know that I love you and want to be with you [he took a deep breath] what I want to say is I have only booked a double room for us both, if you want me to change it to two singles, I will but I was hoping that maybe we could, like you know?" She reached up and placed a finger onto his mouth and smiled and said. "It's fine Bobby, you will never know how much I have been looking forward to sleeping with you again, but please no fancy stuff, just good old sex." He put his hands up in surrender and said. "I promise". They had been sat quiet and she began to giggle, he looked at her and asked what she was laughing at, she smiled broadly and said.

"When you started talking I thought that you were going to propose marriage the way you were carrying on, and if you had not booked a double room, I would have jumped your bones in a single bed, which could have been quite exciting, I suppose?" He looked into her eyes and said in all seriousness. "I was going to leave my proposal until next week when we will hopefully be on holiday somewhere hot, but if you can't wait until then I can always go down onto one knee here and now?" She sat there looking at him so he went down onto one knee and asked her to marry him, to which she said that she would be proud and happy to marry him, and they hugged.

Bobby took her hand and led her out of the hotel to the nearest jewellers and spent a small fortune on matching rings in celebration. Rings bought they returned to the hotel and seeing that there was not much time before they left to go on holiday, they both sat and called their parents to much excitement all around, when his mother had calmed down his father asked him if he had opened the envelope yet? Saying that he had not his father chuckled and said. "Congratulations Bobby, enjoy your wedding present."

Bobby went to his car and collected the envelope and sat back down by his future wife and opened the thick envelope, inside were a lot of legal looking papers, but on top was a single sheet of A4 paper with his name at the top, the note read.

Bobby

      Your mother and I have discussed your situation and the Daleridge Estate. We came to the conclusion that we or you would not like to live there after what has happened, so we took it upon ourselves to sell the whole estate, house, school and everything. If you do not agree with what we have done, you have 21 days in which to reverse the decision. To replace the estate we have found you and Philameena a nice place in the Cotswolds, near Broadway [a 14 century manor house with land].

I could see that you two are deeply in love, so I took it upon myself to ask Phil what she would say if you did propose, and she did not hesitate in saying that she would say yes, so Bobby if you have not yet done the deed, I suggest that you get on with it.

Now most of the papers in the envelope refer to your new home and land, we have arranged for certain furniture items to be installed in the new home ready for when you return from holiday, I took the trouble to ask Phil where she would like to go on holiday and when she said Barbados, I took the liberty of booking you both 4 months at the Barbados Hilton, you can make it a honeymoon or just a holiday it is up to you, by which time your new home will be finished and fully furnished to Phil's specification.

I think that you two are made for one-another and the marriage would make us all very proud indeed. If the proposal goes ahead as we hope that it does, we will arrange for the two families to meet when you return from your holiday. Have fun Bobby and good luck, it may not seem like it sometimes, but we do love you.

Your loving father.

p.s. We have sorted your grandfather out very cleverly, we bought an old peoples home and asked him if he would like to live in and look after all of the grounds. When we took him to see the home we were shown around by the Matron and to be honest I can see wedding bells there as well, as she has agreed to feed him and look after him. I will forward full contact details for everyone just as soon as we have all of the details.

Bobby passed his future wife the sheet of paper, she read the note and placed her hand over her mouth and gasped as she finished the note, her mouth hung open as she looked at Bobby and said. "My god Bobby 4 months in Barbados and a new house, [she looked at him and continued] well go on then, ask me"

He looked at her and she said. "For an intelligent man you are a bit slow sometimes. "She went down on one knee and said "Bobby Francis, I know that you have proposed marriage to me and I have accepted your offer, will you marry me before we go to Barbados, so that we can use the holiday as a honeymoon?" He smiled and slapped his head and said. "Yes, I will marry you just as soon as we can arrange it as long as it is before we go on holiday." They hugged and kissed in the reception of the hotel, she moved her mouth to his ear and said. "Take me up to our room, rip my clothes of and ravish me." He looked into her eyes and took her hand, they walked quickly to the lift, he pressed the number for their floor and was about to grab her when she placed her hand on his chest and nodded to the camera watching them, he took her to their room, opened the door and then stood to the side to let her past, he hung the do not disturb sign on the door handle, when he turned around she was almost naked, he stood and watched as she undid her bra and showed him her firm tits, she then pushed her wet pants to the floor and stood there with her legs wide open and one hand on her hip staring at him.

 He just stood there and studied at every inch of her perfect body, his eyes locked onto her hairless fanny and her swollen lips, she rubbed her fingers along her fanny lips and began rubbing her clit ever so slowly, he looked into her eyes and she said. "Well, you don't seem very interested so I thought that I would start without you and let you catch up." He suddenly realised what she meant and began tearing at is clothes, he was soon stood there naked his hard cock standing before him, now it was her turn to stand and stare, she looked into his eyes and said.

"Was it that big before Bobby" He smiled and nodded his head, he took a step towards her and she took a step back towards the bed, both of them were smiling as she reached the big soft bed with the back of her legs, he was two paces away from her, he took another step and she lay back on the bed her eyes staring into his, he took another step and she lifted her legs and opened them at the same time, he gripped his giant hard cock as he took his last step, she closed her eyes and arched her back as he entered her, stretching her, just like he had done the first time he had fucked her.

As he took hold of her inner thighs he began to ride her slowly but firmly, she knew instantly that this was a new Bobby, if this was Bobby in love then this is how she wanted him, but there was no doubt that when needed, he would spread his feet and ram his big cock into her. That time was fast approaching for her, she felt him increase his pace as he took her through her orgasm, her tits were bouncing back and forth in time with his strong strokes, she lifted her hands and gripped her tits and squeezed them hard, her strong orgasm brought back memories, as she thrust her hips up to meet his powerful thrusts.

Each orgasm always ended with her smiling up at him and him smiling down at her, the old Bobby used to fuck her, fuck her hard until she was ready to give in, but this Bobby had turned into a lover, he took his time and made love to her, he wanted to please her, to give her pleasure that she will remember forever, he would take his own release when the time came but until that time, his thoughts were all about her, this woman that he had loved from the first time he had ever seen her.

On and on he made love to her, until they exploded together, they gripped hands and pulled against each other, grinding against one another until they were finally sated. They stayed locked together until he slipped out of her, she slid off the bed and went down to her knees and showed her appreciation for his tenderness in his lovemaking, by showing him that she too could show tenderness as she licked and sucked his tender knob. They spent the night in each other's arms, they would sleep and make love and then sleep again.

They married in a registry office before they left to go on holiday. When they returned to their new home, his parents were there waiting for them, they had some sad news and some good news for them. Firstly his grandfather had passed away 8 weeks before and the good news, well because both family's had missed out on the wedding and reception, another wedding had been arranged with the permission of Phil who had been in secret talks with his mother. The wedding was very special for everyone involved and a day that will be remembered by all. But Philameena stole the show when she announced that she was with child.

THE END.

www.ingramcontent.com/pod-product-compliance
Lightning Source LLC
Chambersburg PA
CBHW070354200726
48294CB00003B/909